Rory frowned at her. Poor lass must have cracked her head during the fall. Or perhaps he had.

"I'm sorry. What did you say?" he asked.

Her lips quivered into a half smile and she leaned closer so no one would overhear, her turquoise eyes bright and hypnotic. "I want you to be my husband. I'm looking to remarry as my husband passed but a year ago, and I hear you are also on the quest for a wife. Perhaps we could come to an agreement that benefits us both."

While Rory wasn't a man of many words, it was by choice, not because he had nothing to say. Except for this moment. Her words dumbfounded him. He knew his chances of finding any woman who would agree to marry him were slim at best.

"Do you know anything about me, miss?" he asked.

"Aye, my laird, I know who you are and that you are ill. Dying, they say, but I believe you look quite healthy. Perhaps it is all a rumor to create a more mythical presence about you." She bit her lower lip and peered closely at him. "Are you truly sick, or is that just nonsense?"

"Are you always so direct, Mrs. Fraser?" he asked.

Author Note

Moira and Rory's story was born as a whisper of an idea that I submitted for the Harlequin Historical Warriors Wanted Blitz back in the summer of 2020. The idea of bringing together a hero desperate to live while being destined to die and a heroine who wished to hide from her own life intrigued me, especially during a pandemic.

As many of us have learned through this challenging time, life is a precious and fragile gift. I wish you all health, happiness, hope and, most of all, love.

I hope you enjoy Moira and Rory's story set amid the Scottish Highlands in the fictional castle of Blackmore set off the western coast near Oban. Happy reading!

JEANINE ENGLERT

Eloping with the Laird

Recycling programs
for this product may
not exist in your area.

ISBN-13: 978-1-335-40765-8

Eloping with the Laird

Copyright © 2022 by Jeanine Englert

This edition published by arrangement with Harlequin Books S.A.

For questions and comments about the quality of this book,
please contact us at CustomerService@Harlequin.com.

Harlequin Enterprises ULC
22 Adelaide St. West, 41st Floor
Toronto, Ontario M5H 4E3, Canada
www.Harlequin.com

Printed in U.S.A.

Jeanine Englert's love affair with mysteries and romance began with Nancy Drew and her grandmother's bookshelves of romance novels. When she isn't wrangling with her characters, she can be found trying to convince her husband to watch her latest *Masterpiece* or BBC show obsession. She loves to talk about writing, her beloved rescue pups, and mystery and romance novels with readers. Visit her website at www.jeaninewrites.com.

Books by Jeanine Englert

Harlequin Historical

The Highlander's Secret Son
Eloping with the Laird

Visit the Author Profile page
at Harlequin.com.

To my mom and dad, whose own love story is fifty-three years young. Thank you for always reminding me of the importance of hope, love and never giving up, even when you seem to be facing the impossible. Happy anniversary, and I love you.

And to my husband, Brian, every book I write is because of you. I love you.

Chapter One

Argyll, Scotland, October 1740

Scores of men competed in the vast open field in various tests of skill and strength that Moira Fraser's father, Bran Stewart, the Laird of Glenhaven, held each autumn. The annual Tournament of Champions had been a tiresome tradition every year, with this year being even more bothersome than most for she had to select a husband.

'Who is it to be, sister?' Ewan Stewart, eldest of the siblings, approached and settled next to Moira. He leaned against the trunk of one of the many rowan trees surrounding them.

'I choose none of them. Is that a fine enough answer for you?' Moira Fraser faced her favourite sibling and frowned. She attempted to be cross with him, which was impossible.

'Nay, sister. You must select a husband and soon. Tomorrow is the last day of the tournament and then these lairds and their eldest sons will scatter back to

whence they came. If you do not choose, Father will
do so for you. Is that what you wish?' His warm brown
gaze settled upon her. His sympathy sent an undercur-
rent of panic beneath her skin.

They both knew how her last marriage had ended.
Badly.

'You know what I wish,' she whispered. She clutched
at the bark of the tree until it impressed itself upon the
soft flesh of the inside of her wrist. 'Why can I not just
be left a widow? Why must I remarry?'

'It is the best way to protect you.'

'Is that what my last husband was doing?' She sti-
fled a laugh.

Ewan reached out and touched her hand. She flinched
involuntarily, a gift from her first husband. Touch sometimes sent her back to a place she never wished to be:
her memories. 'Moira, you know what I meant. None
of us knew. If we had…'

The familiar agony emerged again.

She smothered the shame and interrupted him. 'I
know that. But that does not mean that I wish to ever
be bound to a man that way again.'

'Father has given you the option to choose this time,
sister. An option a woman usually does not have. Take
that chance. I know it isn't much, and it doesn't undo
anything that has happened, but seize it before it is
gone. Otherwise, he will merely choose the laird with
the largest coin and castle in hopes it will secure your
future.'

Just like the last time.

She studied the field. The two dozen lairds and their

sons looked like reasonable, average, perhaps even kind men, but one couldn't see everything about a person until they were alone with them in the wee hours of the night consumed in darkness. That was when their monsters emerged.

When a large stone caber crashed to the ground, she startled and stared out at the sea of men. 'How can I possibly know if any of these men will be good to me, Ewan? They all seem…the same.'

And she no longer trusted her judgment. She'd met Peter Fraser at a gathering such as this. Father had introduced them, hoping for just such an attachment to form. The eldest son and soon-to-be laird over his clan had wooed her with his kindness and charm. His attentions had been gentle, steady and predictable, and over three days she had fallen for all he had pretended to be. They were married but a month later, and within a few weeks of their vows, Moira had wished she were dead.

Well, more specifically, she wished *he* were dead. She never told anyone all that happened on the night he died, and she never would. Some secrets were meant to be buried, and her secrets were buried with Peter.

'Shall I give you some recommendations? I have spent time with some of these men and can tell you their virtues and vices. Will that help?' Ewan offered, hope dancing in his features.

'Aye.' She would humour him. 'Tell me your top three choices. I will speak with them, make my decision and report it to Father by the end of the day on the morrow.'

His eyes narrowed on her. 'You will?'

'Aye, brother. Now go on,' she answered. She had to placate Father. He was ill and his worry over seeing her settled was taking a toll on him. Heaven knew he also blamed himself for what happened with Peter even though he'd never said as much. She'd promised to provide him a name for a future husband by the end of the tournament, and she would keep her promise, even if she dreaded becoming a bride once more.

'Your first candidate in the northwest corner preparing for the caber toss is Phineas Grant, eldest son of a large estate north of Loch Ness. Strong, capable and fairly clear-headed.'

'And?' She sensed his hesitation.

'He is a bit of a gambler from what I hear, so you'd need to mind the purse strings of the clan, for your children's sake, of course.'

'Not a chance. Who's next?'

He sighed. 'Sean MacIntosh to your left, also an eldest son, lining up for his next shot for arrows. A bit young for you perhaps at three years your junior, but your strength could be a virtue for him. Smaller estate though, near Inverness on the Moray Firth. You'd need to pack your furs, sister. It's a bit blustery in the winter with the wind coming in from the sea.' He shivered.

She frowned as MacIntosh missed his mark entirely. 'Is he blind? I could have hit that target blindfolded.'

He laughed. 'Perhaps he does have a vision issue, now that you mention it. He's never been good at shooting either. My top choice for you would be Garrick MacLean. He's next up to shoot. Garrick was a second son, but his older brother died a year ago from fever. He's now set to inherit a sizeable estate along Loch Linnhe, a day's ride from here. He's a good man, Moira. One of the best you'll find.'

She watched the handsome, sandy-haired man, as the shooting paused and new targets were placed closer to the grove. What did Ewan *really* know of him? She'd have to find out for herself about the man before the sun went down tomorrow. Otherwise, Father would make the choice for her. Her stomach curdled.

Her gaze skipped along other men dotting the field like a rock skipping along water before clunking into the abyss. A man she'd never seen before sat alone far off from the crowd atop one of the last of the timbers the soldiers had set out for those who wished to watch the men compete. The man's dark features and flat brow read boredom and his scowl irritation, which was exactly how she felt. For a moment, at least one person shared her disdain for the day, which warmed her spirit.

'What of him?' Moira squinted and quirked her lips. 'The one sitting alone in the back. He wears a noble crest on his overcoat. Who is he?'

Ewan shook his head. 'Laird Rory McKenna? Nay, Moira. He is not an option. Have you not heard about Black Rory?'

'Black Rory? What are you talking about?' She watched the man, and he stiffened as if he'd felt the intensity of her gaze. She stepped back to shield herself in the shadowy leaves of the rowan tree.

'They say he's ill, gravely ill.' Ewan dropped his voice low. 'Some sort of family curse. He grows weaker by the day. His uncle is eager for him to marry as Rory is a laird and has no male siblings or cousins, but no one wishes to bind their daughter to a dying man.'

Moira perked up, raising her head higher, boldly staring at the man as he stood. Rory McKenna was tall and wore grey trews that showed his rather muscular legs. A black collarless frock coat with large cuffs detailed in silver buttons covered an equally pleasing upper torso. Not exactly the look of a dying man. His dark hair was wavy, perhaps even a bit long for fashion, but it flattered his sharp features. He had a commanding air about him, and his scrutinising eyes didn't seem to miss anything. 'Are you making this up to trick me? He doesn't seem ill. He's quite fit. And you and I both know curses are nonsense.'

Ewan leaned closer, dropping his voice to a whisper. 'Every single direct male descendant of the McKenna family has died before the age of four and twenty for generations. Ask anyone. And if that isn't a curse, what is?'

'You just stated his uncle lives. Doesn't that in itself prove the curse to be untrue?' She frowned at him and crossed her arms against her chest. She knew it seemed too perfect an option to have merit.

'It is long rumoured that his uncle was sired by a man other than a McKenna. He has never made a claim for laird either, so it is largely accepted as truth.'

Her curiosity peaked. She studied McKenna's easy fluid movements as he approached the edge of the field where men were practising shooting at various targets. 'His age now?' she enquired, a bit breathless and eager for her brother's answer. Maybe he could be an answer to her prayers after all.

'Three and twenty. They say he only has months to live.'

Her stomach fluttered and flipped. Those were exactly the words she longed to hear.

She much preferred the idea of being a widow than a wife.

She sucked in a steadying breath, squared her shoulders and pressed a kiss to Ewan's cheek. 'Thank you, brother. I believe I have just found my future husband.'

'You can't be serious?' Ewan cocked his head.

'And why wouldn't I be? He is a laird, pleasing to look upon and days away from death.'

He clutched her arm. 'You cannot throw away your future because of the past.'

'I won't be,' she whispered. 'This, *he*, is how I shall seize my future without having to comply to the demands of a husband for the rest of my days.' For what man would have her after burying two husbands before the age of five and twenty? They'd believe *she* was cursed, and she would fan such gossip until it burst into flame.

'Moira, you aren't thinking clearly. There is no future with a dying man.'

She shushed him and walked through the rowan trees towards Black Rory, ignoring her brother's protests. Oblivious to anything other than the dark, mysterious man who would solve all her problems, she lifted her skirts and moved with purpose out of the grove and into the open field. Rory McKenna, Black Rory she would call him now in her heart, met her gaze, and she smiled.

'Hold fast!' he called, thrusting out an arm to halt her advance a few paces away.

Confused by his call she carried on, unburdened by his words. Alarm lit his features and he ploughed into her as an arrow hissed by her ear. They hit the ground hard. She gasped, unable to take in air, as he lay atop her. The weight of his muscular body a reminder that he was strong and formidable, despite what Ewan said.

'What were you thinking? You could have been killed,' he stated.

When she struggled for air, he moved off her but kept hold of her hand. A soft prickle of awareness as his warm, calloused fingers wrapped around her own travelled along her arm and she shivered. She pulled her hand away. His touch sparked an odd, unfamiliar sensation she hadn't felt in ages: safety. She shifted away from him. She knew far better than to believe such.

'Give it a moment. You had the breath knocked out of you, is all.' His grey eyes were hard and unflinching. His voice commanding and certain. She believed his words despite not knowing him at all, which was ridiculous. 'Take one slow breath in,' he ordered.

Air rushed into her lungs, and she coughed and sputtered. A crowd formed around them. Their faces peered down at her. 'Are you well enough to stand?' he asked.

Indeed, she was well enough to rise…and die from embarrassment. Her face flushed with heat and she nodded. He stood and offered his hand. She hesitated, but accepted it, as she couldn't gain her footing on her own. Pulling her up easily alongside him, he muttered, 'Here, sit a spell.' He gestured to a nearby timber. He attempted to guide her by the elbow, but she shifted away from his touch, and his arm fell back to his side.

'Give her some air,' he commanded, his clear tone cutting through the throng of people with authority.

The crowd dispersed. Ewan stood back, watching. He began to approach, but she shook her head to stave him off before glancing away.

She struggled to regain her composure, her thoughts and her voice. Her heart hammered in her chest and her back ached from the fall. Her lungs brought in uneven breaths, and overall she was plain startled by what had happened. She could see they had moved the target now. How had she failed to notice earlier? She had never been so careless before during a tournament. What had come over her?

She frowned. Her urgent desire to find a suitable husband had blocked out her reason. If he hadn't intercepted her, she'd have an arrow through her chest, or worse. She rubbed her arms.

'Is this your first time here as well?' he asked, glancing over. He leaned forward on his elbows, assessing her.

'Nay. I have been at these as long as I can remember. I am Mrs Moira Fraser, daughter of the Laird of Glenhaven.'

His face paled. 'Whom I have just tackled unceremoniously to the ground.' He cringed. 'My apologies. I've never attended the tournament before and arrived only today due to an unexpected delay. I've yet to meet everyone. I'm Rory McKenna, Laird of Blackmore.'

'You saved my life. I should thank you.'

His brow crinkled. 'So, if you know a great deal of tournaments and shooting, why did you charge head-long out into the practice field where the targets were? You could have been killed.' He held her gaze awaiting an answer.

'Honestly, I wished to speak to you, my laird. Urgently.'

'Oh? Why is that?'

'I wished to ask you to be my husband.'

Rory frowned at her. Poor lass must have cracked her head during the fall. Or perhaps he had.

'I'm sorry, what did you say?' he asked.

Her lips quivered into a half-smile and she leaned closer so no one would overhear, her turquoise eyes bright and hypnotic. 'I want you to be my husband. I'm looking to remarry as my husband passed but a year ago, and I hear you are also on the quest for a wife. Perhaps we could come to an agreement that benefits us both.'

While Rory wasn't a man of many words, it was by choice, not because he had nothing to say. Except for this moment. Her words dumbfounded him. He knew his chances of finding any woman who would agree to marry him were slim at best. He was a dying man after all.

'Do you know anything about me?' he asked.

'Aye, my laird, I know who you are and that you are ill. Dying, they say, but I believe you look quite healthy. Perhaps it is all a rumour to create a more mythical presence about you.' She bit her lower lip and peered closely at him. 'Are you truly sick or is that just nonsense?'

'Are you always so direct, Mrs Fraser?' he asked.

As much as he should be annoyed by her enquiries that bordered on rudeness, he found her directness quite refreshing. Most of those around him walked about as if nettles were underfoot as they never wished to discuss his sickness, let alone his looming death.

'My past experiences have taught me that sometimes there is no time for subtleties and hints, or reasons to be so. Directness suits me quite fine. I hope you don't find it offensive, my laird.'

'Surprised, but not offended,' he offered. 'The rumours you have heard are true. My physicians seem to think me but months from an unfortunate demise. That is why I am here. My uncle wishes for me to find a bride, as do I.'

She lifted her eyebrows at him in encouragement.

'In hopes of somehow siring a child, a direct descendant, to carry on the family name…before I die.'

'Even though you may not live to see the birth of your own child?' Her eyes widened and softened. 'Seems a rather sad mission to attempt to fulfil.'

'Aye, perhaps. It is all a bit of a last attempt to secure a strong future for our clan, but he asked me to try.' He shrugged. 'So I am here to honour his wishes. He has cared for me since I was a boy. I owe him a great deal.'

'Then maybe we could make an arrangement. One that could please us both in our current and unfortunate circumstances.' She played with the end of her long raven plait of hair. The woman was a beauty, but he'd been fooled before, and he'd not be mesmerised by a woman's physical charms again.

He sat back and crossed his arms against his chest, clearing his throat, commanding himself to focus once more on her words. 'I'm listening.' And he was. He was intrigued by what the lass would say next, as it was never quite what he expected. For the first time in ages, he wasn't bored.

'I have been married, but now find myself a young widow without children. After my husband died,' she began quietly, 'I left the Frasers, my husband's clan, and returned here, my childhood home. Now that more than a year has passed, my father grows weary of me putting off his attempts to find me a new and suitable husband. *I* weary of trying to find one. I have until the end of the tournament tomorrow to tell him my choice. Otherwise, he shall choose for me, as he did last time.' She laced her hands together in her lap so tightly that her knuckles whitened.

The hitch in her voice and her pinched features made him curious to know more about why she would leave her married family to return to her father's home and why the idea of remarrying was so objectionable, but he set it aside for now. He needed to know if the lass was serious. He'd not the time to waste on whims of fancy.

'Am I your *last* choice for a husband, then?' he asked, wanting to get to the crux of the truth.

'Nay, my laird,' she answered, gifting him a full smile that finally reached her eyes. 'You are my first.'

Chapter Two

First?

Rory McKenna had never been anyone's first choice for anything, let alone a woman's first choice for a husband. 'I'm sorry, did you say I was your *first* choice?'

'Aye,' she answered. 'My brother Ewan has apprised me of some of the other...options for a husband, but I believe you and I would suit one another, quite well actually.'

'How could you possibly know that when we've never met before?'

She hesitated and a slight flush rose in her cheeks. 'Because you are dying, my laird.'

What did one say to that?

'And here I believed you might be intrigued by my title, estate or good looks,' he teased, rubbing the back of his neck. 'I must say I have never met anyone quite like you, Mrs Fraser.'

Her blush deepened and her shoulders rolled in, reminding him of a raven tucking in its wings. 'You must think me a horrible person. Now that I've said it aloud, I realise how awful it sounds. I don't *wish* for you to die, my laird. I'm not that kind of person. Truly.'

He studied her for a moment. Though she didn't *seem* that kind of person, one could never tell, could they?

'Your logic intrigues me,' he stated. 'Why do you wish to marry a dying man? How could that possibly benefit you?' He angled his body closer to her, hoping she would open up once more. He didn't quite know if he should believe her or not. She had just absorbed a hard fall. Her logic could be impaired.

'My laird, I have no fantasy of love. Mostly I wish to have a simple, peaceful life and future of my own choosing, but as a woman that is not an option. If I must select a husband, then knowing it will not be for long…would be strangely comforting.' She shifted on the timber as she stared out in the distance, her features flat and pale.

Something deep inside him shifted, and his body tightened; his initial shadowy thoughts about her reservations to remarry came into sharper focus. *What had happened to her?* He wished to reach out and touch her, comfort her, protect her, but he ran his open palms down his trews instead. He didn't trust himself. He had little to offer her and from the looks of it she deserved everything.

Or perhaps he was being a fool once more.

He stiffened his spine. His past failed engagement had taught him that women had more layers than the Scottish Highland soil, most of which perplexed him and couldn't be seen until he was far too entrenched to regain his footing. He narrowed his gaze on her.

'Why not align yourself with another man who could offer you a long, happy life with a family and security?' He gestured to the field teaming with future lairds and a handful of second sons. 'There seem to be many prospects.'

Ones that might live longer than a year.

Her bright blue eyes flashed and met his gaze, piercing through him, challenging him. She had not taken the bait to shift her attentions to another. She'd given them nary a glance. None of it made of whit of sense. He didn't trust it as it seemed far too easy.

'I know my own mind, and *you* are who I wish to affix myself to even if it seems illogical to everyone, including you. I have to provide my father a name of my choice of a husband by the end of the tournament tomorrow. If you could consider it, give it some thought before you bat the idea away entirely, I would be grateful.' Her gaze flitted to him one last time as she stood. 'And thank you for saving my life.'

Before he uttered another word, she was gone. He watched her quick, purposeful strides, her dark gown disappearing into a dot along the horizon. What in the hell had just happened? He'd come here in search of a bride and a willing, beautiful lady had fallen in his lap, eager to be just that.

And he'd let her leave, not trusting the bit of luck that had blown his way.

She'd made an utter fool of herself. That was evident in the dumbfounded look he'd given her as she'd left. What did she expect? She'd walked headlong into a target practice, almost got herself killed and then launched quite unceremoniously into a pitch about how perfect it would be for him to marry her, as she hoped to marry a man who wasn't going to live very long.

Poorly done, Moira.

She cursed herself and her spontaneity. If she'd waited and been more thoughtful in how she'd broached the subject, she might have convinced him. Now, she'd dashed her best option for a suitable husband by being far too bold, brazen and clumsy in her approach. He most likely thought her a bit touched in the head.

She began to wonder if she was too.

Ewan jogged up alongside and fell in step with her. 'Moira? Are you well? What happened?'

'I made a fool of myself, that's what happened. Why can I not be a normal, docile woman who thinks before acting?' she grumbled, picking up her skirts and her pace through the open field leading to the castle.

Her brother chuckled. 'Because that is not who you are, sister. You did just run straight into a target practice.' He embraced her in a tight side squeeze and released her.

'I may have survived that near-death experience, but I have just ruined my chance with Laird McKenna.' She frowned as they descended into the small soft dip of the meadow.

'A bit of rest before the dinner may help. You did, however, do a fine job of soliciting added attention to your person. Garrick was quite concerned about your fall and well-being—asked me about you directly.' Ewan smirked. 'You could do worse. He is a kind man, sister.'

'Oh, but that's just it, Ewan. I don't wish to marry at all. If I must, which I know I must, I would rather it be…brief, as it would have been with Laird McKenna. That way no one is disappointed, and no expectations are left unmet.' She kicked a tuft of grass and huffed in frustration.

Ewan stopped and faced her. 'When have you, Moira Fraser, ever given up on anything? You still have time to win back Laird Death, if you wish.' He winked at her.

She gasped. 'Don't say that,' she hissed. 'That is a horrible thing to call him!'

'Says the woman counting on his demise.'

She frowned. 'You have a point, but what can I do to win his favour? Help me, brother. Please.'

'You will not speak to him this night.'

'What? How is my ignoring him going to help win him over?'

Ewan shook his head. 'He will believe he is out of the hunt, which shall make him more eager to win your hand.'

'Perhaps the fall has impacted me more than I re-alised, for absolutely nothing you just said makes a whit of sense to me.' She crossed her arms against her chest.

'Men are rather competitive creatures. Has that somehow escaped you all of these years?'

'Evidently.'

'The night before your engagement was announced to Peter, he battled for you.'

'What?' Her mouth fell open. 'He battled for me?'

'It's true. Two other lairds had also expressed interest in your hand, so Father had them fight for you. The winner by sword, Peter, was allowed to offer for you.'

'They did not play to the death, did they?' Her gut swirled at the thought.

'Nay, of course not. Just until first blood was drawn.'

'Is that normal? It sounds ridiculous. And I can't believe Peter did that. For me.' She rubbed her arms, shivering. His name still sent a chill along her flesh.

Ewan sobered. 'It is why we were all so sure he cared for you. Why we believed you would be safe.'

'I believe it was his desire to possess, not love, which drove him on for that fight, but none of that matters now.' Moira didn't wish to hear any more or linger further in the murky memories of the past. She had to focus on finding a suitable husband before Father selected one for her. 'I have less than a day, brother. What else can I do?' They began their walk once more, climbing the last stretch between them and the castle in a comfortable silence.

'Keep trying,' Ewan finally answered. He bent and grabbed a handful of grass, selected one green stalk and blew on it, sending a trill whistle in the air. He handed her a bright shiny blade of grass. She sighed. Despite the thousand times he'd tried to teach her, she could never get it. What would make today any different?

'I know that look. Just try, Moira.'

She rolled her eyes, pressed the stalk between her fingers and blew. A bright trill sounded for the first time, ever. She stopped, laughed and faced him.

'See? Do not give up so easily. Oh…' He jogged up the castle steps, smiling. 'And by all that's holy, have

Brenna dress you. Do not attempt to select your gown yourself.'

She stopped cold and looked at her walking dress. 'What's wrong with my gown?'

'Do you really wish for me to tell you?' Brenna called from the top of the castle steps. As if on cue, Moira's younger sister chimed in, popping her hands to the tiny waist of her immaculate sky-blue gown. She tilted her head full of dark curls and smirked.

Moira glanced up at her sister's outfit, assembled to perfection, and down at her now grass-stained day dress. 'Nay,' Moira answered, rolling her eyes heavenward. Her shoulders sagged as Ewan chuckled and entered Glenhaven Castle without her.

Could she endure the incessant fluttering and fussing of her younger sister for an hour to attempt to ensnare Laird McKenna into being her husband?

Aye, if the man was certain to not live for long, she could.

Chapter Three

The groan of the heavy wooden door as Rory entered his guest chamber at Glenhaven Castle matched his fatigue. Had he truly arrived this morn? His body claimed otherwise.

'How goes the hunt for a bride, my laird?' Angus asked from deep within the chamber. His manservant blacked a pair of Rory's leather boots, using the light from the westerly facing windows on the far side of the room. The familiar swish-swish of the brush and tang of soot and beeswax acted as a balm to his frayed nerves. Finding a wife was difficult work.

When Rory didn't speak, the old man paused his work and set his steely eyes upon him. His furry, grey eyebrows furrowed as they had done a thousand times before. Angus had cared for Rory since he was but a wee lad. They had more of a father and son relationship, and Rory valued his wisdom as well as his candour.

'Ye look like the devil, if ye don't mind me sayin'.' Angus set down the boot and brush on the window ledge, approached Rory and began helping him out of his overcoat.

Rory chuckled and winced as he twisted his torso to free himself from the woollen sleeves. 'Aye, and I feel it, but it was for a worthy cause. Seems the laird's daughter forgot about one of the most important rules of shooting.'

'Oh?' Angus eyed one of the new grass stains on Rory's coat sleeve.

'She walked headlong into the line of the target and almost got herself cleaved in two by an arrow.'

Angus paused and lifted his brow. 'Surprised to hear a lass raised in these halls is no' aware of such basic rules. Is she hurt?'

Rory shook his head. 'Nay. I pushed her out of the way in time, but I may have bruised a rib or two from the fall.' He winced as he tugged his tunic from his trews and glanced down. A dark purplish splotch was already forming on his side from where he'd landed.

'Is she daft?' Angus spat on the grass stain and scrubbed it in the material along the cuff.

Mrs Moira Fraser had seemed anything but. 'I don't believe so, but she proposed to me, so perhaps she is.' He chuckled and walked further into the chamber decorated with dark wood and the rich hues of burnished reds and bronze that reminded him of the Highlands in autumn. He met his manservant's slack-jawed gaze.

'She…*she* proposed to *ye*? What do ye know.' Angus's eyes widened as if he'd just spied Cook pulling a tray of fresh black buns from the ovens at Blackmore.

'Aye, she did. I had much the same response to her

proposal.' Rory sank into the large chair before the lit hearth. The warmth of the fire and the softness of the cushions soothed his throbbing limbs as it often did at this time of day. He allowed his head to loll back and his eyes to close. The ache in his muscles and joints a dull, rhythmic reminder of the curse he seemed unable to escape and of the limited time he had left to secure a continuation to the McKenna bloodline. Although he'd given up on any chance of happiness after his recent failed engagement, he *could* try to secure his lineage.

'And ye said…?' Angus asked.

Rory smiled. 'I said nothing, and she left. I was a bit shocked.'

'Does she know of yer…erm…difficulties?'

Rory lifted his head and nodded. 'Aye. My imminent death seems my most appealing quality.' He tugged his cravat loose.

Angus stared blankly at him as if stricken by a palsy. Rory hoped he hadn't given Mrs Fraser the same look upon her proposal, but most likely he had.

'Seems she would prefer to marry a man with frailties and a short lifespan. I don't understand it, but it's what she claimed. There was something in the way that she spoke of her first husband that made her appear quite…fragile. It unsettled me. Perhaps he is the reason she desires a husband who will not live long.' He leaned over and tugged off a boot.

The same flicker of protection and concern for her when she'd spoken of her late husband flamed within him once more. The way her features had tightened, and the hesitant pitch in her voice, told him more than any other words could. Her husband had not been the man he should have been. There seemed little doubt on that account, but would he be any better? He'd only become weaker and needier as the illness further claimed his body.

But the selfish, desperate part of him had sung at the feel of her soft, pliant, yet strong frame beneath him when they'd collided to the ground. She might bring him some whispers of happiness in his last few days of life as well as an heir, and his money and clan could protect her. It seemed more than what she had now, didn't it? It was far more than *he* had now to be sure. He tugged off the other boot and let it clunk to the floor. Perhaps they could each be a brief means to an end for their less than desirable situations.

Or he could be making yet another poor decision led by his heart and be on the verge of making an arse of himself over a woman. Again. He frowned. The woman could be barren for all he knew and this a ruse. She'd had no child by her first marriage. This could be yet another bloody trap.

'So, what is your plan?' Angus gathered the boots at his feet.

'I will speak with her further at the gathering for dinner. A private word will help me see how serious she is about her offer to marry. She may be under delusions as to my illness, and I don't wish to have another… misunderstanding.' He gritted his teeth at the memory of Lorna's 'misunderstanding' which led to the end of their brief engagement last spring. Seemed she thought she could marry him *and* carry on with other men. She was mistaken. He cast aside his cravat and ran a hand roughly through his hair. The memory of her limbs wrapped around another man at his own home made his abdomen lurch. Fidelity would be a requirement of his future wife. It was the only thing that could ensure his heir would be legitimate and that the McKenna name would continue on long after him.

'Perhaps a rest before the evening meal, sir?'

Rory sucked in a breath and nodded, trying to quell the cramp that tightened and pulled his stomach. 'Aye. Please rouse me in an hour.'

Rory leaned back in the large chair and propped his legs up on the small bench that acted as a footstool. He closed his eyes and took even breaths as he counted to five. After he reached the fifth round of counting, his abdominal spasm had subsided. He would use this evening to discover the truth as well as the charms of Mrs Moira Fraser. Although she didn't appear to be the kind of woman to keep secrets or be deceptive, he'd been wrong before.

But he wouldn't be fooled again. Even if he was a dying man.

Rory searched for Mrs Moira Fraser everywhere. He'd not had a chance to speak with her all night. They'd been on opposite ends of a long banquet table, and she'd been immersed in the attentions of a Laird Garrick Something-or-other.

After a long, tedious meal full of bland grouse and rather disappointing fig sauce, he needed to speak with her. He'd suffered through the idle chattering of a dull older woman he'd prefer to forget and an additional grating half hour of ramblings from the young MacIntosh lad on his clan's new agricultural plans. He thought the poor sot would never cease talking. The lad was so eager to impress that he didn't realise he'd made an arse of himself by telling a room of lairds and their sons the basic concepts regarding crop rotation they already knew. At least the whisky had helped to drown out some of the words.

Finding Mrs Moira Fraser would make the suffering of the evening worth it. *If* he could locate her in this labyrinth of a castle before the eve was over.

It was as if she had disappeared into the walls of Glenhaven. Was she serious about her offer to marry him? If so, did he wish to propose to her? Neither would be possible to discern if he had to wait until the tournament was over, and by her words, she had less than a day remaining to make her choice of husband. Once again, time was against him.

He scrubbed a hand through his hair and continued down another long corridor, frustration simmering within. Where could she have disappeared to? When the group had reconvened in the Great Hall and she wasn't with the ladies, he thought he'd go mad, right then and there. He had to admit that she was an enchanting prospect for a wife. One that had garnered the gazes from many of the lairds this eve as they dined, and he didn't like their lustful looks one bit.

Which was ridiculous. He barely knew the woman. Perhaps exhaustion was crushing his logic.

Out of the corner of his gaze, a vibrant swath of a

forget-me-not-blue gown disappeared around the corner at the end of the long hall ahead of him. *Moira.*
He recognised the unique shade of blue after catching
glimpses of it all evening. He advanced along the hallway with purpose and speed. Few torches lit the walls
of this rear portion of the castle, most likely because it
wasn't often utilised, so he tried to blunt the sound of
his approach as best he could. He didn't wish to frighten
her away after finally locating her.

The soft tendrils of her voice halted his progress at
the open doorway. She talked to someone in a way he
dearly wished to be spoken to. With reverence, kindness and…something else he refused to name. His pulse
picked up speed, blood thrumming through his body.

'How are you, my dear?' she murmured.

Rory strained to hear the answer, but nothing came.
He clenched his teeth, his muscles coiling tighter. Who
was she meeting here under such mysterious circumstances?

'You are divine, my love,' she whispered.

Or was she meeting a lover?

His jaw clenched. He fisted his hands by his sides.
Had her speech to him earlier in the day been a farce
and she'd already secured a match? Or did she pursue
multiple interests as Lorna had?

He held still, but there was still no answer. Unable
to stand it a moment longer, he inched his head around
the doorway, gripping the moulding until he thought
it might crumble beneath his hold. What he saw stole
his breath.

And confused him.

She appeared to be murmuring with such affection and reverence to…*plants.*

She sat curled up on a dark well-worn leather chair running her porcelain fingertips along the green leaves of seedlings. The small stalks poked through the dark soil nestled in three identical clay pots along the windowsill. Her hair hung in dark curls along her back, down the side of her blue bodice, and danced along her creamy white skin.

The urgency to find her rushed out of him. He was mesmerised. Mrs Fraser continued to surprise him in every way imaginable and beyond even that. And the last thing he wished to do now was invade this private moment. She was so peaceful, serene and…happy. All because of these three little potted plants on a windowsill. It was the most joyful he'd seen her. He felt like a cad for believing her capable of meeting a man for some secret tryst when she had all but proposed to him earlier in the day. She was not Lorna, and he shouldn't believe every woman would be. Inching away from the doorway, he leaned back against the cool stone, letting his heart regain a more regular rhythm. Her sweet humming made him smile.

After a minute, he started off quietly down the hallway to return to his chamber. He was more determined than ever to speak with Mrs Moira Fraser on the morrow. He had to know if she was serious about a future union with him. And whether he wished to make this mysterious woman a proposal to become his wife and Lady of Blackmore Castle.

Chapter Four

The next morn, Rory stepped out of the side door of Glenhaven Castle, and the brisk, biting air filled his lungs with calm, certainty and quiet. He adjusted his dark overcoat collar to shield his neck from the cold. The golden leaves of autumn would be falling soon, and the first snow would be upon them in a few weeks. The serene waters of the loch beckoned him, the foggy mist hovering over the meadow and kissing along its banks.

A bark sounded off in the distance, and he spied a woman playing with a wolfhound along the water's edge. *Moira.* She was out on a morning walk as her maid said she would be. His chest constricted and he opened and closed his hand by his side. *It was now or never.* It didn't matter that most of the household slept and such a private meeting might be seen as a bit untoward.

But if there was a woman who was a bit unconventional, it was Mrs Fraser.

He began his descent to the loch, cutting a silvery path through the heavy dew-covered grass. The unabashed contentment in her movements and her relaxed features made him realise that the woman he'd seen yesterday at the tournament was but a shell of the woman she might be, and he hated whatever had made her that way. He clenched his jaw.

The dog spotted him first, as Rory expected, and the large grey beast galloped towards him barking in alarm and greeting. Moira turned, shading her eyes. Her body tensed and then relaxed. She readjusted her ebony cloak and pulled it around her shoulders as coils of her breath filled the air between them.

'Good morn, my laird. I am surprised to see you so early.' She gestured for the dog to sit by her side, and he did, his tongue lolling out of his mouth as he swiped a haphazard kiss to her hand.

Rory cleared his throat, attempting to regain his purpose. 'Good morn to you, Mrs Fraser. Your maid told me you often take your exercise early. I'd like to discuss your proposal further, since we weren't afforded the opportunity last evening.'

Lord above, he sounded quite rigid and fussy. He frowned and shifted on his feet. Something about the prospect of her refusing him or somehow being wrong about her intentions bunched his reason in knots.

The full smile she gifted him made some of his doubt melt away. 'I am pleased to hear that. I was afraid my rather abrupt mentioning of it had ruined my chance.'

'Nay.' He offered her his arm. 'Care to walk with me while you tell me your terms?'

Her eyes clouded, and she hesitated, biting her bottom lip. She squared her shoulders and then tentatively slid her hand around the crook of his elbow to rest on his forearm. Her hold was stiff, tension resonating through her. He wished to put her at ease, but didn't know how.

The hound ran alongside them, crashing haphazardly into his thigh, before bounding down the hill and sending a flock of starlings scattering into the air.

'Is he yours?' he asked.

'Nay. He is my brother Ewan's, but I adore him. Rufus!' she called.

The hound barked a reply and chased after the birds that had long disappeared. 'Leave the poor dears alone.'

She laughed and her touch lightened along his arm. Rory smiled. When was the last time he felt this relaxed?

He couldn't remember, which made him uneasy.

'Did you enjoy the dinner?' she asked.

'Not really, but that is a reflection of me and my distaste for formal events more than anything else.'

She chuckled. 'Nor did I.'

'You pretended quite well.'

'Aye, as did you.' She stopped as they reached the loch's edge, removing her hand from his arm. Her shoulders rose as she took in a deep breath and released it, crossing her arms against her chest. 'But surely that is not what you came to discuss with me.'

He could have answered, but he didn't.

'You should know that I fear...' She stared out into the distance. 'I fear I will not be a good wife to you. I was never quite as good at it as I thought I'd be despite how much I believed I loved Peter the day we married. I did not enjoy...' She paused again and a flush filled her cheeks. 'Many of my wifely duties. I wish my next marriage to be more contractual, an agreement to serve each other for what we need and require of one another. Nothing else. So, if you would tell me what would be required of me as your wife, before we discuss a possible arrangement any further, I would appreciate it.'

Dear God. She spoke of marriage like it was akin to going before the gallows.

But he'd never been married before, had he? Perhaps it was.

He swallowed hard, holding her turquoise gaze, wanting to be clear, honest, and yet not make things sound any worse than they would be. He cleared his throat, nesting his hands in the pockets of his trews. 'As you know, my main goal in this marriage is to... achieve an heir...before I pass, which, of course—' he paused again, shifting on his feet '—would require your participation. Other than that, and your fidelity to me while I am alive, I am happy to leave you to your own whims to create what happiness you can.'

She studied him, cocking her head to the side. 'You would allow me the choice of where to occupy my time outside of such evening—' she rolled her eyes heavenward '—requirements?'

'Aye. Unless you wished to spend more time with me, of course.' He tugged at the sleeve of his coat. Had he ever had a more awkward conversation? The silence stretched out. But there was more to say and he intended to say it. 'And what are your terms, Mrs Fraser?'

''Tis odd to think upon. No one has ever asked me before.'

'A shame.' How many of her thoughts, ideas and

opinions had gone unexpressed? More than he dared imagine.

She cut her gaze to him. 'May I have my own chambers?'

'Of course, as long as you promise your fidelity. Blackmore is rather large. No concern there.'

Her head lifted a tad higher. 'And may I have a small patch of garden? I have longed to grow my own plants and flowers.'

'Aye.'

She rubbed her hands together, a dare reaching her eyes. 'And may I read whatever I wish?'

Unable to stop himself, he took another step. The smell of her, some combination of rose and dew, tantalised him, drawing him closer still, until he stood but a whisper from her body, his coat brushing along her cloak. He could kiss her right now, press his lips to the soft full pink wonders on her face, and taste her. But he wouldn't, not until he was certain of their arrangement. Certain of her.

'Aye. I've an impressive library,' he answered. 'All of the books are yours for the taking.'

Her eyes glittered in the yawning light, her mouth parting before she shuddered. 'I believe we have an agreement.'

'Well then, Mrs Fraser, will you be my wife?'

Her chest rose and fell, her words falling in a breathy whisper of an answer. 'Aye, Laird McKenna, I will.'

And there it was.

Moira had dreamed of finding herself a husband of

her own choosing before the end of the tournament, and she'd found the perfect one: a man who wouldn't live for long. Yet, now she stood dazed, staring at him, with the sun glowing around his tall form and dark features, as if he were a Celtic god of the past. Now she wasn't sure this union with Laird McKenna was such a great idea. The last thing she wanted was for her next marriage to be complicated by feelings of any sort. It should be a transaction, an exchange of goods and services mutually agreed upon. Nothing more.

Loving a man tended to turn out poorly for her. Her marriage with Peter was proof of such.

'I'd like to speak with your father as soon as possible. Is he early to rise?' Laird McKenna shattered the silence.

She cleared her throat. 'He is, but I will speak with him first, so he knows you are my choice.'

'Then I shall walk with you back to the castle.' He offered his arm, and she accepted it, sliding her hand slowly inside his warmth as she had before. But this time a shiver ran along her arm and throughout her whole body.

'You are chilled to the bone. Here.' He removed his coat and draped it around her. His hand lingered along her shoulder before falling away. Her body tingled from his brief contact. Peter's touch had never made her body awaken in such a way. The scent from his coat cocooned her with every step back to Glenhaven, some heady mixture of mild soap, tallow and a spicy musk that sent her body into another quake.

She hadn't seen this coming. Not at all. Sure, Laird

McKenna was an attractive man, but to have one's body quiver at the slightest touch and smell of him? *Ridiculous.* Perhaps she *should* see a doctor. Could her fall yesterday have affected her sense of smell and nerves? Was such a thing possible? She nibbled her lip. She should ask Ewan.

She imagined her brother laughing aloud at her question. Snorting even.

Or perhaps not.

Surely time would unwind this odd situation, for she didn't wish to be attracted to him or attached in any way, especially if he was not long for this world. They climbed the hill to the castle in silence. Stealing a glance at him, she balked. The man who had seemed so bored and irritated with the world yesterday appeared to be smiling. It was not a broad toothy smile, merely a small upturned quirk of his lip, but a smile all the same. This morn was full of unexpected surprises.

'Moira!' Ewan called to her as he jogged down the castle stairs.

She paused, her body prickling in alarm. Her brother rarely rose in time to break his fast before the sideboard was cleared let alone by sunrise. Something was wrong. Very wrong.

He skidded to a stop in the wet grass. 'My laird.' Ewan nodded a greeting. 'May I steal you away for a moment, sister? It's quite urgent.'

'Is Father unwell?' she asked.

'Nay, nothing like that.'

She exhaled in relief. 'Continue on, Laird McKenna. Once I speak with my father, I will join you in the main hall to break my fast. We can make our announcement then if you wish.'

He hesitated for a moment, but relented. 'Aye. Thank you for the walk, Mrs Fraser. Until then.' She returned his jacket and his fingertips skimmed her own, and she curled her tingling toes in her walking boots.

Lord above. What was wrong with her?

After he'd reached some distance from them, Ewan clutched her by the shoulders. 'Please tell me you have not already secured an arrangement with Laird Death?'

She frowned and squirmed from his hold, straightening her cloak. 'As a matter of fact, I have. We are to be married. He shall even allow me to have my own chambers, and a garden, and I shall read whatever I wish from his library. It will be a fine union as it is an agreement, not some attempt at a love match.'

Especially since it would be brief.

Ewan groaned and scrubbed a hand down his face. 'Blazes.'

'What has happened?'

He slumped forward. 'You must know that it seemed like a grand idea at the time…'

Oh, no. She cringed. Ewan's well-intentioned 'ideas' often left a wake of destruction. Like the irrigator rod that had drowned her seedlings two summers ago.

'Brother, what have you done?'

He chewed his lip. 'If you hadn't been such a bonny lass last night this wouldn't have happened. One could say it was partly your fault.'

'What? I only did what you said. I ignored all of the most eligible lairds, and I allowed Brenna to shove me into a rather too small gown. Those were *your* ideas.' She popped her hands to her hips. 'Now speak. What did you do?'

'I talked at length with Garrick about you after dinner, and after far too many tankards of ale, I might add. It seems he has already spoken to Father and offered for you.'

Moira's heart picked up speed. She was missing something. 'But that should not matter. I have until the end of the tournament to make my choice of a husband and tell Father.'

Ewan pulled at the cuff of his wrinkled coat, avoiding her gaze. 'Aye. He had *originally* agreed to that.'

She batted him on the arm. 'And *why* would he no longer be honouring such a promise?'

'I told him you were considering McKenna. We agreed you might be suffering from some melancholy after your fall yesterday…and that he should decide on a husband for you.' His words rushed over her like ice cold floodwaters.

'Melancholy? Because I selected someone you both did not approve of?' She crossed her arms.

'Nay, because you chose to attach your future to a dying man. Who does that, Moira?'

'A person who doesn't wish to be married in the first place,' she hissed. 'And now, instead of being promised to one man, you have made it so I am promised to two.'

Chapter Five

'Why bother pretending to provide me a choice of husband when all along you and Ewan had planned to make the selection for me, Father?' Moira called out her question even before she'd breached the threshold of Laird Bran Stewart's study.

Ewan hurried after her and grabbed her arm. 'All we want…' he began.

Moira stopped and sent a lifted brow in his direction. He knew better than to grab her in such a fashion.

He let go of her arm and lifted his hands in supplication. 'All we want is for you to be happy, safe and protected. We didn't think you were serious about wishing to marry Laird McKenna. He's *dying*.'

'Why would you not think I was serious?' she countered, whipping around with such speed that her cloak spun out, the heavy fabric pulling her backward. She yanked on the cloak's closure until it gave way and tossed it upon one of the chairs opposite her father.

'I truly thought you weren't thinking clearly,' Ewan

countered, running a hand through his mussed hair. 'With the fall and what it may have triggered and...'

'And what?'

He flushed and dropped his gaze. 'Nothing.'

'Both of you will sit. *Now.*' Father's voice cut through the room. He'd yet to glance up from his ledger. Typical Father.

Moira sat with a huff. Ewan frowned and settled in the chair next to her. It was as if they were eight and ten years old again and being scolded for having a shouting match about who would be first to try Mother's new harp. She had a feeling the answer now to choosing her own husband would be the same answer she had received then.

Not now, Moira. Not yet, Moira. Not ever, Moira.

As in she would never be allowed to make a decision for herself despite being a grown woman of almost five and twenty.

She couldn't wait a moment longer. 'Was this but a ploy to distract me while all of you conspired to pick out the man *you* wished for me to marry? Was even Brenna instructed to dress me in Laird MacLean's favourite frock colour, so I would be more suitable?' Fire burned beneath her skin and she wished to scald someone with it. It mattered not who.

'The door.' Father lifted his gaze to glare upon them.

Moira's shoulders sank as did Ewan's. The closing of the door *never* led to anything good. They met each other's gaze, and Moira sent her brother daggers. His eyebrows gathered in, and he gifted her a pained expression. He attempted to utter something to her before cursing under his breath and rising to shut the study door.

She smiled. At least she had won *that* small battle.

She faced Father and the ire on his face melted the smile from her lips. Shifting in her chair, she squared her shoulders and schooled her features to prepare for whatever unpleasantness was sure to come.

Father rose and stared out the large twin windows that looked out upon the loch. How long he stood in silence, with his arms crossed against his chest, watching the morning sunrise dance along the meadow, Moira didn't know.

'I often wonder what your mother would think of us. What would she say now?' His burr rolled softly into the air as it often did when he spoke of Mother. He faced them, his grey eyes bright with emotion. Agony reflected in his drawn features at the mention of their mother, who had passed before Moira had married, and sorrow burrowed its way into her irritation, loosening her anger.

She studied the lines of her palms, not wishing to dare answer such a question. Her beautiful, petite, fair, soft-spoken mother had always been quite the foil to her tall, dark-haired, brusque father. She had been the constant, steady voice of reason amongst them all. Slow to anger, quick to understanding, and astute to the ways of each of them as if she could pluck the goodness out of them as she did her harp. Her soft lilting voice could silence any argument, and one gentle glance from her could rescue their father from his anger and worry when the clan had faced difficult times. Without her, their family had run adrift more than once. Tradition and her memory moored them together most days. Without

Father, Moira didn't know what would become of them or the clan. Ewan hadn't settled into the idea of becoming laird or husband, Brenna lived in a day-to-day existence unaffected by the challenges of the continued political upheaval that lay rife upon the Highlands and Moira wanted to flee from all expectations of anyone.

They were a fine mess and Father knew it.

Moira sighed and finally lifted her head to discover both of them watching her with interest. She balked. 'What?' she asked.

Father approached and leaned on the edge of his large desk. 'What would you have us all do, Moira? Allow you to throw away your last chance at happiness?'

'Last chance?' She blinked back.

He shook his head and then set his full force upon her, his voice booming under the tufts of his dark beard now peppered with grey. 'Aye, daughter. It is. You are almost five and twenty. And you…' He cleared his throat, focused on a spot off in the distance and continued. 'And you produced no heir for Peter.'

She blanched, feeling the colour and warmth drain from her face. Ewan reached out and squeezed her hand. *The fall.* Her earlier confusion evaporated. Now she understood why Ewan had thought her unsettled from yesterday and what he'd attempted to explain minutes before. She'd had a fall before, one similar to yesterday, but the loss had been much greater. She'd lost the babe she had carried. It had been early in her pregnancy and Peter had not even known she was with child when he'd shoved her away in anger, causing her to fall hard on the castle stairs. When he'd learned what he'd done, what his rage had cost him, he'd left her alone for a time. There were even a few weeks when he had been kind to her. But as all things were with Peter, they did not last. She swallowed her emotion, blinking back such ugly memories and thrusting them deep down, far away, as if they belonged to someone else altogether. She released Ewan's hand and smoothed her skirts before daring a glance at Father.

'You may not wish to acknowledge it, Moira, but this *is* your last chance to secure a union where you will be properly cared for and bring some semblance of honour to the clan by gaining us another ally. Do you understand?' Father's tone had dropped in pitch, but its message still stung.

He viewed her as an old widow, a burden, and almost beyond redemption.

In his eyes, she held little value.

She felt sick.

Her cheeks heated, and she dared a glance to Ewan, who watched her with empathy and concern, his eyes wide and rounded. All traces of irritation erased from his features. *Fool.* She understood now. Ewan hadn't betrayed her in teaming up with Father against her in selecting a husband. Her dear brother had attempted to spare her *this* conversation, this final humiliation, this painful opening of old wounds by manufacturing another outcome their father would approve: a union with Laird Garrick MacLean.

'Then why pretend to grant me any power over my future at all, Father? Such a promise, to be given, and then snatched away...' Her words strained to escape her throat. 'It is a cruelty of its own.'

He shrugged. 'Ewan believed it would help your spirit. I believed you would just yield to my suggestion in the end. You have always done so in the past.'

Had she? Aye, she had.

'Perhaps I no longer wish to.' Her words sounded small and hollow.

He released a hearty laugh. 'Now that we have secured you a match with a fine man and laird, you decide to ignore it to marry some dying man? You cannot be that daft, Moira.'

She pushed up from her chair, her heart pounding in her ears, anger raging through her limbs. This would be it. Her final stand. It was now or never to secure her future, even if it meant disobeying her father. 'Nay, I will not be as daft as to follow your directive again. I almost died by the hands of your choice of husband last time. I will not risk my life to soothe your pride.'

Father stood, slamming his palm on his desk with force, rattling its contents. 'And soon, *daughter*, I shall not care which man I secure for you, but you *will* have a husband before this tournament concludes.'

'Aye, Father, I will. A husband that I so choose, not you.'

'Moira, if you'd just listen,' Ewan pleaded.

'Let her be, son. You'll get nowhere while she's in such a temper.'

'This may be one thing we finally agree upon, Father.' She grabbed her cloak, spun on her heel and headed out of the study.

She would marry Laird Rory McKenna. She would finally create her *own* future.

But how?

She walked down the long hallway, heading to the alcove which led to the outdoors. Fresh air would clear her mind and then she could concoct a plan. The wheels in her mind spun.

All she needed to do was secure her engagement with Laird McKenna while kindly and gently depositing Laird MacLean's attentions elsewhere. Then he would withdraw his intentions and proposal on his own. She sighed. It would be nothing short of a miracle if she could manage it. Lairds were not known for their flexibility or willingness to withdraw from anything.

She huffed out a breath. Of all the foolish things to have happened. Just when she had things as she wished for them to be and had gained a smattering of control over her own future by securing a match of her choosing, Ewan and Father muddled up her efforts.

Moira struggled to wrap her cloak around her while walking at such a brisk pace and, flustered, left it half on and half off, the material trailing behind her on the floor. She thrust through the side door to the alcove with the sight of the outdoors and fresh air just within reach. She had but half a day to create and implement her plan and no firm idea as yet on how to do it. Her cloak tail wedged itself in between the flooring and the base of the open door, pulling her backward. *Blast.* She paused, bent down and yanked with all her might to free herself. The material popped loose, and in her haste to carry on out of doors, she walked backward and right into a man's chest. Strong hands grasped her forearms.

'Oh, I apologise…' Her gaze made contact with the man's own. The blood drained from her face.

Curses.

'Mrs Fraser.' Laird Garrick MacLean smiled at her and nodded. He released his hold and stepped back. Warmth registered in his eyes. He was as genuinely pleased to see her as she was horrified to see him.

She busied herself readjusting the cloak now threatening to spill to the floor. Of all the people to find herself with at this moment. Why could it not have been Laird McKenna she'd walked headlong into?

'Laird MacLean,' she responded in a light tone.

'I am pleased to see you this morn. I enjoyed speaking with you at dinner.' His brow wove concern around his pale green eyes. 'You seem a bit distressed. May I be of help?'

His kindness, so unexpected, left her speechless. She couldn't tell him that *he* was the source of her distress. She floundered for a response. 'I am in desperate need of some fresh air, but I am battling with the closure of my cloak and, in my haste, have tangled myself within it at the door.'

Drat.

It was a ridiculous excuse, but his smile only faltered a moment before he took the clasp in his hands and fastened it for her. 'There. Set to rights, I hope. Let us take some air.' He gestured for her to walk alongside him, and she sighed when the first breeze cooled her cheeks.

'Thank you. You are very kind, my laird.' She swallowed back the emotion thickening her throat. This morn, these past few days, had worn upon her. Tears threatened and she forced them back.

He studied her face. 'I know what it feels like to be thrust into a situation one does not want. I can only imagine you might know something of that as well.' He nested his hands in his coat pockets and his sandy hair shaded one of his eyes as they walked side by side in the meadow.

Her stomach dropped and she stopped walking. His sympathy was her undoing, and one tear raced unbidden down her face.

'I'm sorry. I did not mean to…' He paused, reached for a handkerchief and offered it to her. Something off in the distance behind her arrested his attention as she took it from him. When she heard her sister's captivating laugh, she had a solid guess as to what may have caught his gaze. Perhaps what he'd said just moments before about being thrust into a situation one did not want applied to his attachment to her as well.

The irony of them both being trapped in a situation neither of them wanted almost made her laugh aloud.

She accepted his linen handkerchief and dabbed her cheek. Taking a few deep breaths to calm herself, she stared out at the meadows behind him, where only a hint of the morning fog remained. When she turned her attentions to the castle and the door leading back inside, she saw a flicker of the man she had hoped to wed. Laird McKenna stood watching them from afar at the threshold. The intensity of his gaze sent a flutter through her and she clutched the handkerchief tighter.

Heat flushed her cheeks. How would she explain what had happened with her being promised to Laird MacLean? After all her words of certainty at being able to make her own choice of husband? She was making a muck out of not only her plans but *his* plans as well.

'Ah, I see.' Laird MacLean's words were low.

Moira turned and met his gaze.

'Forgive me. What is it you see?'

'I did not know, Mrs Fraser, that you had already formed an attachment when I offered for you.'

She started and flustered an attempt at a reply. 'I…' She chewed her lip. What did one say? They didn't have an attachment, but an understanding, a business agreement, a verbal arrangement, nothing more. How did one explain that to the other man Father had promised her to? Her mouth closed.

She couldn't.

'You need not explain, as I understand one's heart often attaches itself to an unattainable situation, but I assure you that we will be happy. I will care for you, honour you as a good husband and laird should. From what I know…' He glanced away and a muscle flexed in his jaw. 'From what your brother has shared with me about your first husband, you deserve a good man, and I will be that man, I promise you. You will never have such worries again.'

She sucked in a breath as emotion battled with embarrassment. Who knew what Ewan had told him when he was deep in his cups? Had the poor man offered for her out of pity or a sense of protection?

Brenna approached them, and Moira pressed her

lips into a tight smile. Her sister looked as ethereal as a wood nymph, with her flowing lilac and white gown, and her dark curls loose and bouncing in the breeze. Despite the gown being totally unsuitable for the weather and season, she was stunning, as always. Laird MacLean's eyes softened as he greeted her, and Moira couldn't help but note the catch in his voice as he gave a slight bow. 'Miss Stewart. You look lovely this morn. Are you here to watch the final day of events?'

'Sister.' Brenna smiled at her briefly before turning her full attentions upon him. 'Aye, Laird MacLean, I will be enjoying these final events this morn.' She shivered. 'Although it has become a touch colder than I expected.'

Without missing a beat, Laird MacLean offered her his overcoat. 'Please,' he requested, shrugging out of his coat sleeves. 'I am overwarm.'

Brenna's cheeks flushed as he wrapped it around her shoulders. His lingering glances and touches made Moira sigh in relief. Her escape had just been gifted to her from the heavens. There was a way out for all of them, but as a gentleman, the laird would not seize it unless Moira freed him from his duty.

'Brenna, may I speak with Laird MacLean for just a moment, and then I will send him on to you to watch the events.'

Confused, her sister hesitated but then agreed. 'Of course. Thank you, my laird, for the coat.'

'Aye,' he answered before bowing slightly and facing Moira.

'May I speak frankly?' Moira asked as the plan, her escape, etched its way into her mind even more vividly.

Laird MacLean nodded.

'Why would you offer for me when you are in love with my sister?'

The poor man's features stilled, the colour rising high in his cheeks. He looked away and sighed. Shifting on his feet, he shrugged.

The agony of answering seemed beyond even his own kindness and upbringing. Unwilling to watch him suffer further, Moira stepped closer and dropped her tone to just above a whisper. 'My laird, if you will set me free from your intentions to me, then we will both have what we want, will we not?'

His gaze slipped away and followed the slow movements of Brenna across the field. When he met Moira's gaze once more, he seemed tortured. 'But to allow you to pursue an attachment with a dying man, after all you have suffered. What kind of man would I be?'

She smiled at him. 'A good one. A man who would be allowing me to finally have a choice in my future. I have no desire to be a wife, sir. I find marriage did not suit me. It would be unkind for me to allow you to marry me and keep you from your heart's desire. Do you understand?'

He studied her. 'You are sure?'

She nodded.

After an agonising minute, he answered. 'I will agree to release you from our engagement upon one term.'

'And what is that?'

'You will promise me that if your situation with Laird McKenna changes, even in the slightest, and you are in need of me for protection in any way, that you will send word. Immediately.' His voice was hard, unflinching, and his features tight. 'Do you promise?'

She swallowed hard. Such an offer was unimaginable, but he was a gentleman, a protector, and he seemed unable to offer less. 'I do not entirely understand why you feel so bound to grant me such protections, but aye. I agree to such a term.'

He released a breath. 'Then I release you, and I will tell your father, so you can make your own choice. And I wish you every happiness, Mrs Fraser.'

'And I you, sir.'

With a quick bow, he was gone, and she stood stunned. She watched him disappear through the meadow, walking with ease through the tall grass. His solid, steady form assured of his future. Still clutching his linen handkerchief in her hand, she stared blankly after him. What would it feel like to be so sure, so very certain, of one's future? To know that it bent to your pleasure? She shoved the handkerchief into her dress pocket, determined to find out. Moira turned and stared back towards the castle, eager to find and speak with Laird Rory McKenna, but he was gone.

Where had he disappeared to?

Her stomach dropped and her fingers tingled. What would she do if she suddenly went from having two possible husbands to none? While she might have wished such just an hour ago, now fear had replaced those wishes. Father was desperate to secure her a union. He no longer cared who with, which meant she could end up with a man as horrible as Peter…she swallowed hard…or, heaven help her, worse.

Chapter Six

Rory blanched and breathed in the cool, crisp autumn air outside Glenhaven Castle. He sucked in air through his teeth willing the abdominal spasms to pass. Breaking his fast with a plate of boiled eggs and sausage after meeting with Mrs Fraser this morn had seemed a good idea at the time, but now he wasn't so sure. He wasn't used to such a feast and then seeing Laird Garrick MacLean so openly attending to Mrs Fraser right after consuming such a meal had left him unsteady and uncertain, a feeling he despised. He'd carried on his walk to the other side of the meadow to distract himself and to disappear from her sight while he collected his thoughts and his stomach.

Before the first tournament event of the day began, he had hoped to speak with Laird Stewart to ensure his engagement to Mrs Fraser was secured. But keeping down his morning meal was a requirement for such a meeting. The old man was no fool and from what Rory had heard the laird had a temper. He'd waste no time on a man who was not only dying but casting up his accounts on his castle floors.

Clenching his fists by his sides, Rory swallowed down the sickness which burned the back of his throat. These bouts had become more frequent over the last year. Rory's bitter memories of watching his father waste away to nothing when he was but a boy washed over him in a chilled wave. All the desperate prayers he had spoken hoping his father would be healed. Whispered pleadings with his uncle to explain why his father would never be well. The tears Father had ordered him not to shed after his passing and the promises that he would not have a similar fate still echoed in his ears. Father had been so certain that the curse would stop with him and that Rory would have the life of happiness he and Mother had missed out on.

'Do not worry yourself, my son. You will live the lifetime I have not. Have the brood of babes your mother and I were meant to. Happiness will be yours. Forget about this nonsense of curses. You are strong, Rory, for you are our boy. Our son. This will not be your fate.'

Rory could still feel the trembling, frail fingers of his father lightly touching his cheek, the cool signet ring chilling his skin before his father drifted away from him for ever. A breeze ruffled his coat and Rory shivered. Yet, here he was. A grown man who was sick, anxious and unable to control his body, his health or his future.

Rory swallowed hard. He was a mirror of his father.

Mrs Fraser carried on in the distance into the fields heading towards the next competition where men were readying themselves for the hammer throw. Determination carried her along. He could spy it in the furrow of her brow and rigid, strong set of her shoulders. Her cloak whipped behind her as it caught another breeze. Seeing her with Laird MacLean had thrust an unexpected question upon him. One he'd not really thought upon, mostly because he had not wished to. And he wondered if his father and those McKennas before him had experienced this same moment of hesitation, guilt and uncertainty before they'd met and bound themselves to their future wives.

Did he have the right to bring his sickness and the agony of his untimely death upon Mrs Moira Fraser? While he had felt so certain and sure that he was doing something to help her and fulfilling his duty to secure an heir, was he lying to himself? Was he doing it so he wouldn't be alone in his final days? And didn't a lovely woman such as her, who held hidden sorrows from her first marriage, deserve more?

Aye. She did.

Yet, he'd made a promise to her, and he'd not break it unless she too did not wish to go further in their arrangement.

'Seems you have made quite an impression upon my eldest daughter.'

Rory stilled and then turned slowly. Laird Bran Stewart stood beside him and studied the horizon. Perhaps he'd been watching Rory stare out upon his daughter with questions and concerns about her future as well.

'Laird Stewart,' Rory answered in greeting. 'It is she who has made quite an impression upon me. Mrs

Fraser is a remarkable woman. One that I hope to one day soon call wife.'

The old man sniffed, but continued to gaze far out into the distance as he crossed his arms against his chest. 'What kind of man proposes to a vibrant woman knowing full well he will die, leaving her unable to care and fend for herself?' He turned, setting the full ire of his scowl upon him.

Rory nodded and met Laird Stewart's glare, determined to ask the question he most desired an answer to, although he doubted the man would give it. 'And I wonder what would make a woman, as intelligent, kind and beautiful as she, so willing and so eager to accept *my* proposal. The proposal of a dying man.'

Laird Stewart's brow rose and colour flushed his neck. 'I'd be careful of how you speak of my daughter.'

Rory hadn't expected to hit quite a nerve. His curiosity won over any desire he should have held to please a possible future father-in-law. When the man didn't say more, Rory pressed on. 'I think quite the world of her, sir, despite our limited encounters, otherwise I would not have proposed. I am just unsure of why she wishes to abandon any hope of a more permanent union with a man who could provide her a longer commitment. We spoke openly of my situation, and it seems she finds my limitations the most promising of attributes of all the men at this tournament. It came as quite the surprise, even to me.'

Once again, Laird Stewart stood quiet and resolute as the Paps of Jura, their rippling grey peaks far off in the distance. He seemed just as unwilling to provide answers. 'You need not worry about why she would accept you. She will be marrying Laird Garrick Mac-Lean. Whatever agreement she made with you has no bearing. I am her father, and she will do as I command. She will not wed you. I forbid it.'

Rory smirked. The more agitated Laird Stewart became, the calmer Rory felt. The man was grasping for a way to undo their engagement, which meant Mrs Fraser had spoken with him. He was taking it seriously by being so threatened and determined to undermine their plans. She had pushed forward with their arrangement despite her father's objections. A bit of joy calmed his roiling stomach. 'I was under the impression you had allowed her a choice in who to marry. Was that untrue?'

'Just words,' he answered. 'Like many women, she does not know what is best for her. She chose poorly in accepting your proposal. I will correct her mistake.'

Rory paused before squaring his shoulders, raising himself to his full height, which surpassed the laird's own. 'Since *she* has already accepted *me*, there is nothing to be done or to be corrected. She is a woman of age and her own mind. I wish to marry her as she does me.'

Laird Stewart set an icy glare upon Rory once more. 'Do not underestimate me, McKenna. A half-day remains of the tournament, which leaves me more than enough time to cast you from Glenhaven, undo what she has done, and confirm such a union with a more suitable and hearty man.' He scanned Rory's form and laughed. 'One who looks like they might live through the winter.' He walked past Rory, clipping his shoulder hard with his own.

Rory clenched his jaw, absorbing the outward show of disrespect and challenge, and knowing full well from the glances from the men downfield that they had seen it and perhaps even heard part of their exchange. When his gaze caught Mrs Fraser's own though, he held it and nodded. It would take more than a threat from Laird Stewart to deter him from her and their plan. For the first time in quite a while, he had something and some-one to fight for. While her father might believe her in-capable and uncertain of her own mind, Rory knew it was the furthest thing from the truth.

Just as he knew she deserved to have someone be her champion.

So instead of shirking away at the challenge Laird Stewart had thrust upon him, Rory charged headlong into it. The hammer throw, the final event of the Tour-nament of Champions, was scheduled to begin. He hadn't planned to take part, but now he would. He might not win, but he'd show the laird he wasn't as near death as the old man hoped.

He also wanted to show Mrs Fraser that he would fight for her, for them, for the future they both wished to have, despite how temporary it might be. He strode down the hill towards the circle of men preparing for the event. Rory had changed into his kilt after he'd spo-ken with Mrs Fraser at the loch, as was expected on the last day, and now he was grateful he'd followed suit. While it had been some time since he'd taken part in the hammer throw, he knew he would prefer the free-dom his kilt would allow versus the restriction of his trews when he bent to throw.

Mrs Fraser watched his approach and smiled in greeting. 'Are you to join the games this morn, my laird?'

'Aye,' he answered. 'I had hoped to win the favour of a lass I have had my eye on.' He winked at her, and she blushed before whispering a reply.

'You may have forgotten, but you have already won my favour, for we are still engaged, are we not?' She bit her lip and a ripple of doubt creased her brow.

'Aye, we are, Mrs Fraser...' He dropped his voice. 'For now. Your father seems determined to find you a new match.'

She sighed. 'I'm sorry.' She worried her hands. 'He and my brother are of their own minds and disagree with my choice.'

'I hope to show them that I am worthy of you.'

'You have nothing to prove to me.'

'Perhaps it is for myself.'

'Even so.' She paused and pulled a green ribbon from her hair. She closed the space between them. He felt the heat of her body and the sweet smell of lavender from her dark hair as it rippled in the breeze.

'For luck, my laird.' She wove the ribbon neatly through the silver broach that held his plaid in place at his shoulder, and his chest tightened as if he were but a lad about to earn his first kiss. He had never wanted to be a champion more than this moment, so that he could prove his worth to her, to everyone, and to show her that he was a man capable of protecting her, even if it was from the memories of her past. He longed to give her the hope that she had just given him.

She *believed* in him, a dying man. That he could indeed perform well and impress against a sea of lairds. It had been a long time since anyone had placed their faith and belief in him, and he hoped beyond measure he didn't disappoint her.

He swallowed hard as she smiled at him and stepped away. The horn sounded and the men competing approached the burly man who had run each event. Laird Stewart and the other spectators watched from the side far from the throws, in case one went astray and out of the marked area. Rory scanned his competition. He appeared to be one of the oldest men competing, despite being only three and twenty, and cursed under his breath. The hammer throw was usually a younger man's challenge, but what Rory didn't have in age, he could make up for in strategy.

Most likely, he was one of the few men here who had ever thrown. He was one of the last to throw, and he'd use that to his advantage. Unlike the Braemer, or stone-throw, the hammer-throw required balance. Making four revolutions with the large hammer and releasing it so it travelled as straight as possible to gain distance was no small feat.

The first three men had fair throws and polite claps affirmed they were no threat to Rory. The young Mac-Intosh laird, the youngest of the men here, took his stance. While his turns seemed promising, he failed to release his hammer at the right time, and it went crashing into the trees. An awkward silence followed. Finally, weak clapping commenced and a brief pause was called as a handful of the servants out tending to the guests were gathered and sent into the woods in search of the Stewart hammer.

After it was located and wiped down, the competition resumed. Laird Stewart's son, Ewan, was next. He performed admirably, and his throw earned him top position. The following three men had throws falling just short of Ewan's and then Garrick MacLean walked up to the mark. The sandy-haired man was formidable. Rory could see it in the set of his posture and his eyes. If there was a competitor to beat, it was him. The man completed his turns, released his hammer and a yell. The hammer sailed past even Ewan's mark and skidded into the grass.

Wild cheers erupted from the crowd, and Laird Stewart shouted his support.

Bollocks.

Rory ground his teeth, but clapped Garrick on the shoulder to congratulate him when he stepped away from the throw line. It they hadn't been pinned against one another in pursuit of Mrs Fraser, they might have even been friends. But now they were competitors, which made them enemies. Rory stepped up to the line and stabbed the toe of his boot into the dirt to gain some added traction. He met Moira's gaze. She smiled at him, and he pressed a hand to the smooth ribbon woven into his broach. Whatever pain he might feel tomorrow would be worth her favour today. He returned her smile, settled into a low posture and turned.

After making four revolutions, he set the hammer free, releasing his own groan of effort. His eyes followed the iron maiden in its flight, and he willed it to carry on. *For Moira.* His heart pounded in his chest from the exertion and the desire for it to land, just a thumb's width ahead of Garrick. He didn't need to win by much, but he needed to win.

The hammer landed hard and skidded into the dirt. It stopped right before Garrick's bright green marker of plaid. Rory shook his head and cursed under his breath. Being second would bring him little this day. But he lifted his head and walked over to congratulate the winner.

'Well done, MacLean,' Rory offered, extending his hand.

Garrick shook it, smiling in return. 'You weren't far behind, McKenna. I thought you had me beat.'

'Seems today was to be yours,' Rory answered.

Garrick's voice dropped. 'In the end, I think it is you that has won.' He gestured behind Rory and then left.

Rory turned. Moira had left the crowd of spectators and seemed headed his way. Determination lanced her furrowed brow as if she had decided something. Rory was intrigued to find out what.

'Congratulations,' she offered. Her turquoise eyes shone as clear as a cloudless summer sky.

'Thank you. Second best, it seems, but I gave my all.' He rolled his shoulder. 'I know well that I will feel my efforts on the morrow.'

'You shall never be second best to me, my laird. As I've said before, you have always been my first choice. That shall not change.' She pressed a kiss to his cheek and left.

He stood gobsmacked. A blush warmed his cheeks.

Her outward affection had caught him, and everyone else, it seemed, quite off guard. Even her father seemed at a loss. He merely stared blankly at him and then after Moira as she walked away.

But she lifted her skirts and climbed the hillside with ease as she held her head high and met every gaze.

By God, he had never seen a woman more determined or more brazen. And to risk all for him. And in a moment of panic, he wondered if he had the ability to be the man she needed, the man she deserved for him to be, at all.

Chapter Seven

'Sister! Sister!' Brenna called.

Moira hastened her steps through the grass, ignoring her sister's shouts from behind her as well as the desperation in her voice. A hand clamped around her arm jerking her to a stop.

'What?' Moira demanded, attempting to wrench free of her sister's hold.

Brenna released her and then balked, crinkling her face. 'What *are* you doing? What was *that*?' She lowered her voice, but the judgment in it could not be disguised. 'Kissing a man in public whom you are not betrothed to? No one will wish to marry you now, and you can't possibly wish to marry *him*.'

Moira groaned in frustration and crossed her arms against her chest. 'But I *do* wish to marry him. That was the entire point, sister.' She huffed. 'And we are already engaged. It is Father who stands in my way.'

Brenna froze, her face a pale blank palate.

'Why are you looking at me like that?'

Her sister shook her head. 'Ewan and Father are right. You *have* lost all reason. You are…' She faltered.

'I am what?' Moira demanded, stepping closer. Her heart thundered in her chest. Aye, she'd been impulsive. Aye, she'd done something some might view as reckless, but she'd never felt more alive in her life.

Because she had made a decision and acted on it without fear of the consequences, namely her father.

Brenna's eyes softened and filled with unshed tears. 'You are…unwell. Otherwise, why would you openly choose such misery by marrying a man knowing full well he will die.' A tear fell down her cheek. 'Has losing one husband not been enough?'

Moira's throat tightened. Her flighty sister who never had a care in the world was in tears. Brenna's emotions made Moira shift on her feet. Did they truly think she was unwell? That she could no longer make her own decisions? There was nothing wrong with her. She merely didn't wish the future they chose for themselves. She didn't want a lifelong husband, a family and all of the trappings they desired. All she wanted was to choose her own path, for once.

And she wanted peace. Quiet. Safety. Why could they not understand?

'He is my choice. You, Ewan and Father need to let me make it.' She started from the harsh sound of her own voice and all the desperation and frustration that burst forth from her words.

Brenna stepped back, and Moira continued on through the meadow. She'd not be chastised by anyone, least of all her sister, who knew nothing of the ways of the world, nor of the shackles of marriage.

She reached the steps of Glenhaven quickly, her pace and anger driving her on, and she entered the quiet halls of the castle. She smiled at the fact that only servants remained roaming about since all the guests were out of doors enjoying the fine weather and final hours of the tournament. Her feet carried her to the peace and tranquillity of the one place in the castle where she was never found, never interrupted and, above all, never judged. And before she knew it, she stood at the threshold of the library on the western wing of Glenhaven, where only books, cobwebs and her wee plants resided. She stole a deep breath, revelling in the earthy, musky smell of books and undisturbed air. She willed her heart to slow. Here, she could settle her mind for a few hours before finding Laird McKenna to make plans for their future.

She slung her cloak over the top of a high-backed chair before she sat and curled up in the oversized, sunken worn leather chair she preferred. It was closest to her three wee seedlings that sat perched on the windowsill. Her fingers skimmed their bright green waxy leaves, and she sighed.

'You look as if you have grown even since I saw you last eve, my darlings.' She smiled at each of them and then rested her head on her arms that cradled the top of the large cushions. Would there soon be a day where she could while away a morning in her own garden and a luxurious afternoon of reading all of the books on plants she could find?

A girl could dream. She sighed aloud. Bliss filled her heart with the mere thought of it.

'One day you will be settled in the dirt in the most beautiful of gardens, and there you shall live out your days and grow and live far beyond me.' She gave each pot a quarter turn, so they would have even exposure to the sun's rays.

'I thought I might find you here.'

Moira froze.

She knew that voice. But how could it be? Hardly anyone knew of her hiding place.

She turned and sucked in a breath. Laird McKenna filled the doorway, his hair a bit mussed, and the wind having brought colour into his cheeks. His Adam's apple bobbed in his throat and he swallowed, his full heady gaze taking in the sight of her.

She struggled to untangle herself from the chair and stood, attempting to straighten her skirts. 'My laird. I am surprised to see you. How did you find me?'

'A lucky guess perhaps. May I?' He smiled.

'Aye. Come in.' She knew it was no lucky guess, but his presence stole her reason. She also wasn't sure if he was eager to see her or angry. Men had a changefulness that she couldn't often understand or anticipate. While he seemed kind and reasonable, she didn't truly know him, did she? And now they were alone, very alone, in a far-off portion of the castle.

He closed the space between them and reached out to her. But as he studied her, he paused, letting his hand fall away. A frown replaced his earlier smile. 'What troubles you?'

Everything.

She cleared her throat to give herself a moment before answering. 'Uncertainty, I suppose. While I am quite certain my father and Ewan will be cross with me for what I have done at the fields, I do not know if you are pleased or upset by my actions. And you turning up here unexpectedly has unsettled me. How did you even find me? Only the servants know of my preference for this part of the castle.' She wrapped her arms around her middle and nibbled her lip. Fear began its quiet steady advance, but she commanded herself to hold her ground.

Her earlier bravado had withered away. The old familiar bubbling in her gut began, as it had a thousand times before. She swallowed the acid in her throat and willed her heart to cease its hammering.

He is not Peter. Not every man was, but her body, her mind, had much to unlearn.

For a long minute, he studied her, taking in every feature. His assessment an intense peering in, as if he was climbing inside of her mind, sifting through her thoughts, her feelings, and the moment she felt she could endure not a second longer, he finally spoke.

'Mrs Fraser. Moira.' His hand reached out and brushed her own. She trembled unbidden by the intimacy of his brief touch and use of her given name.

'Whatever the past has been…' He faltered. 'I cannot undo. But I will promise to cherish you and care for you in every way a man and husband should, even if ours will not be a love match. When you showed your promise to me openly on the fields, I could be nothing other than filled with pride and gratitude. To choose a dying man as your husband in front of everyone…to choose me knowing full well of your father's displeasure in such a choice, is no small gesture.'

He stepped closer, so close that she could feel the weight of his plaid pressing into the folds of her skirts, his boot touching the kidskin of her own. The warmth and earthy smell of him enveloped her, and she felt herself softening, leaning into him like one of her tiny seedlings would towards the promise of a few sparse rays of sun. It had been a long time since a man had touched her in kindness and her body longed to be reminded of what that felt like.

He cupped her face, letting his thumb caress her cheek. She expected he might press a kiss to her other cheek. The closeness of his warm breath and skin still cool from the outdoors made her body shiver in delight, rather than trepidation this time. But there was no kiss, only words. Words that stole her breath just the same. 'And while I walk this earth, I will endeavour to deserve you.'

And then he was gone, and she found herself disappointed, and surprised that she longed for a man's touch, his touch.

Steady.

Why had he said such foolish words to her? Perhaps his illness was making him addled.

Rory continued on along the winding maze of hallways back to his own chamber. His body buzzed from his exchange with Mrs Fraser. *Moira.* His mind tripped over all of the questions and concerns now forming. The fear that had shone back at him when he'd found her had gutted him. Whatever had happened to her would take time to unwind. And sadly, time was not on his side.

He needed to return home and secure a path forward for them both. One that allowed her all of the autonomy and quiet she desired while providing him the best chance of achieving an heir before he died. He ruffled his hair. The odds were not in his favour, but now that he'd found her and they'd committed themselves to one another so publicly, he'd not back down. He refused to be another one of her many disappointments.

Another unexpected revelation and rather irritating development. He *cared* for her.

He hardly knew her, yet he wished to give her…everything. They were the fluttering thoughts of a fool caught up in romantic notions, not the cool, calculating thoughts of a laird in need of securing a future for his bloodline. He needed to focus on achieving his goal. Moira was no more in search of a love match than he, and feelings and expectations always brought complications, as if he needed more of those today. It would be challenging enough to find a way for them to marry without interference from Laird Stewart.

Rory threw open the guest chamber door with such force that it clapped back into the wall, and Angus turned from his place near the wardrobe where he was packing Rory's meagre belongings. 'Make haste with that,' Rory ordered, his voice harsher than he intended. 'We will leave at the first opportunity. I've much to attend to.'

'Aye, sir. Has something happened? Has the lass declined?'

Rory frowned. 'Nay. She has accepted, and we have a wedding to plan.'

'Then why do ye look as if you've swallowed butterwort?'

Rory collapsed into a chair and allowed his head to loll back and his eyes to close.

'Laird Stewart has not exactly given his blessing to our union.'

Angus's silence confirmed what Rory already knew.

'Aye. I know. The last thing I needed was another complication, but here we are.'

'Did yer father ever tell ye of how he and yer mother met?' Angus asked.

Rory opened his eyes and sat up. The old man rarely spoke of Rory's mother, and he felt a flutter in his chest when he spied Angus staring into the hearth where a small fire still flickered and flamed. He was pale, his eyes wide, and Rory swallowed to quell the dread creeping along his gut. What other surprises was he in for today?

'Aye. They met at a ball, as I remember.' He steeled himself for whatever was to come next.

Angus faced him while resting a weathered hand along the mantel. 'There was a wee bit more to the story.'

'Go on.' Rory gripped the arms of the chair.

'She was promised to another when they met. A man of greater means and wealth that her father had arranged when she was in braids.' He chuckled. 'I remember going along with yer father to that ball, and the night he met her, I knew he would do everything he could to win her. I'd never seen him in such a state.'

His father? In love? He couldn't imagine it. His father had always been focused, serious, determined. Not emotional or romantic. While he'd always spoken fondly of his mother, who had died shortly after Rory's birth, he'd never shown any of this heady show of affection Angus eluded to now. His father had worked through the days of his life as if he was moving through a list of items that needed to be completed in haste before his demise.

Just like I am.

Rory's chest tightened at the realisation. Angus's next words yanked him from his thoughts.

'He did not tell her of his ailment. He feared the truth would set her afoot, as well it most likely would have. He wooed her to elope with him. They lived in happiness for a while until she realised he was ill.' Angus shook his head. 'Went into a deep quiet after that. The shine gone from her eyes. Ye brought it back though. When ye were born, it was like ye brought the sun and the stars back into her heart. She cherished ye so those days.'

'Before she died?'

'Aye,' Angus answered, his voice so low that Rory almost didn't hear it.

'Well, I have hidden no such truth from Mrs Fraser and she still wishes to marry me. I'm unsure why you told me such a story.'

'Because, my dear boy, a hasty but planned exit and

elopement may serve yer purposes if the father will not yield openly to the union.'

Elopement? 'How could I possibly even get her out of here for such a purpose?'

'It depends on how desperately Mrs Fraser wants out of this castle.'

'I'm listening.'

'There are a handful of servants here who would be more than eager to leave this post if they could be promised future work at Blackmore.'

'And?' Rory rested his hands on his hips.

'So, they might be more than willing to smuggle the lady out through the servant's entrance to our carriage without anyone being the wiser.'

'You suggest I steal my future wife?'

Angus lifted his hands in defence. 'Ye make it sound more sordid than it is. Ye cannot steal anyone or anything if they come willingly.'

Rory shook his head, scoffing at the man's reasoning, one he used oft before.

'Angus, this is not a long-lost ewe that has followed you back to the barn and that you are adding to our herd. This is a woman.'

'As far as I see it, we'd be aiding her escape from a place she no longer wishes to be at. And from the looks of it, she isn't the only one,' he added under his breath.

Rory rubbed his temples and began pacing the room, his boots scuffing the ornate rugs that covered the stone floors. 'This is madness. Why would Laird Stewart not storm Blackmore to bring her back? The man is possessive. Stubborn. And proud. I cannot imagine he would see such actions as anything other than a slight to him. Inciting a dispute with him and his clan, let alone any allies he may have, is not exactly what I had in mind in forging a relationship with a new father-in-law, despite how brief it might be.'

'Any better ideas?'

He sighed and met Angus's stare. 'Nay.'

'Then write her and make haste about it. I will deliver the message to her maid myself.'

'You think she will agree?'

Angus's eyes softened. 'If but half of the gossip I have heard about what has befallen the lady is true, then aye, I think she will come without question. I also know that once ye leave this place today, the laird will not allow ye to return. Seems he has a loftier match than ye in mind.'

Rory didn't doubt a word, but the blunt truth of it still cut like a dirk to his chest.

If it was now or never, then he would choose now and seize his moment, no matter how brief and flickering it might be.

'Give me but a minute, then,' he answered. Rory settled in at the writing desk and gathered parchment, ink and a quill ready to draft the first note to his soon-to-be wife. His fingers tingled as he gripped the quill. What did one say upon such a note when so much depended on her agreement?

He scratched the first word of his message with certainty. He would tell her the truth. Well, most of it anyway.

Chapter Eight

Moira sat curled up in her favourite reading chair in her chamber, trying desperately to focus upon the words of the page on the history of violets she'd reread several times now. Laird McKenna's words and the memory of his touch in the library just the hour before still had her in knots. She wasn't entirely sure why, but there was no disputing the man had an effect on her. She frowned. Was that good or bad? She desired a marriage of convenience and solitude. Feelings and expectations only led to disappointment.

She snapped the book shut and set it on the nearby end table. *Disappointment.* A feeling she knew well. Father had already expressed his displeasure at her actions. She'd been fetched from her quiet, peaceful reverie in the library by poor Enora, her lady's maid, who told her she had been ordered to bring her to her chamber, where the laird bid her to stay for the remainder of the tournament.

She'd been locked into her room as if she were a petulant child.

She pounded the armchair in frustration. She was no child, even if she felt like acting like one right now. Father had no right to order her to do anything. She was a grown woman with her own mind and her own choices to make, no matter what he believed.

The outer chamber door of her rooms opened quickly. Sweet Enora, who had been off seeing to the repair of her grass-stained gown from the day before, scurried in and then closed the door securely before clicking the lock in place. The poor lass looked behind her as if she were being chased by the devil himself before she continued on through the chamber, rushing to Moira's side. Brushing aside tiny pale strands of hair that had escaped her linen headpiece, Enora clutched the arm of Moira's chair. Panting out a breath, she pulled correspondence from her apron pocket and pressed it into Moira's hand.

'What has happened?' Moira asked, sitting up straight. Enora's odd countenance sent Moira into high alert. 'You look as if you've seen Nan's ghost.'

'Nay, miss.' She chuckled at Moira's reference to the old folktale. 'The laird has sent word.' The young girl's blue eyes were wide and her breath uneven.

Moira sighed. 'What does my father command of me now?'

'Nay, not from yer father. It is from Laird McKenna,' she rushed out.

Moira's heart faltered. 'Laird McKenna? Has something happened?' Her nerves pricked to attention. Had he changed his mind or been forced to by her father? She knew just how persuasive he could be.

'His manservant gave it to me directly. Asked that I give it to ye meself and await yer answer.' She stood with her arms behind her back and nibbled her lip.

Moira stared at her maid dumbfounded. What could he possibly be writing her about when he was still within the castle walls?

'Well, hurry,' she urged. 'Please read it, miss! I can take no more.' She shifted on her feet.

Moira started from the urgency in Enora's voice and hurriedly opened the letter.

My dearest Mrs Fraser,

My manservant has told me of your father's plan to keep me from you once I depart today, so I have a bold proposal for you to consider: escape and elopement.

We have a way for you to leave with us unseen, but only if you wish it. And if you dare not risk such a scandalous and hasty separation from your family, I understand, but I cannot ensure that I will be allowed to return to Glenhaven and wed you formally as I had hoped.

It seems not everyone is so eager for you to accept a dying man's proposal.

Yours,

Rory McKenna, Laird of Blackmore

'Lord above,' Moira murmured, allowing the letter to rest in her lap. The man couldn't be serious. Elope? As if they were vagabonds, criminals or lovers, but they were none of those things, were they?

'What does it say?' Enora asked, energy bubbling out of her.

'He has asked me to elope with him.'

Enora froze. 'Elope? Why?'

'Father has forbidden him to return, it seems. His manservant overheard some exchange between Father and one of his men.'

'But if ye are engaged, he cannot object, can he?'

'Aye. As my father and laird, he can.'

He can do whatever he wishes to, unlike me.

'Once Laird McKenna leaves, I will not be allowed to see him again and our engagement will be nullified by Father. It will not matter what words were spoken between us.'

'What will ye do? What message shall I relay?'

Moira's heart pounded in her chest. This was the moment she had dreaded, yet desired since Peter's passing. She had been given a chance to take the reins of her own future, but she had to be brave enough to seize it. Finally, the choice was hers. She swallowed hard.

Would she falter or take that first step forward?

'Give me a quill and ink as well as that parchment, Enora. I will add my answer.'

Rory paced his chamber. By all that was holy, what was taking so long? He ruffled his hair and tugged at his cravat. If they were to leave unseen, it had to happen sooner rather than later. Time, like usual, was not on his side. He frowned. A knock sounded from the outer door, and Angus hastened to open it. Rory froze. Surely, this was his answer.

He squeezed his eyes shut.

Be brave, Moira. Be that brave, fearless woman I have seen glimpses of.

The door closed and Angus rushed to him, handing him the same folded parchment he had sent to Mrs Fraser. The seal didn't even appear broken. 'Did she even read it?'

Angus smiled. 'Open it.'

Rory broke the wax seal and opened it, noting the added heaviness of it.

'Clever lass. Her maid said her missus added her reply below yer own and affixed the seal atop her own, so that if one of her father's men seized it, it would appear unopened and unread.'

Rory shouldn't have been as surprised by her intrigue, but he was. She was indeed clever. He scanned the letter and discovered her script curling like flowery vines beneath his own.

Name the place and time. I will be there.
M

Those nine little words made him light on his feet and his fingers tingled. She had said yes. She was coming with him after all. Why had he doubted her? She was no wilting primrose. He'd do well to remember such.

He grinned over at Angus. 'Ready whatever remains, and notify those eager to leave that they have a position at Blackmore if they choose it. It seems Mrs Fraser has more gumption than even I believed. She has agreed to elope with me. We just need to name the place and time.'

Angus clapped Rory on the shoulder. 'What did I tell ye?'

'You believed it far more possible than I. If I didn't know better, I'd say you were a hopeless romantic.'

Angus shrugged. 'It wouldna be the worst name I've been called in my time.'

Rory chuckled and the hope that had been so long out of reach was within his sights. He'd not lose it. 'And your plan for stealing my bride in the full light of day?'

'Simple.'

He scoffed. 'I doubt such a feat will be simple.'

'It will be if we create one hell of a distraction, my laird. And I know just what will put Laird Stewart at odds.'

'Oh?'

'He has a love for good horseflesh according to his men, so if the barn doors were to be left adrift and his favourite stallions and mares sent loose, well, that would turn his head.'

'You believe he would leave his home and go in search of his animals with his guests during the last few hours of his tournament where he hopes to secure a husband for his daughter? I cannot imagine him to be such a man.'

'There's only one way to find out,' Angus answered with a full smile, revealing the gap between his front teeth.

'And if you're wrong?'

'We'll create an even bigger distraction.'

'Such as?'

'Ye will know it when ye see it. Bid the lady be ready at the front of the castle in an hour. Hopefully she can pack quickly. I'm off to enlist the servants' aid in liberating the laird's animals.' Angus winked and hurried off before Rory could ask any more.

Rory scribbled the time and place on the letter and folded it over before handing it back to Mrs Fraser's lady's maid, who waited just outside the chamber door.

She bobbed a curtsey and disappeared down the long corridor in haste. Rory hoped an hour would be long enough for Mrs Fraser to prepare for a rather hasty and most likely permanent departure.

Rory shouldn't have doubted Mrs Fraser's readiness to leave Glenhaven. She stood at the top of the castle steps holding a single embroidered bag in her hands staring out at the drive awaiting his arrival. If he didn't know better, he would have thought her awaiting a carriage after a ball. She was poised, quiet and certain—all qualities he failed to possess at the moment.

As he approached, her shoulders rose as if she sensed him from behind without even seeing him. He stopped by her side and smiled down at her. 'So far, so good,' he whispered. 'Where is everyone?'

It was quiet. No servants were afoot and no carriages, except for his own, were stationed in the drive that made a smooth arc before the castle steps.

She turned to face him. 'It looks as if someone left the barn door ajar. Horses are on the loose and livestock is everywhere. *Tsk. Tsk.* Only we remain. Everyone else is out assisting my father in hopes of securing greater favour. Well, except for us.' She chuckled. 'Quite a ploy, my laird. I almost find myself enjoying such a ruse.'

'Shall we?' he asked, offering his arm, uncertainty banking in his gut. They had come this far, but doubt still courted him. Was he doing right by her? Did he have the right to let her make this choice? Choosing him and running off in such a way would damage her relationship with her family. One she would need to depend on when he was gone.

Guilt wracked his body.

She released a breath, tucked her arm through his own and smiled. 'Aye. I am.'

'Sister!' Ewan called from behind them, panting.

Confound it.

Rory clenched his jaw. They'd been so close. A few more moments and they would have been on their way without incident.

Moira paused. Her arm went rigid in his own, and Rory held his breath.

'Aye, brother?' Her words were high and brittle, but her face held no emotion.

'Where are you going?' His breath came out in spurts as if he had traversed the whole meadow in a sprint. Perhaps he had spied them while out looking for those escaped animals.

Her gaze flitted to Rory, her brother and back to him again.

'With me,' Rory answered. His words were far more cool and even than he felt, which he was grateful for.

Ewan balked and made a sour face. 'Why?'

'I have proposed to her, and she has accepted.'

Ewan's crinkled brow eased. 'Then stay. Let us celebrate together.' He gestured back to the castle.

'Brother, Father will not allow us to marry, you know that. I either leave now and we elope, or I continue to be prisoner in these walls and married off to another. And I choose the former.'

Ewan's eyes widened. 'You know how Father will react,' he stated.

'Aye.' She held her brother's gaze and squared her shoulders. 'But I still choose this.'

If she had physically slapped him, Ewan could not have appeared more stunned. Her brother blinked back at her. 'You choose him over us? Over family?' he faltered. 'Over me?'

Moira's grip on Rory's arm tightened, and he placed a hand on top of hers to try to will her his strength. 'It is not like that, brother. Do not make it so.'

'You know Father will forbid us to see you.'

'But you do not have to yield to his commands. You will be laird soon. You can make your own decisions. We will only be estranged if you choose it.'

He shifted his gaze to Moira, his eyes softening on her. 'If you change your mind, sister, I will come for you. Always. Just send word.' He hesitated, perhaps hoping for a change in heart from her.

'You will always be welcome at Blackmore,' Rory added tightly, despite the growing sense of protection and irritation he was beginning to feel. Her brother had no right to put her betwixt them.

Ewan glared at him. 'Perhaps I will take you up on

your offer to visit, long after you are dead.' He turned on his heel and left them.

Rory started after him on instinct until Moira tugged him back, tears filling her eyes. She blinked them back and met his gaze. 'He is going in to find help to stop us. If you still wish to leave, we must go now.'

Her turquoise eyes pleaded with him, and he reminded himself that he had promised to care for and protect her. Her family was of little consequence for now. This was their window of escape, and they had to seize it.

'My laird,' Angus called from the drive, holding the carriage door open.

'Aye,' Rory called to him and nodded. 'Then let us go. At once.' He lifted the bag she carried from her hand and escorted her down the steps.

He began to hand off the small satchel to one of the drivers to be settled in the back where all of their bags were stacked and tied through, but she pressed a hand to his arm. 'Please. May I keep this with me?'

The emotion in her voice caused him to pause, smile and return it to her. 'Of course.'

'Yer other belongings, Mrs Fraser?' Angus enquired.

'My maid has packed all I require.'

'Just the one satchel and trunk?' he asked, lifting his brow.

'Aye. The rest can remain.' The tightness in her jaw and set of her chin told him there was far more meaning in her reply.

She sniffed and forced a smile as she accepted Angus's hand and stepped up into the carriage. Rory followed suit and settled into the bench seat opposite her. When the carriage door closed, and the horses settled into a smooth cadence, Moira sat back and sighed.

'I thought you were mad to suggest such a hasty departure, and I had every reason to believe it would never work. Yet, here we are on our way,' she said wistfully.

'You will soon learn that a man like me who has a finite amount of time makes a habit of getting things done quickly.'

'I suppose you have a point.' She stared out the window, her eyes following the landscape as the carriage continued to pick up speed. To his surprise she never looked back to Glenhaven on the long winding drive out of the castle grounds, not even once. She only looked forward.

Chapter Nine

Surely she had lost all reason. Why else would she be fleeing with a dying man in broad daylight to marry him when marriage was literally the very last thing she wished to ever do again?

Perhaps Ewan and Father *were* right. She was being rash in suddenly affixing herself to this man whom she did not know, but her gut told her she was doing the right thing. Leaving her future in the hands of her father and brother seemed reckless, especially after her first attachment. She squared her shoulders. And while it had been some time since that quiet voice within herself had been loud enough to hear, she wanted to listen to it again and trust herself and her judgment. If this were to fail, she wished to be the cause and blame of it. She no longer wished to be the dutiful daughter following commands, especially when none of those commands had her best interests at heart.

If only Ewan could understand. But how could he? He would never know what it felt like to be her. He was a man and a man had options. As a future laird, he had options in spades. Moira's heart pulled at the memory of Ewan's face when he had pleaded with her on the castle stairs. Why couldn't he understand that *this*, this man, was her chance at the life of peace and quiet and solitude she craved? She could be married, have the protection of his clan and his people, and then after his…demise, she could pursue the remainder of her days whittling away in her garden, in the library, and choosing her own pursuits. The mere thought of such a future filled her with hope. A feeling she had not had in quite some time.

A feeling she had missed. She clutched her bag tightly and then cringed, relaxing her hold. If she wasn't careful, she would crush the wee things.

She glanced up to find Rory studying her with a rueful grin. He pointed to her bag. 'Shall I ask what it is you guard with your very life? Family jewels perhaps?'

A nervous laugh escaped her lips. What would he think? Did she dare show him now? Perhaps she should wait until after they were wed to be sure he didn't change his mind.

'You will think me mad.'

'Then that shall make two of us.' He winked and leaned forward, his knee pushing into the folds of fabric of her gown, eliciting a tiny trill of awareness. The heat of him had an oddly comforting and terrifying quality, which she couldn't quite yet manage. Although she knew she should pull away and create more distance between them, her body craved the gentleness that emanated from him. A kindness she didn't understand, truth be told, but one she wished to.

But if they were to be married—and they were at this juncture, weren't they?—she might as well attempt to *begin* in truth. 'Try not to laugh.'

'I promise,' he answered, pressing his lips together in a thin line, his mirth replaced by an earnest attempt to be serious.

She lifted the metal closure and opened the bag, so that he might see within. The sight and smell of her sweet leafy babes snug side by side in the makeshift box carrier without a frond out of place made her sigh in bliss. They hadn't suffered from her hurried packing or from her clutching them for safety as they'd begun the journey.

He leaned closer, so close that his form shadowed her tiny plants. After seeing them, he lifted his head, met her gaze and smiled. Deeply. Her whole being tingled in response. His lips and mouth mere inches from her own.

'You never cease to surprise me in the very best of ways, Mrs Fraser.' He reached out and ran a fingertip gently over one of the green fronds, and she sucked in a breath as if he had stroked her own cheek.

Why did he affect her so?

She swallowed and tried to think of what to say. Absolutely nothing came to mind, so she dropped her gaze and stared back down at her beloved plants. 'I could not bear to leave them.'

'Then I am glad you brought them. We will find a special place for them at Blackmore until a proper greenhouse can be built for you come spring.'

'Greenhouse?' she stammered. 'You would build such for me?' Could he possibly mean it? The carriage wheel hit a hole and jostled them within. Both of them reached for the bag to steady the plants, his hands covering her own. The feel of his strong, certain, capable fingers on hers eager to protect what *she* cared about most in the world sent her heart hammering in her chest.

'Have you got them?' he asked.

'Aye. Thank you.'

He eased his hands away, and she realised she hadn't minded his touch.

'How long will it take to reach Blackmore?' she sputtered out, eager to distract herself from her thoughts or what they might mean.

'We will be home before nightfall. It is but a few hours northeast of here along the shore near Oban. Perhaps you've been there before?'

'Nay. This will be the farthest north I have ever travelled. What is it like?'

He stared out the window and an easy, soft wistfulness came into his eyes and the lines in his brow melted away as if the mere thought of his own home transported him there.

'In a word, lovely. It is a short distance from the coast. It sits high upon the hillside and overlooks the sea. The sunsets are beyond compare. I believe you will find it quite pleasing.'

'It means a great deal to you and your uncle.'

'Aye.' He faced her then.

'Will he be surprised by our arrival?' She hadn't even thought about whether anyone would even be aware of them coming. And, more importantly, would they be pleased about it?

'Aye. I sent word by messenger ahead of us. Uncle will be expecting us. I must warn you that the household will be turned upside down with excitement upon your arrival, especially since I gave them such little notice. I hope they do not overwhelm you. They have long been in hopes of having a lady to grace the castle walls.'

'I hope to meet their expectations.'

As well as yours.

'I am quite certain you will achieve that in spades. And Uncle will find you most intriguing. I will be curious to see what you think of him.'

'That's a mysterious statement to drop without explanation. Anything I should be warned of?'

'Nothing you can't manage. He's just a bit eccentric, but he has a propensity to some of the things I know you adore.'

'Such as?' she asked, curious to hear what he believed he already knew about her preferences.

'Hounds and books.'

She laughed aloud. 'Then I believe I shall get on with him quite well.'

Truly, she hoped she would too. She had many questions about this mysterious uncle and what his claim might be for the lairdship. Could he be as kind and driven to serve his nephew as he appeared to be, especially when he could just seize the lairdship himself with Rory being so ill? Would it matter if he was illegitimate if no other heirs remained?

'I will give you a grand tour of the grounds tomorrow once you have rested. You can also begin thinking of where you would like your guests to stay.' He nodded to the bag that held her beloved plants.

'I would like that. And Enora? Will she be joining me?'

'Aye. I took the liberty of extending an invitation to her and a handful of other servants who seemed less than eager to continue their employ with your father. They shall be joining us on the morrow. Angus has arranged for their transportation.'

'What?' she stammered. Father would not be pleased. 'Did you bribe them?'

'Nay.' His brow furrowed. 'They were eager to help us in our ploy to aid our escape and I wanted to ensure they had employ afterwards. I had a suspicion they would be cast out as soon as your father discovered their role in your hasty departure.'

'Aye. They would have been. Thank you for looking after them.' Rory was unlike any laird she had ever met, and it confused her beyond measure. He was worried about servants he'd never met.

'I also hoped seeing a few familiar faces might bring you some comfort. If it unsettles you, I'm sure we could make other arrangements for them.'

Another unexpected kindness. She worried her hands along the closure of the bag. 'Nay. I am pleased they will be joining us. I am just surprised.'

'Oh? By what?'

Why was he being so nice? So kind? Was he like Peter and this was a trick? Had she merely traded the past for an identical future of uncertainty?

'What has you worried? I can actually see the thoughts

moving across your brow.' He made a line across his forehead with his finger, teasing her.

'Your kindness is, well, unsettling to be honest. It makes me worry that there are more expectations involved in this marriage than I was aware of.'

Or that you have a changefulness like Peter. One I cannot see just yet.

'Nay. Only those we discussed before. Nothing has changed. I would not deceive you, Moira. Despite what you might believe, women are not tripping over one another in haste to marry me.'

She nodded and chuckled at his self-defacing humour, but she still wasn't sure. She wanted to believe him, but she'd believed once before and been very, very mistaken.

'Although we should discuss *when* you wish to marry. I know a more formal wedding similar to the one you had in the past is no longer possible, but I do wish to make it a happy day for you. What is it that you would like? And is there anyone you wish to invite? I know your family may not wish to attend, but if there are friends you have that might wish to come.'

Her throat dried and she fidgeted with the closure on the bag once more. *Fool.* Of course he would want to know when, so they could begin that task of…begetting an heir, but she'd had less than a moment to think upon it. She shrugged and risked the truth once more. 'Since we have been engaged less than a day, I suppose I have not given it much thought. And I lost touch with most of my friends after I married years ago.'

He studied her. Heat flushed her face. She was grateful he did not ask as to why that was, so she didn't have to explain.

He nodded. 'You make a fair point. Well, have a think upon it and let me know.' He settled back deeper into the seat, his boot sliding forward on the floor and up against her own. The slight friction a welcome anchoring to the present to remind her she was really here with him embarking on a new future.

One of her own choosing, and the realisation of it made her heady with excitement. She smiled and tied back the small curtains on the windows further, and the warm, bright sun streamed in the windows.

'Beautiful, isn't it?' he murmured, staring out along the rolling hillside. They were travelling northwest towards the coast, the hillsides climbing higher with each passing minute. It was gorgeous. Even in the autumn, the hillsides were alive with heady greens, golds and shades of auburn. She'd forgotten the beauty that lived outside the walls of Glenhaven. It had seemed the only beauty within those walls had resided in her plants.

'Aye. Odd, really. I just realised I have not been this far from Glenhaven since I returned over a year ago. I have no idea why.'

Why had she never left?

'Grief has an odd way of wrapping its tentacles around you. I would not question it too much.'

Grief? She almost laughed aloud at his suggestion. She squirmed in her seat instead. If Laird McKenna only knew. She had shed tears of *joy* at the escape Peter's death had granted her, not tears of sorrow at his passing. Perhaps that made *her* the devil, rather than her late husband?

She rubbed her forearm and studied a tiny pull on her cloak. She fiddled with the thread and wondered if her cloak would unravel completely if she tugged upon it, much like the truth of her relationship with Peter if she were to share one morsel of the real aspects of her sordid marriage with her future husband, Laird McKenna.

Glancing up, she was startled by the full, assessing gaze of her soon-to-be husband and felt the flush of heat rise once more from her neck into her cheeks. She said nothing but held his pensive stare. He wished to say something, ask something. She sat frozen like a deer awaiting his words, hoping they wouldn't smite her in two.

'As a man with my own secrets, I want you to know that I respect yours. But I also want you to know that I would not judge you if you chose to share them with me.'

Her eyes filled suddenly, unexpectedly, and she looked away to blink the tears back. 'Thank you, Laird McKenna.'

He chuckled. 'Perhaps now that we are to marry you could endeavour to use my given name and I yours?'

'Aye.' She smiled. 'Thank you, Rory.'

The more time he spent with his future wife, the more Rory realised he was completely out of his depth. He watched the gentle sway and pitch of her upper body as the carriage rolled along its way trimming the distance between her past and her future. What woman would be so at ease with such a drastic change in her circumstances in such a short time? What woman cared more for the welfare of three potted plants than the rest of her belongings that remain hitched to the outside of the carriage?

This one.

But who was she? With every answer he gained, twelve more questions edged their way into his mind begging to be asked.

'Tell me more about Blackmore,' she asked, and he cut his eyes to her.

'Not a great deal to tell, really. It is like most castles of its age. Large, a bit draughty, and full of stories and heritage. It has been the heart of Clan McKenna for centuries. Since it is along the coast, many of our clan make their living farming, fishing and mining for slate. Perhaps a bit more rugged terrain than you're used to, but other than that I think you will find it comfortable and comparable to your own home. I know you'll love the wildflowers and plants that grow along the hillsides. You can see them nowhere else.'

'Then perhaps a hillside shall be the perfect spot for our vows.'

'Outside?'

She shrugged. 'I have never been married outside. It shall just be us and those needed to witness our hand-fasting and declarations, I suspect. But if you prefer a chapel, perhaps you could—'

He reached out and squeezed her hand. 'Nay. The hillside shall be perfect. I know just the spot as long as the weather cooperates.'

She stilled and slid her hand from his, and a blush warmed her cheeks. He would need to take great care with her. Now, if only he knew how to do that. He wasn't exactly practised in caring for people. He didn't really have friends any more as he'd pushed them away to protect them. He knew the agony of loss and he wished to keep them from it if he could. And, well, most of the people he had ever loved had died.

Just like he would soon.

And what would become of her?

He shoved the thought away. He cared not to think about leaving her when he'd just found her.

He scrubbed a hand through his hair. He needed to watch himself. Feelings, caring for her, was *not* part of his plan. Gaining a wife, producing an heir and leaving Blackmore with some sort of a future was what he needed to focus on. Everything else was just a distraction. One a dying man like himself didn't need.

Chapter Ten

'Moira?' Rory's voice and a gentle touch to her shoulder jostled her to wakefulness. 'Moira? We are almost there.'

Good heavens. Moira squinted and blinked open her eyes, startled and confused. Where was she? Slowly the earlier memories of the day snapped neatly into place and she remembered. She was engaged to be married to this man and headed to Blackmore. She struggled to sit upright. When and how had she fallen asleep? She wasn't one to ever be lulled to sleep along a bumpy journey, yet here she was. She attempted to smooth her skirts and noted her lap was barren. Where were her plants? She scanned the small compartment.

'Don't worry. I've kept watch over them.' Rory smiled and patted the seat next to him where her bag of plants sat carefully nestled between him and the carriage door. 'When you fell asleep they began to slide, and I didn't want to risk them falling.'

'Thank you,' she murmured, rubbing her eyes. What

a picture she must paint. 'I'm sorry. I'm not prone to falling asleep in carriages.'

Especially with a man who is little more than a stranger, even if he is to soon be my husband.

'It has been no ordinary day. I will admit that I was envious of how soundly you were sleeping.'

Heavens, what he must think of me.

She could only hope she hadn't dozed off while he was speaking to her in mid-sentence. The last thing she remembered them speaking about was Blackmore.

She patted her hair, which was now a bit mussed, and grimaced. And she'd be meeting his household in minutes. *Ack.*

'You look absolutely perfect. You need not worry.'

'I'm sure I look something quite short of perfection, but thank you.'

'Here we are.' A full smile lit his face and eyes as he pointed out in the distance to a large dark towering castle that rose like a phoenix from the grassy hillside surrounding it, emerging as if it were part of the cliffs itself.

Whatever Moira had expected Blackmore to be, this was not it. It was absolutely stunning and larger than any castle she had ever seen. She couldn't help but gasp at the sheer size of it.

Heavens above. Two Glenhavens could fit within it and have a touch of room to spare. She swallowed hard. 'You didn't tell me your estate was quite so…expansive.'

'Well, it wasn't originally so large, but over the years there have been additions and improvements.'

The driver slowed as they eased their approach to

the castle. There were no cobblestones along the drive, but a smooth, level sheet of rock perfectly fit together. She marvelled at how she could scarce tell they were even moving. How long it must have taken to level out the dirt and create such an exquisite entry she couldn't imagine.

'Is there a village below? I haven't seen any other cottages or buildings.'

He chuckled. 'You were sleeping as we rounded many of the cottages that sit tucked in along the hill-side and the village proper. There are also extensive pathways that lead from the south end of the property to the larger farms as well as the mine below it.'

'I'm sorry to have missed it.'

'You'll have plenty of time to see everything. Do not worry yourself.'

She marvelled at the beauty of the trees, shrubbery and plants that framed the castle walls. The leaves were burnished and turning, casting a golden glow amongst the dark castle stone. 'It must be absolutely gorgeous in the spring and summer when all is in bloom.'

'Every season has its own beauty. I believe you will favour them all.' He met her gaze. 'Welcome to Black-more, your new home, Moira.'

Home.

Her chest tightened. She never thought she'd have a home other than Glenhaven after Peter's death, yet here she was about to be mistress of this huge, sprawling estate. 'Perhaps I should pinch myself to ensure I am not still dreaming.'

He chuckled. 'I assure you that you are awake and

that this is no dream, merely your new life. One that I hope will bring you some joy and happiness.'

The carriage rolled to a stop and before she could respond, a young servant opened the carriage door.

'Mrs Fraser.' He bowed and offered his hand.

She smiled, accepted his hand and stepped down from the carriage. Soon that would be a name long forgotten, as a part of her past would be, or so she hoped. She was ready to let Mrs Fraser fade into the mist and embrace a new version of herself and eager to become a McKenna. Perhaps as a McKenna she would be the Moira and the woman she'd always hoped to become.

The line of servants was impressive, and their friendly, flushed faces brought a smile to her lips. While she was horrid with names, she was wonderful with faces. She'd learn them all and their duties in due time, and she was grateful that they seemed as eager to meet her as she was them.

Having greeted all of the Blackmore household staff, she took hold of Rory's offered arm and walked with him side by side up the ripple of stairs that graced the large, wide doors of her new home.

'Everyone here is quite warm and lovely,' she murmured to him.

'We are a bit more informal here and many of our staff are from families who have been serving Blackmore for generations. For what we lack in longevity within our own line, we have in loyalty from those who serve our family. I'd dare say they view you as a precious and welcome addition. As do I.'

She tightened her hold on his arm as a flush of happiness warmed her. It was quite the contrast to the rather cold welcome she had received when she had joined Peter's household. She almost wished to pinch herself to wakefulness as she crossed the dark, smooth stone floors which swallowed the sound of her footfalls.

The main hall was impressive and quite taste-fully decorated. Colourful tapestries dotted the walls amongst paintings of what she would only assume were past McKennas who had graced the castle before her. One portrait arrested her attention and she paused. A woman with flowing auburn hair sat resting under a tree reading a book. She was surrounded by lush greenery and a sea of purple heather that almost seemed to be in motion behind her.

'My mother,' Rory stated, emotion filling every syllable.

'She is beautiful. I almost feel like she is here.'

He nodded and smiled to her. 'I have oft thought the same. I will not reveal how many hours I have spent staring upon it over the years.'

Moira squeezed his arm. 'I do not blame you. She is absolutely captivating.'

A door slammed from the other end of the castle and a loud cacophony of barking sounded, jarring Moira from the moment. Rory bent down to whisper in her ear. 'Maintain that tranquil peaceful thought. You've yet to meet my uncle and his many hounds.'

She relaxed her hold on his arm and chuckled. 'I wondered when I would get to meet him.'

Nails clicked along the stone floors and around the corner came a trio of wolfhounds in a full sprint.

'It seems you shall meet them all at once.'

'Cease!' an older man commanded as he rounded the corner into the hall behind his furry beasts. The grey wiry trio of hounds skidded to a haphazard stop and sat obediently on their haunches not far from where she and Rory stood. The dogs' huge pink tongues lolled out the sides of their mouths and they whined, desperate to greet them.

Moira gave a hearty laugh. 'They are dears. What are their names?'

'I have many ill-tempered names for them, but most days I call them Hamish, Rab and Tam. My pack of hounds are quite harmless, despite their excessive affection. You must be Rory's new bride. I am Leonard McKenna.' The older man rushed forward with flushed cheeks. 'Poor Sean had to come find me deep in the woods to tell me of your blessed news as I was hunting, my boy. I've just now returned and look the worse for it. My apologies, Mrs Fraser, but I did not want to miss a minute of your arrival by cleaning up before greeting you.' He grasped her hands and pressed a kiss to her cheek. 'Welcome to our family.'

Moira's cheeks warmed. 'You are too kind. I am so pleased to meet you, sir.'

'Ah, such formalities. Call me Leo.'

'Thank you, Leo.'

'It is I who must thank you for bringing some cheer, life and loveliness to our home. You must be exhausted from your journey.'

'I am a bit tired, but nothing a bath and short respite before dinner won't cure.'

'Of course, my dear. I'll leave Rory to get you settled in. Until this evening.' Before he departed, he gave Rory a tight hug, whispering something in his ear so low she couldn't hear it, but the words brought a smile to Rory's lips.

Then he was off, sending a shrill whistle as he left that sent his dogs clambering behind him. As quickly as they arrived, they departed.

'Shall we?'

'Aye.'

A whisper of envy went through her as she realised she wished to be the one to make him smile so. She shook her head. What a ridiculous thought. The journey must be wearing upon her. Rory offered his arm, and they walked on down a long corridor that led to a set of large twining stairs. 'This is the main staircase to the family chambers. The one next to mine has been prepared for you. I hope it will be to your liking.'

He paused outside the chamber door, the second one on the landing, and opened it.

Sweet heather.

Her hand fell away from his arm, and she took a step into the beautiful green-and-white chamber. Soft white linens and laces graced the two windows that filtered the afternoon light into the room. Even without candles, it was bright and welcoming, and the view stole her breath. She went to the windows like one of her wee plants, eager to feel the warmth of the sun and light on her face. While her old chamber at Glenhaven had been beautiful, it was nothing like this.

Nothing.

Lush green rolling hills went as far as her eyes could see and then disappeared at the cliff's edge. The dark sea glimmered in the distance like glass. 'Absolutely beautiful,' she murmured.

Rory settled in by her side. 'Aye.'

'I see why you are reluctant to ever leave.'

'She has her charms.'

'Her?'

'My uncle always explained to me that Blackmore was to be referred to as a she for the life she gives, breathes and cares for within these walls. Just like a mother would, he'd often tease.'

'In that case, I am quite enamoured by her and her charms as well.'

His eyes met hers and an intensity settled in the warmth of his gaze. 'It means a great deal to me that you find it as beautiful as I.' He lifted her hand to his lips and pressed a soft lingering kiss along the ridges of her knuckles. A flutter of awareness hurried along her skin.

'I will leave you. Dinner is at seven. Tressa will assist you until your maid arrives. She'll be up shortly. Until then.' He let go of her hand and left the room, closing the door behind him.

As soon as he left she realised she hadn't thanked him or said anything at all before he'd left her. *Curses.*

She rushed out and spun in the hallway wondering *which* chamber next to hers was his. Trying the knob closest to the stairwell, she discovered what looked to be a guest chamber decorated in gold. She hurried on to the door on the other side of her chamber and it opened with ease.

What she saw there made her freeze in her tracks. Her voice died in her throat and her chest tightened.

'Seems I've overdone it a bit today, Angus.' Rory winced as his jacket was removed from his arms by his manservant. Rory doubled over and clutched his stomach. 'I'm in dire need of a tonic to ease the pain.'

'But ye have done it, sir. She's lovely and a son ye shall have. Blackmore's future has been secured. Perhaps knowing that will ease some of yer pain.' Angus wrapped his arm under Rory's own, and the two staggered with some effort back to the dark settee that faced a matching pair of windows looking out at the same view as her own.

Rory groaned as he settled into the cushions, allowing his head to fall back.

'I'll get yer tonic.' Angus turned to the door and met Moira's gaze, but he didn't falter or acknowledge her presence. 'For now, get some rest.'

Shame burned Moira's cheeks. Why had she just stood there and watched rather than announced herself?

She closed the door, swallowed hard and skittered back into her own chamber. Why had she not realised how sick he was? Her heart pounded in her chest. Why had she not seen it?

It seemed she wasn't the only one keen on keeping secrets.

Chapter Eleven

Every muscle in Rory's body ached and throbbed as he lay in bed looking out at the moonlit sky in the bay of windows before him. *Blazes.* He'd never sleep and movement would ease the pain more than resting ever would, a cruel and certain truth about one facing their untimely death. He threw off the bedclothes and shrugged on his trews. He tucked his nightshirt into them and headed for the study that adjoined the library. Perhaps some mind-numbing hours working through the Blackmore ledgers and a walk through the castle would help loosen his mind as well as his taut muscles.

Stepping out of his chamber, he padded barefoot down the maze of halls that led to the library and study. The cool stone on the soles of his feet seeped through him like a balm. He sighed aloud, feeling the tension ease from him with each passing step away from his chamber. The study and library had long served as his refuge, just as it was for Moira at Glenhaven, and she would love Blackmore's as much as he. The smell of dust, mustiness and leather soothed him down to his toes and the strains of the day fell off him as he crossed the familiar threshold. The fire still blazed in the hearth and the wall sconces flickered as they did each night, as was his wish. He tended to spend more time within these walls than his bedchamber.

He paused in the room and studied it with the new and unfiltered eyes that he believed his betrothed might. His gut tightened. Try as he might, he couldn't quite get used to the idea that he would be a married man on the morrow, but it had been settled at dinner. Married at midday along one of his favourite meadows by the cliffs with his servants and Uncle in attendance. Moira had seemed eager to settle the matter at dinner, and although he didn't know if it was out of urgency to move on to another topic where she was not the focus or out of apprehension for her family not being there. He'd tried to enquire once more if there was anyone they could send word to attend on her behalf, but the request had fallen unanswered. He hoped it was merely shyness, as he noted she often steered conversations about her back to others. A quality he'd never known in a woman before, but he'd never known a woman quite like Moira Fraser.

He found himself smiling like a giddy schoolboy and shook his head. Best not be a fool for her. She'd made it clear she preferred their attachment to be transactional and not emotional. Yet, his thoughts drifted to her beauty, her kindness, and her unique intellect and keen interest in learning, and he approached a section of his library he'd never quite explored: horticulture. There were shelves of books on plants, local and otherwise, botany and all sorts of scientists, and he smiled. She would be in heaven, and he made a note to tell her of it.

Then he frowned at himself.

Keeping his distance would be a challenge, but one he also needed to abide by. The woman was warm, endearing and so damned likable. Everyone in the household would soon be under her spell. Uncle was smitten with her as was the rest of the household and they'd known her for but a day. *Ack.* How did one keep from getting attached to one's wife?

A sharp pain lanced his stomach and he sucked in a breath, willing it to pass. Well, dying was surely one way to maintain distance. He chuckled at his own macabre humour. Perhaps he could simply enjoy what small happiness they could build together over the coming months and set aside his worry. He was close to achieving his goal: securing an heir to maintain Blackmore's future and position amongst the Highlands. All he needed to do was focus on that. The cramp relinquished for a moment before striking once more with an intensity that brought him to his knees. He gripped the rug beneath him with one hand and his side with the other and groaned aloud. No matter how he wished to, he couldn't allow himself to care for her, to love her. She'd been damaged by her first husband somehow and he refused to allow her to be broken by her second.

After the pain finally passed, he gathered his strength and pushed himself up to standing. He made his way to the large chair that sat nested within his desk and pulled it out. Collapsing within it, he sucked in a few breaths to even out his breathing and then opened the large, worn castle ledger with its thick brown leather binding. Work would distract him until sleep claimed him. A stack of correspondence also awaited him. 'Numbers or words?' he mumbled to himself.

Recognising the familiar curling script of his solicitor on the first sealed letter, he grabbed it from the pile and broke the wax seal. *Correspondence it was, then.* Mr Dobbs wasn't a man who often contacted him, so if he had it must be important. He scanned the document and let it fall back on the desk. It was for the yearly assessment of finances and taxes that needed to be paid to the king. Although it wasn't a task he looked forward to, at least this year he would have some positive news to discuss: plans for his new bride and heir to be and how to ensure they were properly protected and provided for. A conversation rooted in hope rather than the usual talk of his imminent demise. He could even speak with him about the cost of plans to update the old solarium next to his study until he could build that greenhouse for Moira come spring. If he lived that long.

Once again he steeled himself. Why did his thoughts always shift to her and her happiness so quickly without warning? He set the correspondence aside and looked at the pile of information that needed to be tallied and updated in his ledger. While running Blackmore wasn't a business, many lives depended on the turnout from the slate mine, the fields and being able to be self-sustaining. It had saved them from ruin a handful of times when the British had pressed closely in upon their land. Continued care and vigilance would keep them safe or at least he hoped it would. The Highlands was a fragile, harsh place given to swift turns in weather and politics. He picked up his quill and ink pot and began filling the blank columns. He'd work until his eyes ached, and then no doubt he'd probably work some more. Sleep was a luxury for the living.

The warmth of the sun on her face woke Moira. Heavens, she'd slept like the dead. She stirred and rubbed her eyes, and then let her gaze scan the chamber, her chamber. It was just as beautiful in the early morning light as it had been yesterday when she'd first laid eyes upon it. She sat up, propped herself up on a few pillows, and stared out at the golden hues of a heady sunrise and the soft rolling blanket of fog that hovered low in the sky above the grassy hills.

In a few hours she'd be a bride...again.

Her stomach churned at the thought of it. *Stop it*, she chided herself. Rory was not Peter, and she was no blushing bride. She knew what his expectations were, and she was going into this marriage with her eyes wide open and clear parameters. Of course, he was human, and he had flaws and failings as she did. And as far as flaws went, she'd yet to really discover any, which gave her great pause. Well, with the exception of knowing he was hiding his symptoms from her. She wrung her hands in her lap and her heart picked up speed. The sight of him struggling to walk to the settee in his chamber the night before had caught her unawares and stopped her in her tracks. He must have been in agony along their lengthy drive, especially after taking part in the hammer throw and the haste in which they had readied and departed. And the man had only arrived the day before. He'd had two long hard journeys in as many days, but he did not complain. She chided herself for not asking and tending to his welfare.

To her shame, she'd never even thought of it. She was distracted by her own worries of her family and the possibility of losing them. It was also hard to remember he was so ill—dying, in fact—when he seemed so vibrant and full of life in all other accounts. But she understood how pride could seal one's lips. She'd suffered in silence for years with Peter and told not a soul. Blaming herself had seemed far easier than the truth. Hiding that truth from her family and friends and letting those ties fall away until she was totally isolated had seemed easier than uttering what her life had become: a nightmare. Perhaps he felt the same way about his sickness.

But no matter. She smiled. It was time to rise and shed her Fraser title for a new one. Moira McKenna had quite a lovely ring to it, and she was eager to start a new chapter in this glorious home full of such warm and welcoming people. Despite its name, Blackmore seemed full of light, beauty, promise and hope, unlike the walls of Glenhaven. Today was indeed the first day of the rest of her life, and she was ready to begin it. She rose from the bed, pulled the cord for Tressa and started her daily ablutions.

Before she had even finished, Tressa flew into the room, her arms brimming with gowns. Moira gasped.

'What are all of those?' she asked, staring upon the multicoloured gowns the maid spread carefully across the bed.

Tressa curtseyed and blushed. 'Laird McKenna bid me pull some gowns of his mother's and others arrived from the village. We have some of the finest seamstresses, and they are so pleased to hear of yer arrival and pending union. They were brought to our doors without even a request. The laird is quite beloved.'

Moira stared at them in awe of their beauty.

Tressa's brow furrowed, and she worried her hands. 'While I know they are ready-made and were not designed for ye specifically, Mrs Fraser, he hoped one of them might suit for yer wedding today.'

Moira skimmed her fingers across the beautiful silk and lace gowns. One was blush, another a soft lilac and another a pale green. Two were off-white with beautiful multicoloured beading with flowers trailing along the bodice. 'They are all absolutely beautiful. How can I possibly select one?' Her brow wrinkled and worry brewed. *Drat.* If only Brenna were here. Moira didn't have the first inkling of an idea as to which one would best suit. 'Will you help me, Tressa? I find it overwhelming. Without my maid, I'm at thistles with this whole process.'

Tressa's worry flew away and she smiled, clapping her hands together. 'Aye. I would love to! Let us try them all on and then decide? Would that do?'

Sighing in relief, Moira nodded. 'Aye. Thank you.'

Tressa guided her through each dress as Moira tried them on, describing what suited her as well as which ones didn't. The green and blush shades were too light, but the lilac wasn't bad as it caught the colour of her eyes. But it was the off-white gown with beading and a series of twisting bluebells and what appeared to be heather stalks interwoven along the bust that fit to perfection. It was as if the gown and cut had been made for her. While it had long sleeves, the tops of her shoulders as well as her collarbone were exposed, creating a beautiful line along her neck and upper body.

'Oh, miss,' Tressa murmured, gathering another looking glass so Moira could see the front and back of it. 'I believe this is the one. Do ye like it?'

Seeing herself at all angles made her gasp. Was this even her? She'd never seen herself look so becoming, not even on her *first* wedding day. 'It's as if it were made for me, isn't it? The proportions are magnificent. Aye. It's the one.' She pressed a flat palm over her stomach and smiled. Perhaps this wedding, this marriage, *would* be joyful. Perhaps this time, her future would be without pain and upset and she'd look forward to seeing the sun rise every morning with Rory by her side.

She swallowed hard and a bit of the joy she'd just felt melted away into the reality that a wedding day led to a wedding night. Her intimacies with Peter had been brief, but painfully and brutally unpleasant. She sighed, resigning herself to the fact that she had to uphold her end of their agreement by being a participant in his attempts for gaining an heir. Enjoying it had not been a requirement, so she would merely await it to be over as she oft had before. It was a small sacrifice for having some safety, security and peace in her life.

'Miss?'

Moira glanced over to see Tressa studying her with a pinched expression.

'Are ye unwell?'

Moira looked to her reflection in the mirror and flattened the pained frown that had initially greeted her. 'Nay. I am fine. A bit of nerves, I suppose.'

'Ye needn't worry a bit. Laird McKenna is a kind and generous man. He will treat ye well. I can also see by the way he watches ye that he is quite taken with ye. Never seen him look at another lass the way he studies ye when he thinks no one sees him.'

He does?

'Now, let us take this off. I shall bring ye a tray to break yer fast and then we shall get ye ready. I've been ordered to bring ye to the carriage at half past ten and not a moment later.'

In a few hours, she would be a bride once more. She released a breath and let her eyes flutter closed as Tressa began the tedious task of unlacing the back of the gown. As the young woman tugged on the laces and buttons, Moira prayed.

Help me to begin a new life and new chapter without fear or at least without as much fear as I held in my last marriage. Help me to be a good wife for the time he remains alive and, once he is gone, let me know the peace, confidence and certainty of independence.

She opened her eyes and then squeezed them shut again and added to her prayer.

And let my father and family not interrupt this union, but accept me and my choice and one day come to my new home at Blackmore.

Part of her worried her last prayer would never come true. Her father might not storm the castle to stop the union, but he'd be slow to forgive her disobedience, if he ever did. She shivered. His stubbornness and pride were traits he shared with her late husband. Traits she prayed her new husband did not possess.

Chapter Twelve

When Rory thought he couldn't bear the wait a moment longer, he heard the slow rumbling arrival of the carriage along the dirt road that led to the designated wedding location on the hillside overlooking the sea. He released a breath. Part of him feared she would cry off, not come and leave him here alone perpetually waiting for his bride. But he should have known better. Mrs Moira Fraser was no Lorna. She was a woman of her word, and she no doubt viewed their union as part of a larger plan for her escape. Just as she served as part of a larger plan for his survival, even if in name only.

Despite Angus's urging not to look back, Rory turned to watch her arrival. His heart roared in his chest and his palms grew damp. The carriage door opened, and he saw Moira, his future wife, emerge. One graceful step, then another until both of her white slippered feet were settled on the soft dirt. When she met his gaze, he felt weak in the knees like a lad. *Good Lord.* She was beautiful, and that dress… His heart may have stopped in his chest. He recognised it from the large portrait in the library. It had been his mother's from her wedding day. The familiar blue and purple curling flowers and green vines along the bodice and the smooth sloping neckline. He'd stared at it for so long as a boy wondering at all he had missed by not knowing her. That Moira would have chosen it amongst all the dresses he and the village had sent to her moved him beyond measure. He swallowed the lump of emotion in his throat as he watched her approach. She smiled, and he commanded himself to return it despite how overwhelmed he felt.

She carried a bound bouquet of pink, yellow and purple flowers and a small necklace with a blue jewel bobbed in the notch of her throat. It was the colour of her eyes, and he willed himself to breathe. Soon she was at his side. For a woman who had left her own home in haste only a day ago, she looked remarkably settled, relaxed and prepared for this union.

Which was more than he could say for himself.

'You look lovely, Moira,' he murmured, cringing at the small crack in his voice. 'Breathtakingly beautiful.'

Her cheeks glowed, but there was a cool distance in her eyes as she replied in even tones, 'As you look handsome, my laird.'

Before he could question it further, Rory turned to face Cawley, the long-standing minister of Blackmore, who had agreed to marry them in such haste casting aside the reading of the banns and any other 'required nonsense' as the man called it.

'Who am I to stand in the way of a blessed union?' he'd always spouted. *'There's God and then there's the law. I always put God first. The rest of it be damned.'*

One of the many reasons Rory enjoyed the wry humour of the tall old man, who was so trim he looked as if he might blow over in a gust of wind. He'd been Blackmore's man of God for as long as Rory could remember. He'd also provided Rory guidance and support through his many losses. He trusted the man with his life and now his future.

Cawley led them through the opening pleasantries, and Rory didn't notice any nerves from his bride-to-be until the handfasting. Angus handed him Moira's wedding band, which he held out in his cupped hand to her. When she extended her hand and placed it atop his own, the tremble was unmistakable. His heart pulled in his chest as he placed his other hand atop her own and hers beneath. As the McKenna plaid was wrapped around them both, he met her gaze. The fear residing there gutted him.

Her hands were ice cold, and Rory realised he'd been a fool.

She wasn't *ready* for this union, but terrified. The three knots were tied to symbolise his love for her, her love for him and the love they shared for those in attendance, and he cursed himself. How else could she feel? She had not a soul here she knew to witness their union. No family, not even her lady's maid had arrived in time. While he knew everyone here, she knew no one, save him, and she'd only known him a short time. He'd have to be more aware in the future, and he needed to do something to help her feel more at ease.

As Cawley commanded their repeating of vows to one another, they each complied in turn. The plaid was removed, and Rory slipped the wedding ring upon her trembling finger. When Cawley announced them as man and wife, Rory smiled at his bride and she mirrored his own, but he noted the smile never quite reached her eyes. His bride was worried, and he had no idea how to lessen the strain. He squeezed her hand and led them through a small throng of McKenna revellers cheering their union. While he felt full of hope, he worried about his bride, who gripped his arm with a fierceness that only rivalled the pit of unease cramping his stomach.

He led her to the carriage and settled opposite her on the bench seats. She gripped her hands so tightly in her lap that her knuckles whitened, and she avoided his gaze.

'I am sorry,' he sputtered. 'I realise you knew not a soul out there but me, and, well, you have only known me two days. I should have delayed our union until some of your family and friends could have arrived.'

She released a small chuckle. 'You and I both know Father would not have come, nor would he have allowed my siblings to attend. I do not blame you for any of it. I knew the consequences of my choice. I chose you willingly. I am just nervous.'

He tried to wonder what would make the fearless and headstrong woman who kissed him in a sea of observers publicly and fled with him, a stranger, in midday in a carriage against her family's wishes afraid. There was something important he was missing.

'Are you uncertain of me? Of being here? Have I done something to make you uneasy?' He leaned forward and reached for one of her hands. She stilled at his touch and a flush filled her cheeks, so he pulled his hand away.

She shifted on the seat as the carriage rumbled along. Blackmore was in full view. Their brief moments of intimacy would soon be over. 'Nay, my lord. It is merely memories.'

Before he could utter another word, the carriage came to a rocking halt, and the door sprung open. Moira smiled and exited. As Rory pushed up from his seat, he wondered what memories she referred to despite the nagging truth echoing in his mind. *Peter Fraser.* He seemed the only man she still feared even though he was dead.

While he'd never known the man, Rory wondered what this Fraser had done to make his wife so fearful of marrying once more. He exited the carriage and frowned. His gut told him he didn't truly wish to know the answer.

The hours of celebration whiled away quickly. The joyous music, flowers and sounds of happiness filled the usually quiet halls of Blackmore. The sheer life of it all filled Rory with more gaiety than he could remember. And the fact that such a union had given his uncle and clan such hope was not lost on him. Even if he could not sire an heir in time, giving his people hope of a bright future was a gift that was beyond his own imaginings. And he had Mrs Moira Fraser, nay, he stopped himself, he had *Lady Moira McKenna* to thank. He spied his bride chatting with his uncle and local women from the clan across the room. She was laughing, smiling and enjoying herself. She'd relaxed since they'd entered the main hall, been announced and the celebration had begun, and he had been pleased to see the ease in which she moved amongst his people, now *her* people.

He approached her and Uncle. 'How is my new bride?' He pressed a kiss on her cheek and pulled her gently to his side. Her body stiffened in his hold, and he relaxed his grip.

'We were discussing her love of plants, and I assured her there were countless dusty leather volumes in the library on botany and agriculture awaiting her in dire need of being read.' His uncle chuckled and sipped from his glass.

Rory released his hold of her. 'Aye. He speaks the truth. The volumes will bloom under your care, as your plants will. Have you found a space for them?'

She blushed and her shoulders relaxed. 'Aye. There is a room next to the library with a beautiful expanse of windows. May I put them there?'

He grinned. 'Of course. That used to be a solarium, and we can update it as such. As I promised, you shall have run of the library and your plants. We will also construct a greenhouse where you see fit come spring once the weather turns.'

His uncle laughed. 'I see you know how to barter, my lady.'

She smiled. 'I do, Uncle. You should see me at cards.'

One of the ladies chimed in and winked at her. 'Ye can't say ye have na' been warned, Leo. And, Rory, ye couldna' have found a more lovely bride. Best wishes for ye both.' She squeezed Moira's arm and left them.

'Shall we retire and leave the rest to celebrate our future?' Rory asked.

Moira's eyes widened briefly before she set a smile to her lips and nodded. 'Aye, my laird. Good eve to you all.'

'Good evening, Uncle.'

He extended his arm to his new bride, and as Moira slid her arm through, it felt as small and fragile as a baby bird's wing against his. As they walked down the hallway, the music began to fade and finally he could hear the sound of their footfalls and the sound of wind whipping up outside. Winter was not far away, but this time of year was his favourite.

'Where are we going?' Moira asked. Her voice sounded small and timid. For a moment he even wondered if the words had come from her at all or had been his imaginings.

'I thought you might show me where you'd placed your wee plants and see all of those dusty volumes Uncle is so desperate for you to read.' He smiled down at her and felt her taut hold on his arm relax. He didn't know why she was so nervous. The hard part of the day was over, wasn't it? They were wed. Her father had not spoiled their union. She was married to a dying man as she wished. Her future was secure.

They travelled down the last corridor leading to the library. The moon shone full and bright along the hallway. They had no need for the wall sconces that flickered along their path at even intervals. At the threshold of the library, he paused. 'Your library, my lady.'

She let go of his arm and ambled along the rows of

books one after another. He found himself staring after her, bemused by her wide-eyed interest in each volume. Her fingers trailed along one spine and then another.

'Why do you have a fire burning in here when no one is here?' she asked, turning to face him.

He nested his hands in his trouser pockets. 'You will know soon enough, but I rarely sleep. I find I wake quite often in the night. I have for some time. This is where I end up most nights, reading, staring into the fire, worrying over ledgers. The staff knows to always leave it lit, for me.'

She straightened and that beloved little notch of interest between her brows formed, one he realised now was meant for puzzling out something. He smiled at her quizzical look, pleased that he knew something of her after so few days between them.

'Willow bark tea?' she asked.

'What about it?'

'Have you tried it?'

'Aye, but I don't like it.'

'Well, I will make you some of mine, which you *will* like. Then you will sleep.' She turned away and began scanning the volumes once more.

He chuckled. 'So easy, is it?'

She shrugged and pulled a volume from the shelf, hugging it to her chest. 'Aye. It could be.' She smiled and whisked past him, her skirts swishing over his shoes. 'Now I must tend to my seedlings.'

He smiled at the ripple of joy in her voice and the lightness in her step. It made him wish he was but one of her beloved plants. He shook his head.

Fool.

He followed her to the room next to the library. It had at one time been a solarium, but no one really frequented it now. He couldn't even remember the last time he'd been in it. Three little clay pots sat like tiny soldiers along the windowsill awaiting their orders from the sun and of course their commander, Lady Moira.

He smiled at the thought of her being in such a role. She fussed over each of them, sprinkled them with water from her fingers from a nearby pitcher, and turned to him. She met his gaze. Colour eased up her neck and into her cheeks as she looked away from him. 'My apologies. I know you have other, er, plans for this eve than me dawdling over my plants.'

'My only plan is to spend the eve with you. To get to know my wife.'

She stilled and nibbled her bottom lip. Her bosom rose and fell quickly, and he found himself entranced entire by the bloom of her skin glowing in the shadows of the flickering firelight.

'You are absolutely beautiful, Moira Fraser.'

She released a breath and the tiny glass pendant at her throat winked in the light. 'McKenna,' she whispered.

'Aye. You are right.' He approached her and took her hands in his own. Once more they were cool, and he realised she must be chilled in her thin gown. The temperature had dropped as the sun had descended, but he'd not been bothered in his tunic and jacket. He clutched her hands in his own, the soft, chilled flesh so welcoming against his skin. He rubbed her hands between his own before lifting them and blowing warm air on them.

She shivered, her eyes widening and chest rising and falling as if she couldn't catch her breath. Slowly, she dropped his gaze and pulled her hands away.

'You're chilled. I'm a fool. Come. Let us get you warm.' He rested his hand along her lower back and she shifted away from his touch. He let his hand fall away. Somehow he was upsetting her, but he didn't know how or why.

They walked in silence back to their chambers, her a half-step ahead of him. She stopped at her door and faced him. 'I shall ready myself, my laird.'

'Moira, I—'

She closed the door before he could utter anything further, and he clamped his mouth shut.

He was somehow making a muck of being a husband, and he'd only been married a mere handful of hours. He ran a hand through his hair, entered his chamber and yanked off his boots, letting them clunk one by one to the floor. He sank in his favourite chair and sighed. He'd given Angus the night off, so he could spend uninterrupted time with his new bride. Perhaps that had been an error. He frowned. She seemed nervous, edgy, as if... He groaned and pinched the bridge of his nose as he squeezed his eyes shut.

He was a fool. A daft bloody fool.

Of course she had been married. She was no virgin or unawares of the ways of the marriage bed, but that didn't mean she wouldn't be nervous about being intimate with him. He was little more than a stranger after all. He'd never even thought of it until now as there had been so many other things to focus on. He should have put her at ease. They didn't need to rush into anything if she wasn't comfortable. Sure, they had an arrangement with terms she had openly agreed to. He needed to sire an heir, but he would need a compliant and willing wife to do that. He rose, poured himself a whisky and paced the room. He'd give her a half hour and go into her chamber. They'd talk it through, so she understood. He didn't wish her to be walking around on nettles fearing that he might ravage her at any moment.

When the clock finally chimed half past eleven, he sighed in relief, set down his almost empty glass of whisky and knocked on the chamber door that joined his room with her own.

'Moira?' he called.

'Come in,' she answered.

He released a breath and smoothed his rumpled tunic. He would talk with her. They'd figure this out.

Steady.

Turning the knob, he entered the room. A chill seized his body and he stood frozen, transfixed at the threshold. He swallowed hard.

He'd never seen anything so terrifyingly beautiful in all his life.

On top of the dark coverlet under the glow of the dim candlelight of the room was his bride. Moira lay stark naked, her eyes squeezed shut with her luscious skin glowing like a pearl along her dangerous and beautiful curves. And he found he didn't trust himself at all.

Chapter Thirteen

Moira trembled. This was it. She'd heard the chamber door open and knew Rory was there, but he'd not said a word and she didn't dare open her eyes. Fear licked upon her limbs and it was all she could do not to flee and run from her chamber. Memories of Peter and their couplings flickered hot and bright in her mind, tripping over one after another as they had for the time she'd lain here awaiting her new husband's visit. While she couldn't bear the thought of seeing Rory standing above her full of expectation, the memories of the past with Peter were more terrifying. Perhaps she should just open her eyes and face the truth of it.

Nay. She couldn't. She clutched the bedclothes in her hands and shivered. The waiting. The moments before it began were always the worst. She clenched her jaw and commanded herself to breathe.

You made an agreement. This is part of it. Just lie still, do as he says, and it will be over quickly.

It always was. She'd learned early on in her marriage to Peter that resistance only made it worse in all ways. A small creak on the floorboards brought her back to the moment. Gooseflesh rose along her skin as she heard Rory's approach. One step and then another. Not boots upon the floor, but a soft padding of feet. Perhaps he was barefoot. Naked even.

She swallowed hard and prayed he wasn't. She wasn't ready, she wasn't ready, she wasn't ready. She squeezed her eyes shut and a tremble seized her once more. This marriage to Rory McKenna was her last chance at some semblance of happiness or at least contentment, and if she didn't fulfil her wifely duties, any hope of a future of her own would be null and void.

Give me the strength.

Soft furs fell over her skin in a smooth ripple, first at her feet and then all the way up her body, settling just along her shoulders and below her neck. She was being covered in a blanket of some sort and her eyes shot open in a panic. Had she already disappointed him? Her eyes adjusted to the darkness, and she noted the back of her husband's tall, fully clothed muscular form across the room. He picked up a chair and brought it to the side of the bed. Settling it on the ground, he sat in it. She was startled by the handsome rugged planes of his face and boyish look of him in his rumpled tunic without his jacket and formal neckcloth. He ran his hands down his trews and rested his weight on his elbows. His tunic sagged open from where it had been loosened about his throat, and she caught a glimpse of his chest and the dark hair sprinkled along it. Worry danced along the shadows of his face and something more potent rested in his gaze.

'Moira...' He linked his hands together, searching her face. 'I...' he began and faltered once more, looking around the room as if his words had been scattered about the walls and he was desperate to collect them.

'Have I disappointed you, my laird?' she rushed out, beginning to sit up, the furs slipping down to her waist leaving her exposed.

His gaze slipped to her breasts and then away to her waist. He scrubbed a hand through his hair. 'Please cover yourself,' he pleaded, his voice husky and deep.

She gripped the fur to her chest, her loose hair spilling about her shoulders. Her heart thundered against her ribs. She could not be banished so soon. Not yet. 'I know Peter said I did not have a very desirable form, but I will try to please you, my laird. I will. Before you cast me out, let me try—'

His eyes widened, and he shook his head. 'Nay.' His brow furrowed and he reached out to her and stopped his hand just short of touching her arm. 'You are beautiful, Moira. So much so that I do not trust myself.' He gifted her a brief smile before it faded away.

Beautiful? She was confused. If he found her so attractive, why had he just covered her from head to toe and pleaded for her to re-cover herself?

'I feel I have faltered somewhere in this. To see you lying here, in such a state, I...' He swallowed hard and glanced away, fixing his gaze upon the candle burning brightly on the table behind her. 'I have not been a husband before, and I did not think how you would feel about this night. You do not really know me.' He met her gaze. 'And despite the urgency with which I wish to sire an heir, I cannot place that ahead of your comfort. I respect you. I have made a promise to cherish and protect you as my wife, even if that is from myself.' He fisted his hand and sat back in his chair, which creaked under his weight.

What?

She blinked and sat dumbfounded, unable to understand his words. *He was worried about her comfort and her happiness over his own needs?* Her gaze narrowed. Perhaps it was a trick. She'd never known a man to put her needs before his own, and she had no idea how to process such a concept. She shifted under the warmth of the soft furs and studied him. Could he possibly be telling her the truth? Was this the real Rory McKenna? She studied his profile as he stood and approached the bank of windows, staring out in the darkness with his hands resting on his waist.

Agony rippled along his furrowed brow and rigid shoulders. Perhaps he *was* being truthful. 'I will not touch you until you are ready, Moira. I have no desire to force myself upon my wife. I will leave you,' he whispered and turned, heading to his adjoining chamber before she could utter a word of reply.

As the door closed softly behind him, Moira realised Rory McKenna was not Peter. He would never force himself upon her. Emotion gathered in her chest tightening her throat and she softly wept.

Thank you, God. Thank you, God. Thank you, God.

Rory had no idea how to be a husband. Why had no one told him what to expect and prepared him? Perhaps because no man he knew well was actually married. He frowned. Uncle, Angus and the few servants who Rory still knew well were all untethered, so he had no experience to draw upon.

He slipped on his boots and headed down to the study. Despite the chill in the air, he'd no need for a jacket. His blood was heated through and through from the sight of his beautiful wife lying naked before him. Although he'd assumed she would be beautiful, he hadn't been prepared for the perfection of her all at once. It had been an assault to his senses and his body had thrummed in kind. As he reached the study, he released a shaky breath, took in the familiar sights and musty smells of the room and allowed it to help slow his thundering pulse and raging desire. He sat on the oversized sill of the large bay of windows that looked out upon the cliffs and sea beyond. Waves crashed in a gentle regular rhythm against the cliff side, and the wind whipped through the trees.

If he'd stayed in that chamber one moment longer, he'd not have been able to walk away. His wife was too beautiful and held the promise of all of the hope of the future he'd longed for. She possessed a wink at happiness, and he'd been alone and full of despair for so long that every part of him had burned to hold her and seize the hope her body held.

He sighed. He'd been a cad to believe she would have been ready for them to make their union official this eve. And the way she had prepared herself for him shook him to his core. The sight of her there naked, waiting, trembling. He'd never be able to forget such an image for as long as he drew breath. What the hell had Peter Fraser done to her to make her believe that she was undesirable and that the act itself was to be feared? He scrubbed his hand through his hair and slammed his fist against the windowpane. He knew he didn't wish to ever know.

But he did wish to turn the tide of her view of it, especially when time was of the essence in his case. Hurrying from the windowsill, he went to his desk and found a blank page of parchment. Unearthing his quill from the correspondence it was buried beneath, he found his ink pot and settled into his chair.

A wicked smile formed on his lips. He would seduce his wife one gesture at a time until she couldn't resist him. He faltered. But *how* did one do that? And should he really do it? He'd never had to win over a woman before, and having to win over his wife was an unexpected complication. It also sounded ridiculous. He was a laird, and she'd agreed to his terms.

The sight of her flashed through his memory once more. This simple marriage was transforming into something else entirely. He didn't wish for their agreement to become more than what they'd intended. He'd tried love before and it had turned to ash and besides, soon he'd be dead.

Dunking his quill in the ink pot, he decided to begin a list of what she liked. No harm could come from *making* the list. He'd probably not even use it.

1) Plants
2) Books

He paused. What else did she care for?

3) Hounds
4)

He cringed at the short list. He'd need to figure out what she cared about in order to charm her, if he *did* decide to resort to such ridiculous measures. Once her lady's maid arrived, he could pry it out of her. He faltered. Why hadn't she and the servants from Glenhaven arrived already? He'd sent a messenger with instructions for their transition to Blackmore, but not a single one of them had arrived before the wedding this morn. His stomach curdled. He glanced at the new stack of correspondence that sat unopened on the side of the desk and prayed that what he now feared hadn't happened.

Sifting through the pile, he saw a thick letter. He split the fat Stewart seal and prepared himself. Enclosed were his instructions to the servants along with a terse note from the laird:

You may have stolen my daughter, but you shall not have my servants.

Enjoy your last days, McKenna. They are numbered, and once you are gone, your clan will be swallowed up by the rest of us.

Rory cursed and tossed aside the letter. Now what would he tell Moira? Her lady's maid and the handful of other servants who'd risked all to aid in her escape were now trapped within the walls of Glenhaven. Most likely, they were being punished for what their role had been in their ruse, or let go entirely without aid. And now how would he discover what she liked and disliked? Trial and error seemed a poor plan, but what else could he do?

He stared up at a painting of his parents. It had been of their wedding day, and he wondered what hopes and fears they had possessed in that moment and whether more of their hopes or fears had ended up coming true. And what he could do to protect Moira from her father. Bran Stewart was known for holding grudges and Rory had no desire to see Moira fall back into the hands of a man who would rule her by control, fear and subjugation. Rory's mind swirled in protest to the strains of the day, his gut burning and cramping from the worry and lack of sleep. He groaned and rang Angus for a glass of wine in hopes that it could at least ease one ache from the budding list of worries from his mind, body and soul.

Chapter Fourteen

Moira woke and shifted under the weight of the soft furs above her and the warm coverlet beneath. Sunlight streamed into her window warming the edges of the bed it could reach, and the smell of something soft and floral, rose tinged with verbena perhaps, lingered in the air. The delicious coolness of the furs along her naked limbs made her sigh. It was a glorious day. Then the dreadful memory of the night before crashed into her awareness. Her wedding night. She covered her face with the furs. *Blast.* How would she ever face her husband again? And when she did see him, what would he say, think or do?

Poorly done, Moira. Poorly done.

Heat flushed her skin at the memory of their meeting in her chamber the night before. Rory had been nothing but kind, patient and gentle, but fear and anxiety had consumed her whole. Her body had quaked at the thought of his hands and weight of his body on her. Her heart pounded in her chest and she bolted upright, gathering uneven greedy breaths, as panic gripped her once more. She counted. One, two, three, and released a breath. Four, five, six, and she breathed in. Slowly, it subsided.

She fisted the covers in her hands. His eyes had seemed equally haunted last eve, and he had resigned his right to try to sire an heir until she was ready. Even now she wondered if she'd heard the words correctly or imagined them. He was laird after all, and he had full claim over her as her husband, but he'd not exercised that right, which surprised her.

He'd been a gentleman. Worry flashed through her once more. What if he cast her out? He could. They'd not made their union official as he had not bedded her. She needed to face the truth of what had happened and speak with him. She wasn't upholding her end of their arrangement, and she knew she'd never find a better situation for herself. An apology, nay, perhaps not an apology, but an explanation was in order. She owed him that at least. She swallowed hard. She'd not tell him the whole truth behind her fears, but enough for him to understand.

She threw off the furs, strode naked over to her wardrobe and looked for a gown to suit. Plucking a deep purple the shade of heather from the armoire, she yanked on the bell pull for her maid. Rushing through her ablutions, she'd just donned her shift when Tressa hurried in. She beamed at her. 'Good morn, my lady. I hope ye slept well.' She winked at Moira, who blushed on cue, but not for the reason Tressa implied. It was from *not* sharing her marriage bed with her husband the night before.

Tressa pressed her lips together and her eyes twinkled with mirth. 'Glad to hear it,' she replied to Moira's non-answer.

'Where might I find Laird McKenna this morn?' Although it felt silly to ask such a question, she didn't wish to waste precious time attempting to find him on this vast estate alone. She needed to speak with him before she lost her nerve.

'He'll be out with the hounds taking some air as he does most morns. South trail to the cliffs.' She smiled. 'Let's get ye dressed, and I'll find yer cloak. It will be cold up along there this morn. The winter winds are blowin' in early this year.'

Moira held fast to her cloak as it buckled and twisted in the high winds. Off in the distance, she could see her husband's strong, unyielding profile. He walked at a decent clip along the hillside playing some game of fetch with one of the hounds. The smallest of the three creatures spied her first, gave a welcoming bark and began a steady charge down the hill towards her. She stopped and let him inspect her. Soon, the hound slobbered her gloved palm and lost interest, racing back to Rory.

She met his gaze and his body tensed. His long overcoat whipped about his trews and high boots. His hair a mussed, boyish rumple similar to the night before. She smiled and waved to him. To his credit, he waved back and began to walk to her. She picked up her skirts and began the small incline, so she could meet him halfway.

'Good morn,' he offered. 'Did you sleep well?' His words held a deeper enquiry and his gaze laboured over her, scanning what seemed every inch of her face. Doubt rested along the downturned corners of his mouth, and guilt turned her gut.

Heat flushed her once more and she dropped her gaze, unable to meet and accept the concern in his eyes a moment longer. She pulled on her gloved fingertips. 'I came to try to explain. I feel dreadful about last night, and I should have told you before of my fears…it wasn't fair of me. I just didn't know how. One doesn't usually speak of things such as…*that*.'

Awkward was one thing. *This*, this conversation, was quite another. She wished to get it over with, but had no idea how to go about it.

Her heart thundered in her chest. How did one speak of a fear of intimacy when one never was supposed to talk of the act and such intimacies in the first place? Despite the chill, she felt an urgency to shed her cloak, although she knew she'd be just as flushed. Embarrassment clawed through her and held fast followed by her own frustration.

He stepped closer. 'Moira.' He paused. 'Please look at me.'

Her body quaked, but she lifted her head slowly and met his steady, unwavering gaze. He reached out and clutched her hands in his own and flickers of desire scattered through her as leather ran along leather. She *was* attracted to him. She couldn't deny it. He was handsome and kind, but it didn't mean she wasn't terrified of being with him. Her body had memories beyond her mind. Ones she still couldn't command or control.

'I don't know what your marriage with Peter was or

was not, but I promise you that I would never hurt you in such a way. My desire to be intimate with you is out of need to sire an heir, as I said before, nothing more. I will make no additional demands of you. No attachments, no entanglements, just as you wished, but I will wait until you are ready and feel comfortable enough with me to follow through on that.'

His matter-of-fact explanation stung her more than she would have liked to admit. And far more than she felt comfortable acknowledging. His words shouldn't have mattered a whit, but they did, which irked her further. While he was attempting to console her, he'd also made her feel little more than a trough of dirt in which seeds would be planted in and that any old fertile ground would do. She slid her hands from his own. 'Aye. I know that. You made such a need clear to me. I just wanted to try to explain. I'll leave you to your walk.'

She turned and began to leave.

'Wait.' He touched her arm gently, and she turned to face him. 'I'm making a muck of what I wish to say. Truth is, I don't understand what has happened to make you fear…coupling. I don't have any idea how to ease your concerns. All I know is that I don't want my wife fearful of me. But I'm also dying. My time is not my own.'

They stood staring at one another as the wind whipped around them and between them. His words echoed in her mind. One day he would be dead, and they both knew not when. Yet, she stood between his clan's successful future and her own.

A memory of another time she'd been far too afraid to do anything seized her.

'Moira, jump in. It shall not be easier by putting in one toe at a time.' Ewan smacked the warm waters of the loch with his arms, sending a cascading arch of water droplets into the air.

She stepped back from the water's edge.

'I can't do it,' she pleaded in distress. *'I don't know what's in there and I can't swim. I'll drown.'*

He laughed at her, treading water in his soaked tunic and trews. *'You're my sister. I'd never let anything happen to you. I might steal your puddings, but I'll always protect you. Jump!'*

The trust in his gaze made her run to the bank's edge, close her eyes and jump in. When the water began to soak her dress, and threatened to drown her, his strong arms pulled her up.

She slapped at the water, gulped in air and strained. *'Help, Ewan. Help!'*

'Stop flailing about like a baby bird. Relax,' he commanded. *'Just float,'* he ordered, turning her on her back.

And the moment she'd stopped flapping her arms and panicking she had rested atop the water like a miracle. That feeling of weightlessness, freedom and the sound of nothing but lapping water against her ears as the warm sun kissed along her face had set her free. A feeling she had never forgotten. One she saved when she needed it.

Just float.

Could this be the same?

'Kiss me,' she whispered, the words rushing out in a flurry.

His brow lifted and his head tilted. 'Sorry,' he chuckled. 'I think I misheard you. Did you say "kiss me"?' He shifted on his feet and tugged up the collar of his jacket about his neck.

Her heart pounded in anticipation. She didn't know if this was the worst or best of ideas to help her repair her fears, but she'd never know if she didn't try. Her chest rose and fell. 'Aye.'

His gaze dropped to her lips and she swallowed hard. Taking a step forward, he paused, perhaps as uncertain as to her changefulness as she. He removed his gloves and came closer, so close that she could see the tiny flecks of gold and blue amongst the light grey hue of his irises and smell the soap from his morning shave. His warm calloused fingers skimmed along her jawbone and she shivered, her lips parting to release a sigh.

He pressed a kiss along her jaw, not once but twice, and then captured her mouth in his own. The soft, warm urgency in his lips sent a swirl of heat through her, an unexpected response. She lifted a shaky gloved hand to his cheek and heard his groan of pleasure against her mouth. A moment of fear gripped her, but she remembered to float and leaned into his embrace as he pulled her against him. He deepened the kiss and her hand found its way into his soft, wavy hair. She felt his smile against her lips as he pulled back and rested his forehead on hers.

'Perhaps we just need a bit of time to unwind some of your memories.'

She nodded. 'And replace them with new ones.'

'Aye,' he answered, stepping away and capturing her gloved hand in his own. When he wove his fingers through hers and squeezed, the memory of freedom she'd felt when she'd floated whispered back to her. Perhaps if she just let go, she could wade back into the waters step by step. There was no need to jump in this time.

'What would you like to do today, my lady?' he teased. 'You have an estate to see, people to meet, and a sea of future plants and books to pour over.'

She chuckled at the ease in which the morning had turned from fear and worry into joy. 'Perhaps them all, but where shall we begin first?'

'I think the weather demands us to return inside. The winds will only worsen until the storm blows through. I can give you the full tour of the inside of Blackmore, and then you can lose yourself in the shelves of the library while I finish up the ledgers. Hopefully the rain will pass and the wind die down for an evening walk.'

The wind ruffled her hair and she instinctively leaned towards him to block the biting gale that chilled her through her cloak. He let go of her hand, unbuttoned his jacket and pulled her under his arm, allowing his jacket to fall over her shoulder. Delicious heat and the feel of the muscled planes of his torso sent flares of warning through her. She should pull back and let go. But part of her craved his touch even though the last thing she wanted was to care for him more than what was required when he would die.

But why not allow myself comfort for a time?

What harm would come from it?

She gave in to that small part of herself that longed to be cared for and cherished, and nestled her cheek against his chest and curled her arm around his back. His side hitched at her touch and then relaxed as he tightened his hold around her waist. They walked arm in arm and the ease at which it happened startled her. While she still didn't feel ready to sleep in his bed, her body and heart sung at the comfort of being understood, and the feel of being cared for, desired and respected that his touch provided.

A feeling she had long forgotten.

Chapter Fifteen

*H*old fast.

Rory sucked in one deep breath and then another as his body thrummed in desire and want of his wife. There was no denying it. The feel of her strong, small frame against him and the slight tremble he felt pass through her undid him. The irony of desiring his wife so much when she feared intimacy was not lost on him. Fate had a grand sense of humour, it seemed. The dying man had finally found a wife, yet he could not begin the act of trying to beget an heir with her.

Another man might have just bedded her without cause and justified it with the fact that he was her husband and the future of a clan was at stake, but he was not that man. Perhaps it would be easier if he was. They began the slow descent to the back entrance of the castle and Rory accepted the truth with each footfall. He would have to be patient. Once more, time demanded more from him and Fate would give him what he desired on Her terms but not a moment sooner.

Moira shifted against him and slowed, turning her face to the west. 'It's beautiful. May I look inside?'

Rory glanced in the direction of her interest and his chest tightened. They should have gone the long way around to the front entrance and risked getting caught in the rain. The painted glass windows of Blackmore's small chapel winked back at him as it caught the sun's intermittent rays, as if daring his approach and mocking his past with it. If it wasn't sacred ground, he would have spat upon it. He met her quizzical expression and realised he'd not answered her. 'If you wish,' he replied, his words sharper than he intended.

'Did something horrid happen here? You're scowling.' She tilted her head and stepped out of his hold. An immediate sense of loss consumed him. Some from the past and some from the present.

He sighed and crossed his arms against his chest. ''Tis not my favourite part of Blackmore.'

'Oh? It's quite lovely. I am surprised you did not wish to have our wedding here.'

'I tried that once before,' he muttered, and started up the worn stone path to the chapel's large, dark wooden doors. With every step, the walls he'd built to keep the loss he'd experienced there fell away until only the feelings of shame and grief remained.

A crack of thunder sounded and the skies opened up, releasing plump, heavy drops of rain. 'Seems the weather has decided for us. Come inside. We can wait out the storm.'

He couldn't prevent the dry, bitter laugh from escaping his lips as he continued on.

Moira walked beside him until they reached the doors where he stopped cold, staring blankly at the barrier standing between him and the past.

To her credit, she didn't move but waited patiently for whatever truth he would give her.

Rory's hand grasped the large metal handle. All he had to do was pull on the ring and the door would open, yet he couldn't quite summon the courage to do so. He hadn't been inside since he'd caught Lorna in the throes of passion with one of his stewards here. He squeezed his eyes shut as the sight and sounds of such a discovery crashed through his mind like it had but a thousand times before. He clenched his jaw. The wedding they had planned to have there but days later had been cancelled, the steward cast from the castle and Lorna not far behind. He gripped the iron tightly. The future he had planned had turned to dust by entering this door. Would it do the same now if they went in?

Moira placed her hand over his own and he started, yanked back from his memories.

'We don't have to go in.' She smiled up at him, and he met the blue depths of her gaze. One filled with concern, empathy and understanding even though he'd told her nothing. Perhaps if he allowed her into some of his pain, she would allow him into hers, and somehow they could find a future, no matter how brief it might be, together.

He relaxed his hold and pushed it open. 'It's time to set aside some of the demons of the past. Come. See the chapel.'

The dank, musty chill of the air startled him. He

hadn't been in this space for over a year, but his body remembered the familiar sights, smells and sounds that he'd cherished as a boy. He smiled. 'I used to love this place. I'd come and sit in here for hours.'

'You did?' She studied him. 'What changed?'

'Her. Lorna. She changed it. We were planning to marry. Thought she hung the moon and stars, and I would have done—' He stopped himself from blathering on, ashamed of how foolish he had been to believe in such love. 'Anyway, we were to marry here, but a few days before our union, I found her here—' he paused, searching for a softer way to say the truth of it '—in a rather compromising position with a steward. Said she believed I would one day be too weak due to my illness and that she needed to make other arrangements.'

Moira's eyes widened in understanding. 'Oh. That is ghastly. I'm sorry.'

'*That* is why I did not wish to marry you here. I have not got over the betrayal in a place I once cherished.'

'Why did you love it so? It is peaceful, but for a child it might be a bit dull, I would imagine.' She twisted her lips and scanned the small and albeit simple church.

Rory's gaze danced along the space. It was still clean and cared for. No doubt Uncle Leo had made it so despite Rory's initial command that it be razed to the ground. He smiled, grateful his uncle never listened to a word he said. 'Father and I came here every week when I was very young and then my uncle continued the tradition. My father used to tell me stories of my mother and we'd pray to her and then walk about the place looking at the carved stones and depictions of all the McKennas before us. Later, Uncle would tell me the stories of our clan, and the hours would just melt away, especially on rainy days such as this.'

He removed his gloves and let his fingers drift upon one of his favourite carvings. A chiselled depiction of a woman with a small babe that measured the length of two hands. He traced it with the pads of his fingertips, allowing them to dip in and out of the crevices. 'Father always told me he crafted this one of me and Mother himself.' He chuckled. 'Although I doubt he did such as he had little talent with drawing let alone stone carvings. But I always wanted to believe it was true. Perhaps more than he even wished for me to.' The soft shadowy cheeks and upturned quirk of the woman's lips always made him smile, as if she held a lovely secret that she would never tell.

'It's quite beautiful. Have you ever thought to carve one yourself? Leave your own McKenna mark upon this chapel?'

He shook his head and let his fingers fall away from the wall. 'Never even thought of it.'

'Well, you should.' She smiled up at him and walked to the small scarred altar that stood resolute at the front of the chapel. Steady rain created a soothing rhythm upon the roof overhead, and he suddenly felt peace rather than anger in this space, just like he had as a child. He walked down the aisle and slid into his favourite pew, the third row centre. The familiar hard, solid strength of the wood against his torso as he sat was a blessed comfort he had missed. His hands relaxed in his lap and he closed his eyes, content to hear the rain and breathe in the damp musty scent of the place.

The pew shifted beneath him, and he opened his eyes to see Moira sliding down to him. She sidled up to him. Meeting his gaze, she said, 'Thank you for sharing this place and what happened here with me.' Before he could say a word, she rested her head upon his shoulder. His chest tightened and a knot formed in his stomach. The harder he tried to keep his feelings for this woman at a distance, the closer she came to his heart as if she were the tide raging in and he the moon above. He clenched his jaw as the familiar pull and burn in his gut took hold of him. He seethed out a breath trying to let go of the pain slowly without jarring her. Another reminder that no matter his plans, Fate had yet another. One he had no control over.

She lifted her head and faced him. 'Are you unwell?'

'Just a stomach ache. Nothing for you to worry over.'

She leaned closer and studied his face. Her lips were so achingly close to his. How he wanted to kiss her again. His gaze fell to her mouth and her eyes widened. This was a moment where he could have what he wanted or protect the fragile trust he was attempting to build with her. He quashed his desire and smiled at her instead. She'd told him of her fears and he had shared his own sordid loss. Perhaps it would serve as the foundation of something more in time.

'You do not have to hide your illness from me.' She chuckled, tilting her head. 'It is not exactly a secret.'

The ease with which she referenced his sickness always surprised him. 'Nay, it is not, but I don't wish to burden you with it either.' He lifted a loose strand of her hair and let it glide unbidden through his thumb and index finger. Her smile flickered and faded as her gaze dropped away from his. He let the strand fall back to her shoulder.

She twisted the edge of her cloak around her gloved fingertip and then met his gaze. 'Perhaps I could make a tonic to help lessen some of the symptoms. I have read many books on herbs and their medicinal uses.'

'I have had my share of foul tonics, but none have helped thus far. If you wish to try, by all means do. I will attempt them. They cannot be worse than the one Cook made for me last year.' He shivered at the memory.

She angled her body to him and her shoulders lifted. 'So, what are your symptoms? It will help me.' She rested a hand on his thigh and then as if startled by her own actions she eased it away. A reminder that she was most comfortable when she was caring for others. If he allowed her to help him, perhaps it would add another layer of trust and companionship between them.

But he'd also be exposed and vulnerable...*weak.* His heart picked up speed, and he shifted on the pew. Lorna's last words to him echoed in his head.

'Think you can dare cast me out? You're dying. Weak. Unfit to be laird. No other woman will ever want you. Not unless they are beyond desperate.'

He cleared his throat and stood, brushing imaginary dirt from his trews to avoid her knowing gaze. 'The rain has stopped. Best we make our way back while we can. Perhaps we can discuss the tonics later?'

'Aye,' she answered, following him out of the pew. 'I've much to see. The tonics can wait.'

They walked back to the castle in silence. He hadn't meant to be abrupt, but the memories of Lorna had pressed in on him so tightly he could scarce breathe. Now that he was out in the fresh air again and not pinned in by the past and his own weakness, his pulse began to slow and the fog of his mind lifted. Moira was a part of his plan to save his clan from being overtaken after his death, and he'd make sure that he didn't let the past dictate his future.

His only problem now was getting his new wife to trust him enough to share his bed and for him to live long enough to sire the heir he needed to secure that future. As they crested the final hill between them and Blackmore, Rory spied a dark stallion being taken off by one of his grooms to be brushed down and his steps faltered. He didn't recognise it.

And the amount of visitors he'd had in the last year that he didn't know could be counted on one hand. He frowned.

'Ewan!' Moira cried out and picked up her skirts to increase her pace. He faced Rory. ''Tis my brother's horse. I had worried that they would not come.' Colour filled her cheeks and Rory could not help but smile back.

'You need not wait for me,' he replied.

'Thank you,' she whispered as she broke out into a run.

He laughed at her mirth. Her childlike eagerness another reminder that she was also as fragile as he, despite her strong-willed and independent nature. He sighed. He had no idea what he was doing when it came to her. All he could hope for was to not complicate things further between them.

He tucked his hands in his trews and revelled in the feel of the familiar smooth stone beneath the soles of his boots as he reached the drive. He jogged up the steps and entered the main hall.

'What do you mean he has forbidden Brenna to come?' Moira's brittle tone revealed her irritation.

'Sister, you knew this would happen. You cannot pretend to be surprised.' Her brother's words were stiff and measured as if he'd rehearsed them on his ride over.

'Of course I am. What else should I be? You are my family.' She popped her hands to her hips and glared at him. 'While he may be angry and refuse to see me, he should not forbid you or Brenna to come.'

Rory almost felt sorry for him. *Almost.* He reached Moira's side and nodded to her brother. 'Ewan.'

'McKenna,' he replied. 'Perhaps we can talk in private, sister?'

She chuckled. 'Why? 'Tis no secret what we squabble over.'

'Fine,' he added and flicked a cross glance at Rory. 'Moira, you can still return to us. It is not too late. All will be forgotten.'

Moira snickered and crossed her arms against her chest. 'We both know that is not true.'

He rolled his eyes and shifted on his feet. 'Perhaps not all, but it can be undone. Be reasonable. You have gone against Father's wishes in a rather reckless way.

You've embarrassed him…and us with your display, but you have not bound yourself to him. Not yet. There is still time to marry another,' he murmured, attempting lower tones. He slid his gaze towards Rory, who glared back at him. Not exactly the warm words of support of a brother-in-law that a man hoped for.

Moira grasped Rory's hand in her own. 'It is you that are embarrassing me, brother. We *are* already wed. And there is nothing I wish to undo. Rory is a good man. This is where I am meant to be. Here at Blackmore. Not at Glenhaven. Father made that quite clear.'

Her brother stood with part of his mouth hanging open for so long Rory wondered if the man had suffered an apoplexy.

'Ewan?' Moira asked. 'Did you hear me?'

He laughed loudly, too loudly. 'I did not think you would truly do it, sister.' He ruffled his hair with his hand before he turned his gaze on Moira. 'You married *him*?'

Moira's cheeks flushed and she glanced at Rory before clutching her brother roughly by the arm and dragging him off. 'What is wrong with you?' she hissed. 'He is *my* choice. Respect that.'

'You could have had any man there, Moira,' he countered, his emotion making his voice carry with ease.

'But I didn't want *any* man. I wanted Rory. He is my choice, my husband, my future.'

Ewan scoffed. 'For how long?'

She didn't reply.

'I never believed you a fool until now.'

Moira released his arm and recoiled. 'I never believed *you* would abandon me until now.'

'Well, I suppose we're both full of surprises. Have a happy life, sister.' He turned on his heel and left her.

Rory shook his head as Ewan approached, moving quickly to the main doors to leave. He grasped his brother-in-law by the arm. 'Do not give up your sister because of your Father's weakness.'

'Do not lecture me on matters of time or family, McKenna, when you have neither.' He yanked his arm out of Rory's hold and left, slamming the doors behind him.

Despite the foolishness of Ewan's words, they still stung. Rory clenched his fist by his side and set his jaw. The man wasn't wrong. Rory had little experience with family and less time left to his name, but he also knew Moira was a rare creature. Ewan would see that in time.

But for now, Rory needed to care for her. He came to her and placed his hand gently on her shoulder. Before he could utter a word of comfort, she crashed into his chest, wrapping her arms around him, and began to sob. Gripping her tightly, he whispered into her hair. 'All is not lost. They will come back to you, Moira. I swear it.'

And they would. He wasn't entirely sure how he'd mend what had come to pass between her and her family, but before his own demise he'd figure out a way to sort it through. Even though at the moment he had no idea how.

Chapter Sixteen

Moira hadn't had such a good cry in a while. Despite being embarrassed by soaking through Rory's tunic, she had to admit she felt a great deal better. One last hiccup, and she met her husband's gaze. He was still holding her and rubbing her back in small circles. His comfort without rebuke had been a heady and welcome surprise. Peter had never been comfortable with emotion and had shied away from her tears, often abandoning her or ordering her to stop her foolishness. Rory wiped away a final tear with his thumb and smiled at her. 'He will realise his error in condemning you. They all will.'

She chuckled. 'You do not know my father. He is stubborn. The only one who could ever soften him was my mother, and now that she has passed he has become as fixed as the standing stones of Nether Largie in his thinking.'

He frowned and his brow crinkled. 'Perhaps now is the best time for me to tell you that I received a letter from him. He intercepted my message to the servants who wished to leave and returned it to me enclosed with his own stating that he would not be allowing any of them to depart. Not even your lady's maid, Enora.'

'Father will make their lives a misery.' Moira slipped out of Rory's arms and walked to the window where rain still fell splattering along the glass. He joined her and slipped the damp cloak she'd forgotten she was even wearing from her shoulders.

'If you figure a way for us to steal them away, tell me. I am not afraid to try yet another ruse at Glenhaven.' He smiled down at her. 'I found the first to be quite successful and worth the risk.'

She chuckled, grateful for his humour as well as his truth. His lovely grey eyes settled on her and another tiny flutter of attraction flitted through her belly. Goodness, he was kind. What in the world would she do with him? She wasn't used to it. She dropped her gaze and shifted on her feet.

A door slammed from far off. 'Rory? Rory? Did you leave the hounds out in the storm?'

Moira smiled. 'It seems your uncle has need of you.'

Rory held a finger to his lips, grabbed her hand and pulled her along as they scurried off quietly along the hallway. Pulling her close to him, he whispered in her ear, 'I will never hear the end of it for leaving his dogs out in the rain. We must escape while we can. Hurry.'

She smiled and nodded, pressing her lips together to smother a chuckle as they moved like mice scampering down one hall and then another until they had safely sealed themselves within his study and library once more.

Rory sighed as he leaned back against the closed door. 'Why don't you peruse all of those neglected volumes while I attempt to gain control over this unwieldy correspondence?'

'A great plan, I think, my laird.' She smiled and disappeared down the second row of books.

'How goes your research? It is nearly nightfall,' Rory asked, leaning around a row of books.

Moira started. *Was it nightfall already?* But he spoke the truth. She looked up from the corner she had parked herself in to read upon the floor and noted the afternoon sun had begun its slow descent along the sky. Heavens, the wall sconces would need to be lit soon. Her cheeks heated as he surveyed the smattering of open books displayed across the floor. She'd made a mess of things. 'I'm sorry,' she stammered. 'I should not have been so careless with them. I wasn't thinking. She shifted to her knees and began to attempt to close and gather the volumes that filled the small aisle.

'Nay,' he interrupted, easing into the fray of knowledge surrounding her. 'I am bored of my letter writing and intrigued by your process. Show me what you have found.' He stepped over opened volumes and settled in next to her on the floor before she could utter a refusal. His large frame filled the small space and his presence made her shy and uncertain. Did he *really* wish to know what interested her and what she had learned? Peter never had, nor her father. Not even Ewan had ever asked to know what she was truly interested in or what latest volume she was devouring. She bit her lip, studying his eyes that settled on her with openness and expectation, trying to determine his sincerity.

She glanced down to the volume in her lap and faltered. Sharing what she cared about with him was a risk. She ran a finger over the safe, tidy words on the page. What if he laughed? Called her foolish? She tucked a lock of hair behind her ear.

'Please, Moira,' he said, resting his hand on the same page, the edge of his pinky finger touching her own, sending a tiny spark of awareness through her. 'Let me in. Tell me what you are reading. What you care about. I would not ask if I did not want to know.'

Something in his words made her want to believe him, yet she couldn't bring herself to let go. Not yet. He lifted the volume from her lap and began to read aloud about the uses of cloves and what it could remedy. He reached the section about its uses for curing toothaches and paused. 'Does it truly do that?'

Moira shrugged. 'So it seems although I have never tried it.'

He shook his head. 'Fascinating.' He flipped the book over and looked at the cover. 'I swear to you I have never seen this book before this very moment.'

She laughed. 'Based on the amount of dust on many of these volumes, I would guess neither has anyone else.'

He answered with a laugh of his own. 'You are quite right.' He looked at the volumes and back at her. 'It brings me joy to know you will use them. I am glad you are here. That you said yes to marrying this almost dead man.' His full smile made her breath catch in her throat. He pressed a light kiss to her cheek and stood, brushing the dust from his trews and jacket.

The clock chimed and he extended his hand to her. 'Care to ready yourself? Uncle shall join us at half past. He prefers to dine early, as do I.'

'Aye,' she answered, attempting to stand. She accepted his hand and grimaced. 'Oh, the prickles. My foot is asleep.'

'Shall I carry you?' he teased, smiling at her, attempting to grab her waist.

She flushed and stepped out of his hold. 'Nay. I shall be fine.'

His smile fell away, and he busied himself with picking up the opened books and stacking them by the window. 'I'll leave these here for you in case you wish to look through them again tomorrow.'

Blast. She hadn't meant to reject him.

She added the final two to the stack and walked beside him back to their chambers. Why had she pulled away from him? He'd not been unkind or untoward. She couldn't shake the reminders of Peter and her shame of the past, but hoped one day she would.

Dinner was most likely delicious, but Moira couldn't taste a whit of it. Worry plagued her throughout the meal. She had to explain to him. To help him truly understand. After all he had given her in bringing her here and providing her a future. He hadn't even plagued her about her reluctance to share his bed. They returned back to their rooms in silence and she thought of screaming just to break the dull throbbing nothingness between them.

She tugged at her hands, restless at her door. Instead of opening it, she faced him unable to suffer through another moment of quiet. 'Care to share a drink with me before bed, my laird?'

His hand faltered on the knob of the door to his own chamber and he met her gaze. His face went slack. His confusion evident and warranted.

She tilted her head and looked heavenward trying to find the words. 'I wish to try to explain to you my hesitation, my reluctance. It's important to me.'

He opened his door and gestured for her to come in. 'Then it is also important to me.'

The scent of soap and tallow assaulted her as she stepped into his chambers, and she took a heady breath of the smell she was beginning to find comfort in.

'Sir?' Angus asked, coming from the back of the room.

'I'll manage on my own this eve. You may take your leave,' Rory stated.

Angus gave a small nod. 'My lady. Ring if ye have need of me, sir.'

'Aye,' Rory answered. He walked over to the glass decanter and poured himself a whisky in his favoured McKenna chalice as well as a dram for herself in a small glass.

She settled into one of the pair of chairs that ensconced the hearth and stared into the embers and flames licking along the fire that burned steadily before her. 'Moira,' he murmured, extending the glass to her. Her fingers slid around it, resting atop his briefly before his own eased away.

He settled into the chair next to her and took a drink from his chalice. The gems encased on the sides of it caught the firelight and glistened at her briefly, daring her to speak.

Just begin, Moira. Just begin.

She cleared her throat and clutched the glass so tightly she feared it might shatter in her grasp. 'I truly believed I loved him at first. Peter, that is. He said all the things a man in love was supposed to say. Did all the right things to appease my family and friends. He made them believe he was a good man and that he loved me, but in truth he was the devil.'

Rory shifted in his seat and when she lifted her gaze to his, she was startled by the hard flint grey of his eyes. He said nothing though, but swirled the whisky in his cup and waited for her to continue.

'For a while, a few weeks, he was that man I had believed him to be. Honourable. Good. Kind. But then…' Her eyes narrowed in on the memory, the memory of the first betrayal, and heat flushed her limbs along with a chilling cold. 'One night, I displeased him. I had a megrim and I refused his attentions when he came to my bed later that eve.' Her heart pounded, a trembling began from within and worked its way out to her limbs. She'd never told anyone about the first time.

Just say it. He deserves to know the truth.

She sucked in a breath and stared into the fire as it reflected and danced in light and shadow. 'As the first-born son of a laird, he was a man unused to being refused, and as he was twice my size, I was not strong enough to fend him off. You can imagine the rest.' She shook off the memory of his breath on her cheek and the force of his hands on her wrists. That same sickening shame slid through her limbs coating her in regret, but she pressed on. 'After that, there were many ways in which I displeased him no matter how hard I tried, and he made no efforts to hide it from me in his words and in his physical treatment of me. Over the few years we were married, I became a smaller and smaller version of myself, hiding away from everyone. There was a time I wished to disappear into the ether to escape him as I believed there would be no other way to end my misery. His death was an unexpected blessing.'

Blinking back the emotion that threatened, she took a longer draw from her whisky and coughed a bit from the heat as it slid down her throat. She'd said it. Well, not all of it, but enough for him to understand her reluctance. 'So you see, my laird. It is not you. It is me.'

'So when I came in that first night and you were there naked. That was what he expected of you?' His gaze was steady, unflinching and without judgment.

'Aye. And I found over time it was easier to simply comply.'

Rory thought he would retch. The acid and sickness churning in his gut at the news of what her husband had done to her during their marriage was more than he could manage. *More than any man could manage.* His sweet, beautiful wife had been forced—he stopped his mind from calling it what it was—by her own husband. Rory swallowed the rage that threatened to burst from him in a series of curses. His dark-haired delicate flower of a wife had been crushed and smothered under the hold of that tyrant for years. He drained the rest of the whisky from his chalice, savouring the burn down his throat, and set it on the table beside him, so he didn't throw it at the wall in anger. He pounded the arm of the chair instead and rose hastily from it, walking to the window to stare out at the moon and the silver-grey clouds slicing along the black skies.

He cursed. 'It is a good thing he is dead, Moira. Otherwise, I would be hanged for his murder.'

'He would not have been worth such a loss,' she answered. She sounded so small, so far away, yet when he turned he found she stood a mere length behind him. His arms ached to hold her, but he didn't dare, not after such an admission. He didn't wish for her to think he wanted to take advantage of her vulnerability, so he held his ground.

'I am so sorry,' he stated, his words slashing the air like daggers. 'So bloody sorry for what he did to you. He was no husband, but a brute and a coward.'

'I know that now. You are teaching me such over the few days I have known you.' She met his gaze then, and her eyes shone bright as bluebells in the reflection of the moonlight. He sucked in a breath. His body shifted from her praise of him, and he opened and closed his fists at his sides. He didn't know what to do. They stared at one another before his body finally breached his command and closed the distance between them, stopping close to her, but not touching her.

'You will *never* fear such from me, Moira. As I live and breathe, I swear it,' he murmured. He risked everything and reached out his hand to her.

She hesitated and then slid her fingertips over his palm, wrapping her hand over his own. 'I know that, and I am so very grateful for it. I know what is at stake for you.'

'We will find our way through this, so everyone gets what they want and yet without anyone getting hurt. I know we can.' He squeezed her hand, and she squeezed back and smiled.

He just wasn't exactly sure how.

His gut twisted, his stomach souring, and he flinched involuntarily from the pain in his abdomen, letting her hand go. Her eyes widened in alarm. 'Rory? What is wrong? Is it your stomach?'

'Aye.' He grimaced, almost doubling over as another sharp pain struck.

'Will lying down help?' she asked.

'Nay, it is worse. Sitting will be better.' He walked hunched over back to his chair with her arm wound around his waist supporting him. He collapsed in the chair and groaned as another sharp spasm seized him.

'Shall I ring for Angus?'

'Nay.' Rory breathed out a gasp. 'But if you'll bring me the tonic by my bedside table. It is in a small flask. It will help.'

She hurried off and returned with it. She twisted off the cap and sniffed it. 'Thistles. That smells dreadful.'

Her puckered face made him laugh, a welcome distraction to the pain. He took it from her and choked down a mouthful. 'Ack.' He shook his head as the foul liquid made its way down his throat. After a minute the harsh pain subsided. 'But it does help to quell the most intense spasms.'

She knelt before him, resting a palm on his knee, her eyes wide with concern. 'Will you finally tell me of this curse of yours? I want to understand. See if I can somehow help with whatever this sickness is. I feel powerless.'

He understood exactly how she felt. So did he. He sighed and covered her hand with his own. The least he could do was share his own horrors, since she had bared her own to him. 'Where shall I begin?' he murmured.

'Wherever you wish.' She squeezed his hand, rose and settled back into her own chair, tucking her feet beneath her. She leaned on her elbow on the arm of the chair intent for him to start.

'I have been told that it is a curse cast upon our families from a healer, a very powerful one, it seems.'

'A healer? Why would a healer curse your family? Isn't that the opposite of their mission?'

'Well, it all began over a century ago, according to legend, with the birth of a small boy named Gabriel. He grew up strong and worshipped his father, as many boys do. His father was one of the finest soldiers and served the McKennas. He died in battle, and his son was determined to serve as well. He became one of my ancestor's most trusted men and served alongside the laird at that time, a Laird Daileass McKenna.

'Daileass was eager to impress his new bride and thus made hasty decisions regarding warfare and infighting in the Highlands. He cared little about the lives of the men who might be lost or the impact on their families. He was not the most admirable of the McKennas.

'Gabriel was sent out to lead a foolhardy mission to overtake a band of soldiers along the border wall and gather riches from them that they had stolen from the British. As you might have guessed, Gabriel and many of his men didn't survive. And even worse, they were never retrieved for burial. They were piked and left to rot along the border wall for days before Daileass sent men to cut them down and gather what they could for their final rest.'

'Let me guess, Gabriel was the healer's son.'

'Aye. So, she put a curse on the McKennas starting with Daileass's son. No McKenna heir would live past four and twenty, the very age of her son at his death.'

'That's quite a horrid tale. Do you believe it?'

He shrugged. 'It seemed fanciful when I was a lad, but look at me. I am dying. How can I dispute such evidence?'

Her fingers stilled and a shiver passed through her. He couldn't. Nor could she, so she chose to ignore it instead.

'When did you begin feeling ill? To believe you might be affected?'

He toyed with a loose thread on his armchair and stared into the fire. 'Hmm. I would say about a year ago.'

'First symptoms?' she enquired.

He lifted his eyebrows. 'Well, Doctor,' he teased. 'Stomach cramps, fatigue, lack of appetite.'

'What does your actual doctor say it is?'

'He's given me a variety of possible diagnoses. The most recent and perplexing possibility is poisoning.'

She sat upright. 'Poisoning. From what? By whom?'

'And there lies the mystery. It is as if my body is turning on me and poisoning itself.'

'That doesn't make any sense. And most poisons are fast-acting with a rather sudden and permanent effect on the body. Does he believe you are having some slow exposure to it? Does he believe that has happened to all of the McKennas?'

He leaned back in his chair, crossing his leg at the knee. 'Why the sudden interest?'

'To be truthful, I have always been interested in healing, but find myself more curious as I get to know you.'

'Oh?'

Moira shrugged. 'I rather enjoy your company, much as it surprises me. Perhaps having a husband and being a wife is not so horrid after all.' She paused and smiled at him. 'At least not with you.'

She dropped her gaze and felt her cheeks flush with heat.

'And I find that you, Moira McKenna, are not so bad to have as a wife either.'

'Will you let me investigate? Do you have any old McKenna family journals I may read or books on poisons? Perhaps we can find what ails you and make you well and whole once more.'

He reached over and took one of her hands and held it between his own. 'I am moved by your desire to help me, but I do not wish my last few months to be consumed with such hope when I will surely die. It is not fair to you.'

'Or you,' she murmured.

'Aye. Let us revel in the blessings we have in finding each other for now. Agreed?'

She crossed the fingers of her other hand behind her back. 'Agreed.'

Chapter Seventeen

Almost a month had passed since their wedding day and still Rory had not pressed her upon joining his bed. His health also hadn't improved. Moira had read dozens of books on poisons, herbs and even a few of the old McKenna journals that Rory and Angus could unearth for her, but nothing had brought them any closer to determining the cause of his sickness or the cure for it.

They'd settled into a peaceful and comfortable routine of walking with the hounds after breaking their fast each morn followed by hours in the study for him and hours in the library or solarium for her. Then they enjoyed supper with Uncle Leo followed by a drink by the fire. Each night, Rory walked her to her chamber door, gave her a light kiss and bid her good eve. She'd grown used to and comforted by his touch. The way his hand would rest on the small of her back when he escorted her anywhere, even if it was only back to her chambers. The feathery feel of his body near her when they stood side by side along the rows of books in the library. His touch no longer startled her. She'd grown to trust it, to trust him, and to look forward to the sound of his footfalls down the hall.

All in all, Moira was content, happy and comfortable, except for the part about her not following through on the terms of their marriage agreement. Guilt was beginning its ugly advance upon Moira's spirit. Sickness darkened his eyes and the way he often dozed in the afternoon while looming over his ledger told her his time on this earth was dwindling away. She was supposed to be helping him in the process of siring an heir, yet she kept to her bed and he never asked otherwise. He'd been true to his word about not pressuring her, but she was doing a fine job of torturing herself about it. His birthday was in mid-March. It was almost mid-November. She bit her lip. Four months wasn't much time.

If she did not make haste, she might be responsible for the end of a clan, and these people had been nothing but kind and welcoming to her. They had accepted her from the first moment, and she'd found herself valued and listened to. She was even making friends and coming out of the shadows she had hidden in for far too long. Shadows she'd become desperate to find and hide in to escape Peter.

Moira secretly watched Rory from the corner of her makeshift desk in the back of the library. The lovely little piece of furniture had been moved from one of the guest rooms, so she could read while enjoying the view of the rolling sea and cliff side rather than reading on the floor as she'd done when she'd first arrived. Rory sat opening correspondence. She'd discovered many of his quirks and what they meant. All in all, she was enjoying getting to know her husband.

'What has you frowning so?' she asked.

He paused and looked up at her through the gaps in the shelving. He smiled at her. 'Are you watching me?' he teased.

'Aye,' she admitted. 'You are a handsome man and you are my husband. 'Tis no crime.'

A sly smile curled his lips and the furrow in his brow relaxed as he closed the letter and rose from his desk. 'Nay, it is not a crime, but now I am curious as to why.' He lifted an eyebrow at her and tilted his head.

She shrugged. 'No reason.'

She smiled and faced her window again and gasped. She flattened her palm against the glass. 'The first snowflakes! I must go outside.' She snapped the book shut on her desk and rose in such haste that her chair almost clattered to the floor.

He laughed, glancing at the wall clock. ''Tis almost dark, Moira. Let me come with you.'

'All right, then. Let's hurry. I don't wish to miss a flake!' She grabbed his hand and tugged him along.

They rushed along the hallway and Rory donned his overcoat and hat and then helped Moira into her cloak. Flipping up the collar of his wool coat, Rory smiled at her. 'Shall we?'

'Aye,' she answered, slipping her arm within his own and following him out the back door of Blackmore. The light dusting of snow on the ground swallowed the sounds of their footfalls as they jogged along the hillside. The sunset was a myriad of bright pinks and purples as the snowflakes blew about them. The snow intensified and began to lay, covering the cold ground quickly.

Moira stopped, tilted back her head and opened her mouth to the sky, catching the cool frozen flakes on her tongue. His laughter echoed. 'What are you doing?'

'Enjoying my first snowflake of the winter for good luck.'

'Then so shall I.' He tipped his head back and his hat tumbled to the ground.

'You have lost your hat, my laird,' she jested, picking up his cap. She stealthily shovelled some snow in it and put it on his head, tapping it into place.

Snow popped out of the sides of his hat and down his face. 'You little minx,' he muttered. He yanked the hat from his head, shook out the snow and gave chase.

Moira laughed and dodged his advance. She'd had much practice escaping the revenge of her siblings in snow battles in the past. After a small chase around the hillside, he finally captured her by the waist in the small copse of trees surrounding the chapel. They tumbled to the ground laughing. After their laughter subsided he looked down at her, his gaze heavy with meaning, and kissed her.

To her surprise, she kissed him back eager for the touch of his lips on hers and soon the kisses deepened. She wound her fingers in his damp hair and savoured his warmth and strength above her and the cool, solid ground beneath. Tingles of snow cooled her face as his caresses banked a fire within her. In the blink of an eye, she wanted him, desired him, and found she was no longer afraid of being intimate with her husband.

The revelation stole her breath even more than her husband's touch. Too soon, he pulled back and smiled at her. 'Best we go in before we freeze to the ground and become covered by snowfall.'

'And what if I said I'd rather not,' she whispered, dragging her thumb across his lower lip.

He stilled, his eyes wide, studying her face as if he were attempting to make sense of her nonsensical implication. Despite the growing shadows as the sun passed its responsibility to the moon and the snow swirling above him, she spied the uncertainty in Rory's face. 'I fear I do not trust my ears.' He ran a hand along her cheek. 'I think my desire and want of you has made me addled.'

She laughed. 'I am asking you to make love to me, husband. Is that plain enough for you?'

His eyebrows threatened to rise into his hairline. 'Here? Now?'

'Aye,' she answered. ''Tis time.'

'You are sure. I don't wish to rush you,' he stammered, running a hand through his hair and shifting his weight onto one side.

'If you do not wish it, then we do not have to,' she answered.

'Nay, nay,' he rushed out. 'I have never longed for a woman as much as I do you, Moira, and the fact that you are my wife makes such desire even more exquisite.'

His muscles tightened, and she could feel the thrumming need pulsing through him as it matched her own.

She removed a glove and slid a hand between them and under his tunic until she could splay her palm flat along his bare chest. He trembled against her and closed his eyes. A small curse of pleasure echoed through his clenched teeth. He released a breath and set his glazed, hooded eyes upon her.

'Then, wife, I shall give in to your command,' he murmured, leaning over her and pressing a trail of urgent and swoon-worthy kisses along her neck. 'Otherwise, what sort of husband would I be?'

This...this is what it must be like to be seduced, desired to within an inch of reason.

And it was lovely.

She trembled against him as his hands caressed her despite the mountain of material that divided their flesh. The soapy scent of him mixed with the vibrant smells of earth, wooded trees and the crisp, cool snowfall lit her senses on fire. This...this is where she wished to first join with her husband. In nature, there were no memories of blankets, beds and hasty couplings. This would be a new memory to stamp over the old. She knew she could never erase her memories of Peter, but she could paint over them one by one with Rory.

Ack.

Rory had never wanted a woman as he did Moira. And now of all places, in the middle of the forest with dusk settling in around them, she finally wanted him. The irony made him wish to laugh aloud. He could scarce think or hear as the thrumming of need threatened to drown out any lucid thought he had.

Steady. Steady.

He wouldn't rush, despite how his body demanded it. He would take it slow, even if he wanted to ravish her. He was not Peter Fraser. This would be his chance to be gentle, take his time and show her of the pleasure she could have. When she lowered her hand to unbutton his trews, he gasped and grit his teeth.

'Moira,' he pleaded. The woman would rush this along if she weren't careful.

She granted him a wicked smile. A beautiful flush from exertion filled her cheeks, and his breath hitched in his throat. Her bright blue eyes and full lips distracted him from speaking.

''Tis not my first coupling. You need not seduce me or tarry. I am ready.' She shifted her leg up and he sighed at the sight of her bare flesh. It seemed he would need to rethink his plan.

Sweat beaded his forehead and his body vibrated at the thought of being one with his wife. She popped one button on his trews and then another. He cursed and tugged up her skirts.

She gasped and he stilled until she pulled him down to her. He kissed her deeply and soon he was joined with his wife as one surrounded by smooth soft blankets of snowfall. The sweet cry of her release followed by his own a reminder that he was still alive and his hope of keeping the McKenna line from dying out was also.

Good Lord.

She didn't know it could be quite like *that*. She sighed with pleasure, sated like a cat having lapped up a full bowl of warm milk. If it hadn't been cold and windy, she might have wished to fall asleep right here and now amidst the forest draped in a blanket of fallen snow.

Moira closed her eyes and clutched her husband's head to her chest. She and Peter had never had such a connection, and the beauty of it created a smooth stroke of bold, bright colour to blot out the dark, muted shades of her past. Their first union had been a grand first step to letting go.

Both of them were out of breath and heated despite the budding cold as they lay on the ground. The temperature had dropped and heavier snow threatened. The moon was now full and climbing higher into the dark night skies. Their breath twined in smoky columns of air reminding her that they would be missed for their evening meal with Uncle Leo soon, and that they truly shouldn't get any colder and damp than they already were by remaining on the snowy ground. She playfully ruffled her husband's hair.

'Now, I believe I am ready to go in, my laird,' she teased.

He rested his chin on her chest and grinned at her. 'I am at your bidding, my lady. Whatever you wish.' He brushed a fingertip to her cheek, creating a single spark of desire in her once more. Surprise rippled through her at her body's response. She had no idea she might crave more so soon. It seemed her body and Rory McKenna were full of surprises.

He shifted and straightened his trews as well as her skirts. Gaining purchase, he reached down and drew her up beside him to standing. They both brushed crushed snow from their clothes and each other, and then headed off to the castle. He tugged her hand as the snow turned into thick downy blankets steadily collapsing one after another upon them as they jogged towards the lit torches flickering outside of Blackmore. Laughter pealed through the air as they climbed the stairs, and for a moment she felt like the newlywed she was and not the widow she had long been. Hope bloomed full in her chest, and for the first time in a long time, she wanted for nothing. This moment was perfect.

Chapter Eighteen

A few more minutes out in the snow with her and Rory might have attempted to make love to his wife once more then and there on the forest floor. He shook the snow from his head and attempted to regain his reason as they stood in the main hall, shrugging off their outer clothes. He felt like a lad having stolen his first kiss. He righted his still twisted trews. In some aspects he most likely looked like one too. He batted away a glob of snow from Moira's backside and she laughed anew.

'Ah! There you are, son.' His uncle called to him from the other end of the hall, splintering their revelry. Their chuckles dwindled away, and Rory cleared his throat.

'Aye, Uncle?' he asked, not meeting his elder's gaze, lest he see a blush on his cheeks.

'We must speak. A letter has arrived.'

The mere fact that he didn't say who'd sent it in front of Moira told Rory it was another missive from Bran and most likely a nasty one. Over the last few weeks, the

Stewart laird had sent regular correspondence deploring what Rory had done in whisking away his widowed daughter and marrying her against the man's wishes. Rory frowned. The laird was hell-bent on making their lives a misery. 'Go ahead and ready yourself for supper,' he urged, shaking out Moira's cloak and kissing her cheek. 'I will speak with Uncle.'

'I shall look in on my lovelies, and then ready myself. Soon, they will need to be transferred to larger pots. They love it here.'

As I love having you here.

The words had bubbled up in his mind before he could even stop them. He watched her disappear around the corner and faced his uncle. 'What has my dear father-in-law demanded now?' he asked in low tones once he was sure Moira was out of earshot.

'Come with me.' Uncle's features were tight and drawn. Rory knew he wouldn't like whatever it was one bit as his uncle wasn't a man prone to scowling.

Once they were sealed in the vault of his uncle's chambers, Uncle Leo turned to him. 'He has made yet another complaint of your hasty marriage to Moira and claims it is not legal. He accuses you of theft of his property.'

Rory blanched. 'What? Moira left willingly. She accepted my proposal. Hell, she initially proposed to me.'

'Aye. I know that, but he claims Moira is his property and that you absconded with it without arranging settlements first. He demands funds from you for the union or he shall take the matter to the king.'

Rory scoffed. 'The king will not care.'

'Nay, he won't, but the uproar Bran will create will undermine us amongst the other clans and weaken our position further.'

'Further?'

'May I speak plainly?'

'Don't you always?'

Uncle set his stare upon Rory. 'This is serious, dire even. There is talk of the Stewarts, the Frasers and other clans making an alliance to undermine you and this clan. To absorb us into their own clans once you are gone.'

'Dead, you mean?'

'Aye.'

'While I understand why Bran is angry with me for whiling away his daughter against his wishes as he is a man driven by control, why are the Frasers now our enemy? Moira was their daughter-in-law, and we have no qualms with them. We never have.' He tugged loose his cravat and set his hands on his waist.

'It seems they now blame Moira for Peter's death and for not producing an heir in the time they were married. They say you are providing her refuge.'

'Refuge from what? What exactly do they insinuate about her being to blame for her first husband's death?' White hot anger boiled within him.

'It is unclear, but the idle talk is spreading like creeping thistle and threatens to smother out the truth.'

'Blame *her*?' He cursed aloud, muttering, 'She was lucky to have survived.'

Uncle Leo's brows knit together. 'What do you mean?' A muscle worked in his jaw.

Rory shook his head. 'I cannot betray her trust by speaking of it to you so plainly, but know that she was ill-used and her husband a brute. He will earn no sympathy from me. Truth be told, if he were still alive, I would kill him myself.'

His uncle slapped the letters down on the table. 'I suspected as much. Why else would she be so eager to…' But he had the kindness to stop himself from saying the rest.

'I know. A woman must have reasons for affixing herself to a dying man. I asked her about it the moment we met. While she hinted at unhappiness, it was not until we were married that she shared the details of what she suffered by his hands. And I am not entirely sure I know all of it. Trust me in that you do not wish to know.'

'Well, what is to be done, Rory? We cannot counter their narrative without exposing Moira to scrutiny, but we also cannot leave it left unanswered. These are serious accusations against her. They will not die out on their own, especially with Bran bent on feeding the flames about us thieving his daughter away without recompense.'

Rory crossed his arms against his chest. As usual, his uncle was right. It could not go unanswered. If there was an inkling of Moira being barren or a whiff of intrigue about her being the cause of Peter's death it would bring her unwanted attention and make the clan appear weak and vulnerable to attack. Without a clear heir, the McKennas already were.

'What are our options?' Rory asked. 'Seek an alliance with another clan? Provide settlements for Bran? Both leave a sour taste in my mouth.'

'We might not have a choice. We must act and quickly. I say within the next few days, if not sooner. Otherwise, it may become something we cannot stop.'

'Let me think upon it. We will come up with a plan, Uncle. We have come too far to lose now, especially to the likes of Bran and the Frasers.'

Uncle Leo nodded and slapped Rory on the shoulder. 'And keep working on that heir, son.' He winked at him and heat filled Rory's cheeks.

It was then he realised his trews were still partially unbuttoned and his jacket askew. Then he laughed a full, deep laugh from his belly, and, rather eager to take his uncle's advice, turned down the hallway and headed towards his chambers. He and his bride would be enjoying supper in their rooms tonight. The Stewarts and Frasers be damned.

Moira swirled her finger in the dark hair peppering Rory's chest and rested her cheek upon his shoulder. After another round of lovemaking, they had enjoyed a quick respite of supper before crawling back into her bed to snuggle together. Snow continued to fall outside and the moonlight reflected against it created beautiful shadows of dark and light.

'I do not know if I have ever felt so content,' she murmured.

'Nor I,' he replied, running a hand over the smooth loose waves of her hair that covered most of her back.

'What news from your uncle? I had never seen him with such a scowl before.'

He stiffened beneath her, and a tremor passed through her. He was keeping something from her, but what? Was he growing sicker?

'You need not shield me from anything, Rory. I am stronger than I look.' She rested her chin on his chest, so she could almost see his face. He ran a hand through his hair and down his face.

''Tis your father.'

Her stomach churned, and she popped up on an elbow as alarm set her heart racing. 'Is he ill?' Perhaps her hasty departure had made his sickness worse.

He clutched her hand and propped himself up so he could meet her gaze. 'He is not unwell; however, he is angry.'

'At me?'

'Nay. At me. I have whisked you away. He claims our union is not valid and plans to make such a case to the king.'

'Then let him. The fool...' she huffed out. '*I* proposed to you. There is no cause for such a claim. And we have already made our union official, have we not?'

'Aye,' he whispered, his voice husky and low as he twirled a lock of her hair in his fingertips. 'That we have. Several times now, which I have thoroughly enjoyed.' He smiled and then his eyes lingered briefly over her body. Her flesh warmed from his gaze. He sighed and brought his focus back to her face. 'Sadly, your word matters little in the eyes of the law. It shall be my word against his, and he has many powerful friends, as you well know, while I have equally few.'

She nibbled her lip, sat up, and clutched her legs and the covers over them to her chest. Just when things had become comfortable, her world was shifting once more beneath her feet.

He followed suit, pulling her back against him. 'Do not worry yourself. Uncle and I are thinking upon a response even now.'

She sighed, turned in his arms, and met his gaze. 'What is it he demands? My return?'

His gaze drifted from her and studied a landscape of the cliffs that hung to the left of her. His lips in a thin stoic line of resistance.

'You will tell me.'

'I don't wish to hurt you. There is no need for you to involve yourself in it.'

'I spent far too long *not* asking and *not* involving myself in matters, and it ended quite poorly for me if you remember. I refuse to become that woman again. You will tell me what he demands. I wish to know everything, no matter how ugly.'

'He wishes financial recompense from me for stealing away your possibilities of marrying another with greater financial means.'

She scoffed. 'Ewan must not have told him of the expansiveness of Blackmore. You have more than abundant financial means.'

Rory nodded. 'Aye. I believe Ewan *did* tell his father of it and that is why this new demand has now surfaced. Prior to your brother's visit, your father's letters were mere vitriolic nonsense from a man unused to being ignored. Ravings he could not express in person.'

Foolish man.

'I am embarrassed by his treatment of you. And of me. I am sorry.' She picked at a corner of the blanket. Why was her father always making a mess of things?

He lifted her chin. 'You need never apologise for others. You cannot control him, nor anyone else. He will do as he wishes. And I believe I will send him coin to cease his complaints. It matters not to me. You are all I care about.'

The buzz and flutter in her belly grew fat and full with desire and longing. She reached for him, kissed him deeply and pushed away the ugliness of the past as she settled happily into the present.

Chapter Nineteen

Another three weeks passed, and Rory found himself content. Dying but still content. How many men could say such? He and Moira were working diligently on begetting a McKenna heir, a joyful daily endeavour. She was a passionate woman who enjoyed his touch and trusted him. A feat he thought impossible on their wedding night. His gut tightened. He worried heartedly that he would muck it all up at any moment or die before he'd secured the heir he needed to sustain his bloodline. Each day his body grew weaker despite taking healthy doses of tonics and medicine, and soon he would be four and twenty. March was three months away, and according to the dreaded McKenna curse, he would be dead before then.

He watched Moira out in the distance with the hounds. He hadn't planned on caring for her as he did, and he wondered if it was even fair to. He would be gone, and she would be here missing him. He sighed. Little could be done on either account. The wife he had

hoped to one day beguile and seduce had done such to
him instead. But he couldn't complain, could he? At
least he would die a happy man, and his wife seemed
happy too. A far cry from the woman he had met in the
tournament field months ago. There was not a cloud in
the sky on this glorious bright December afternoon, but
as with all things in the Highlands, the weather could
change quickly and without warning.

Footfalls sounded down the hallway and Rory
smiled. He'd recognise his uncle's uneven gait anywhere. He rose from his chair and greeted him at the
threshold of the door. His uncle patted him on the shoulder and then settled into the chair opposite the large
desk where Rory sat in his study.

'And what of your journey, Uncle? And the Camerons?'

His uncle paused. 'I met with them. Cunning bas-
tards are the same as always. Demanding the tunic you
wear as well as your trews. They leave a man with nothing.' He smirked and shook his head.

Rory leaned back in his chair. This wasn't the news
he'd hoped for. He forged ahead and asked anyway.
'Have you assured an alliance with them? One that will
keep you, Moira and the clan safe?' *After I am gone.*
He could have added that, but he didn't wish to. 'I need
some assurance that Bran Stewart and the Frasers will
not exact their revenge on Moira and our clan. Despite
the sizeable coin we gifted Bran, he still seems mal-
content, and I would not put anything past the Frasers.'

His uncle's sigh gave little comfort. 'Nor would I.'

'And?'

'In the end, the Camerons will come round, but mostly due to a common loathing of the Frasers, but it shall take more time…and more coin.'

Rory shook his head. 'Coin I have, time I do not. What will it take to secure it?'

'You will not like it,' Uncle Leo answered, dropping his gaze. 'See the amended terms for yourself.' He pulled a rolled parchment from inside his coat pocket and extended it to Rory.

The hardness in his uncle's eyes told Rory that he would more than not like it. He would hate it. He untied it and rolled it out, scanning it as he went.

'They cannot be serious,' he muttered, dragging a palm down his face.

'As a Highland storm, son.'

Rory slammed his fist into the wood and the desk shook under the force, causing the stack of ledgers to slide to the floor. 'This is no agreement. This is thievery.'

Uncle nested his hands in his trouser pockets. 'I wish we had other options, but we have none. The Camerons are the largest and closest of the clans that we could align with. The Frasers and Stewarts hold weight along the Highlands, and to go against either of them has consequences. The Camerons have no current loyalty to either of us, but this…if you agree to this, you will have their influence and Bran Stewart and Tavish Fraser will not.'

'But you and Moira and our people could end up with nothing.' He cursed and released a bellow of frustration. 'And all because I will be dead.'

'You forget that there is a chance they may not be able to make that last claim.'

Rory sighed, pressed his palms flat to the desk and leaned forward letting his head fall forward. ''Tis unlikely.'

'Why? You have bedded your wife. She could be carrying your child even now. You could have an heir, and it could be a boy. And if she bears a male heir, your heir, within a year of your death, then the clan and she and your boy will be untouched and safe under the Camerons' veil of protection.'

'Even if that were somehow a reality and there are many ifs within that, can you trust they will not just slay them both in their sleep to overtake our clan?'

Uncle Leo shrugged. 'The Camerons may be greedy and cunning, but they are not ruthless nor are they murderers. They would not dare it.'

'And we have no other options remaining, do we?'

'Nay, son. We don't.'

'I need more time. I'll not sign it yet.'

'Don't wait too long. Something is in the air. I can feel it.'

'My lady?' Tressa called.

Moira turned and smiled. She walked towards her maid with the hounds bounding before her to greet their newest human companion. 'Aye. What is it?' she asked, pushing a rogue lock of hair from her face.

'A letter arrived for ye, by way of messenger, at the front gate. Sean bid me pass it along to ye.'

'Thank you.' Moira took it and then waved to Tressa,

as her maid began the trek back to the castle. *Odd.*
Moira didn't recognise the curling script and no dec-
oration appeared on the generic wax seal that held it
closed. She popped the letter opened and scanned it.

As she read the meagre three lines on the note again,
her body numbed. Then she broke out in a full run after
her lady's maid. 'Tressa! Who brought this? Who was
the messenger?' She grabbed her maid by the arm.

Tressa's eyes widened, and she stammered. 'I cannot
say, my lady. Perhaps Sean might know.'

'Take in the hounds, please. I must find him. And
quickly.'

Moira ran around the estate to the front gate. Sean
worked alongside the road, and she spotted him with
ease.

'Sean, who was the messenger of this note?' she
commanded.

Sean froze. 'Unknown to me, my lady. He wasn't
local. Didn't give a name, and I didn't think to ask.'

'And the plaid?'

He squinted and paused. 'Could have been a Mac-
Donnell or a Fraser, maybe.'

A Fraser? Ice chilled her veins.

'Which way?'

'My lady?' Sean asked.

'Which way did he go? Leave by?'

'Headed right back down where he'd come up from.
To the village, I would guess.'

'How long ago?'

He blushed and dropped his gaze. 'Brought it by this
morn, but I forgot. Mare was on the loose and I tucked

it away only to remember it when I saw Tressa. I was distracted. My apologies.'

Hours had passed. 'Bring me my mount. Make haste! I must try to find him.'

'But, my lady, you cannot go alone.'

'I can and I will. Tell the laird that I have gone to the village to see the healer.'

He shifted on his feet.

'Now go,' Moira ordered, her tone sharp and un-yielding in the panic of anxiety that pumped through her. She had to find this man. She had to know what he knew and how he knew it before he ruined everything.

'What do you mean she's gone?' Rory growled. He glared down at the lad who dared give him the news he surely didn't wish to hear, especially with dusk but an hour away and a storm settling in. He could see the darkening clouds off in the distance headed their way. It wouldn't be long.

Sean cowered. 'She ordered me to ready her horse, my laird, which I did. I dinna believe I could refuse her. She went to the village for a visit with the healer.'

'So why did she not just say as much to me?'

The lad didn't answer, but his face flushed with co-lour, and Rory leaned closer to him. 'Spit it out, lad. Why?'

He squared his shoulders and straightened up. 'She was upset by the note, my laird. I dinna believe she was travelling to see the healer, but to find the messenger who brought the letter.'

'What letter?' he demanded.

Tressa chimed in. 'Sean was given a note by messenger this morn, and I brought it to my lady later in the day. She opened it and was in quite a state. Wanted to know who brought it, so I told her to ask Sean.' She worried her hands. 'I did not think she would go after the man, especially not in her—' She bit her lip, faltered and blushed.

Lord above. Why was this taking so long? He didn't have time for this. 'In her what, Tressa?'

Her brow wrinkled. 'I'm not sure, my laird, but I think she may be—' her voice dropped to a whisper and her beet red cheeks deepened to scarlet '—with child.'

Joy and anguish gripped him at once and he felt weak in the knees. Uncle Leo rested a hand on his shoulder. She might be carrying his son even now and be in danger. He righted himself, nodded and shoved his fear aside. Finding her safe and alive was most important. 'Get my horse. Ready the carriage. Get Angus and a few men from the house. We must find her. Now.'

Once the servants departed, Uncle faced him. 'You and I both know you are not well enough to ride. Let me take the men to find her. You stay back.'

'You know full well I will do no such thing. If she...' He swallowed, faltering on the words with the emotion filling him. 'If she carries my bairn, I can do nothing else but go and find her. Not only for her own sake but because she carries the future of this clan. You know that.'

'I know that, but I had to try. You are my nephew, and I cherish you above all.'

'I know that, Uncle.' He hugged him and mounted

his stallion as soon as it was brought to him. 'Will you stay here in case she returns before us?'

Uncle nodded. 'The clan will find and protect her. She is family.'

'Aye,' he answered before galloping off in search of his wife and the babe she carried: the very future of Clan McKenna.

Sunset would soon be upon her, and Moira had spent the afternoon searching the village for any sign of the mysterious messenger from Clan Fraser. While a few had seen him on his way through heading up to Blackmore, as he'd stopped to break his fast and rest his horse, no one had seen him return. It was as if he had vanished into the mist. Most likely she had just been too late to catch up with him.

She huffed in frustration and gathered her mount ready to depart and return to the castle. No doubt Rory would have noted her absence by now and be concerned. Along the way, a frigid rain began that pricked her skin even through her heavy cloak. An ice storm was moving in. Her horse neighed, and she patted her muzzle.

'Slow and steady, Clover.'

Her horse leaned into her touch, and they continued on. The storm worsened quickly, with the wind and ice making the steep incline precarious at best. She dismounted and took to the woodland path off the open road for more cover, leading Clover by the reins. It would take her longer, but they would be less exposed to the elements and another hour in the open storm was too much for either of them to endure. Besides, she'd come to know this path almost better than the main road as she loved to walk amongst the arms of the tall trees that climbed high into the sky.

She carried on despite the flush she felt under her skin and the chattering of her teeth. Why was it taking her so long to get home? *Home.* Blackmore. She smiled. Having a home she felt safe and secure in was a gift. One she'd never expected to receive when she married Rory. She'd hoped for a neutral arrangement. One where she would be treated well and live an almost independent life.

What she'd found instead was a love match.

At Blackmore she was respected and cherished. She was an equal. Rory asked for and valued her opinion. He kept no secrets from her. She flushed and her stomach flipped. She had so much to lose by telling him of the note and what it threatened, but wouldn't it be worse to not tell him?

A twig snapped behind her, and she froze.

Clover yanked on the reins and tried to pull away. Whatever or whomever was there was frightening them both. A stag emerged from the woods followed by another of smaller stature. She chuckled at herself and continued on. Why was she so hot? She yanked the cloak from her and draped it over Clover. The instant relief of the cold rain on her helped until it turned to tiny ice pellets minutes later making her skin freeze.

She sighed as she climbed the final hill and saw the lit torches of Blackmore. 'It is her! Help me get her inside!' a soldier called out from the gates. Another shouted, 'Gather her mount!

Sean came to her and soon two more soldiers came running up behind him. One took Clover's leads from her while the other man supported her on the other side as she walked. For some reason she was dizzy, and walking demanded great concentration.

Finally she was inside, but she was still so overwarm. People fussed over her, yet their faces were fuzzy, blurry splotches. A few voices sounded familiar, but they spoke so quickly and with such force she cringed and gave up attempts to answer their many questions. She needed to close her eyes, if only for a moment.

Chapter Twenty

'Moira?' Rory rushed into the main hall, rain still dripping off his cloak.

She struggled to open her eyelids. They felt heavy and gritty. Finally, she did, and her gaze fixed on her husband's handsome and rugged face. Sorrow gutted her. She'd gained so much, but now all would be lost. There would be no escaping her past now. He would know and hate her for what she'd done and for the secret she'd kept from him. She began backing away, and he froze. Angus rushed into the room behind him and Rory put out a hand to halt his advance.

'Moira?' Rory implored, walking towards her slowly with his hands open as if she were some injured animal he wished to capture or soothe, which was ridiculous. She was no such thing.

'What has happened?' he asked in low, gentle tones.

She shivered in her wet gown despite the mad heat flushing her body and clutched the letter in her hand. The letter that threatened her future, their future. She couldn't stop shaking and her teeth chattered in her head creating a dull aching throb in her skull.

The lines of the note throbbed in cadence with the pounding.

I know you killed Peter.
I have proof.
You will hang.

But how could the Frasers know?

This was Moira's secret. Her secret with Peter. The one thing they still shared away from everyone else as past husband and wife. It was a quiet noose hung loosely about her neck. One she did not want, but one she also couldn't escape. Not after what she'd done.

'No one else knew,' she murmured, staring at Rory's dark, distant form as her vision blurred. 'I don't understand.' She shook her head and the few hairpins that had remained in her hair scattered to the floor, allowing her hair to fall in loose, wet waves about her face. She crushed the letter into a ball in her fist. Anger, grief and fear collided within her and a wave of nausea gripped her stomach.

'It is impossible,' she continued. 'And I searched for him, for the messenger. He was gone. I was too late.'

Rory reached her and gripped her shoulders, running his hands up and down her arms. 'You're soaked through,' he murmured. 'Come with me. Please. Let us get you changed and warm you by the fire. Then you can tell me what has happened. You're safe now. That is all that matters.' She met his grey eyes, so full of care and concern rather than anger, and the knot of unease tightened in her gut. They would tell him. He would never understand. She would be banished from here or be hanged.

Or both.

She swallowed hard. 'They will hang me, Rory,' she whispered. 'I am sorry.'

Rory gripped her face with his cool, strong hands. His brow knotted and he frowned at her. 'Moira, look at me. You're not making sense.'

He felt her forehead and cheeks. 'You're burning up. Angus!' He bellowed for his valet, who stood frozen at the threshold of the main hall. 'Get the doctor. She's ill. Hurry!'

'But I am not ill,' she answered. 'I am just...'

'You are just what?' he asked in soft, docent tones. 'Tell me. Whatever has happened, you can tell me. I will understand. I promise.'

She gripped his hands as they clutched her face and whispered the shaky words. 'I am a murderer, Rory. Somehow they know what I have done, and I will hang for it. He shall have his revenge on me at last as he always said he would.'

What?

'Who? I don't understand, I—' he started.

Moira crumpled in his hold, and he caught her before she collapsed to the floor. Nothing she had said in the last few minutes made a whit of sense. He picked up the balled letter that had fallen from her hand and shoved it in his pocket before swooping her up and into his arms to carry her back to her bedchamber. Her head lolled against his shoulder and her arms swung loosely as he walked. His heart hammered in his chest.

What was going on?

Tressa appeared from his wife's chamber. 'What's 'appened, my laird?'

'Moira is ill. A fever, I think. Ready her bed and whatever you feel the doctor will need when he arrives. And make sure someone has gone to fetch him,' he commanded.

Tressa scurried back in the room to turn down her mistress's bed, and Rory laid his wife gently on the covers, resting her head back carefully along the pillows.

Just this morning they had been talking about the future. Of a day when he might be well and they could be a family. Now, she was muttering to him of a murder and hangings? Tressa fussed at Moira's shoes and Rory ordered her away. 'I will tend to her. Gather what the doctor will require. Now!'

Tressa hurried from the room, closing the door hastily behind her.

Rory cursed and ruffled his hair with his hand. While he didn't mean to snap at the lass, he couldn't think with Moira like this. *He* was supposed to be the sick one, not her. She was the one full of life and joy. But this? Her weak, pale form rattled him.

Stop worrying and do something.

Shaking his head, he snapped back into form. He needed to get her out of these wet clothes and warm her. He tugged at the knotted laces of her boots, snapping the ties until he was able to free her feet from them. Her toes were ice cold and her stockings soaked through. Carefully, he rolled her stockings off and rubbed her feet between his hands in a desperate attempt to warm her. Realising she was still wearing a soaked gown, he turned her carefully to unbutton the back of it. *Why were there always so many buttons?* Before he could take a dirk to it and cut them off, Tressa returned. She avoided Rory's gaze and headed straight to her mistress.

'If ye will allow me, my laird. I shall be faster. And yer uncle awaits ye in the main hall. He's returned.'

'Aye,' he answered, relief consuming him. The lass was right. 'Change her clothes. Try to warm her.'

'Aye,' she replied, already beginning the task of unbuttoning Moira's dress. He gave his wife one last lingering glance and left the room.

This couldn't be happening, could it? He jogged down the hallways and rushed down the staircase until he reached the main hall. Uncle, who was shaking off his hat and giving his wet coat and gloves to a servant, faced him.

'I saw Angus roaring down the road on horse to the village despite the ice and enter to find the servants rushing about as if we are to hold a celebration. They told me you've found Moira.' He smiled.

'Aye,' Rory answered. 'She's returned, but in quite a state. She's in a fever. I sent Angus for the doctor. Something has happened. I can't make sense of her ramblings.'

His uncle's gaze narrowed in on him, his smile crashing into a thin line of concern. 'What do you mean?'

Aware that they were being overheard by everyone

and anyone, Rory nodded to his uncle. 'Come with me. We must talk.'

Silently, they made their way to his study. Once inside, Rory dropped the latch to the room, shrugged off his wet coat and pulled the balled letter from his pocket. He pressed the crumpled mess to the desk and smoothed it with his hand. Even though the ink had been smudged from the rain, the words were still unmistakable.

He read the note twice to be sure.

I know you killed Peter.
I have proof.
You will hang.

The three short lines hung heavy with meaning, but Rory stared at them dumbfounded and uncertain as if written in some other language he could not ascertain. His Moira, a murderer? He couldn't fathom it. Her mutterings echoed in his mind.

'They will hang me, Rory. I am sorry.'

He collapsed in his leather chair. Could it be true? Had she resorted to murder to free herself from her first husband? Had it come to that? He fisted his hands. What had her life been to resort to such measures? His stomach curdled and twisted. He couldn't think upon it further. Otherwise, he would be ill or smash his study to bits.

'What's all this?' Uncle Leo asked, his voice pulling Rory back to the present. His uncle stood beside him and stared down at the crumpled note.

'I don't quite know yet to be honest. It has something

to do with this letter she was clutching in her hand when she returned. She was undone by it. Upset, talking nonsense and flushed with fever. Evidently, this is the note the messenger gave Sean at the castle this morn that Tressa passed on to her. The one she went into the village to try to locate and enquire who had sent it without telling anyone here her true purpose, which isn't like her. She's not a liar, nor is she secretive or reckless. But this…this note drove her to search the village and to stay out in the middle of a storm, so it must have some credence. But I cannot imagine it being true.' He stood, unable to sit one moment longer. 'Moira is no killer,' he stated. 'I would bet my life on it.' He paced the length of the room and then stood staring out at the sea as waves crashed against the rocks, dashing whatever was in its wake into ruins.

Chapter Twenty-One

'*Moira, jump in. It shall not be easier by putting in one toe at a time.*'

Ewan smacked the warm waters of the loch with his arms, sending a cascading arch of water droplets into the air. She stepped back from the water's edge.

'*I can't do it,*' *she pleaded in distress.* '*I don't know what's in there and I can't swim. I'll drown.*'

He laughed at her, treading water in his soaked tunic and trews. '*You're my sister. I'd never let anything happen to you. I might steal your puddings, but I'll always protect you. Jump!*'

The trust in his gaze made her run to the bank's edge, close her eyes and jump in. When the water began to soak her dress and threatened to pull her under, his strong arms had pulled her up.

She slapped at the water, gulped in air and strained. '*Help, Ewan. Help!*'

'*Stop flailing about like a baby bird. Relax,*' *he commanded.* '*Just float,*' *he ordered, turning her on her back.*

Moira closed her eyes and floated, enjoying the warm sun and heat on her face until a heavy hand pressed down on her chest, holding her under. She flailed, and grasped at the man holding her beneath the water, but he was too strong. She couldn't breathe.

She opened her eyes and screamed, choking on the water as it filled her lungs.

Peter's face appeared before her and she heard his voice. 'I know you killed me, Moira. Everyone knows. You'll hang, you murderer. You'll hang...'

'Moira! Moira. Stop.' Rory's voice became louder than Peter's, and she flailed about, trying to reach the surface.

'Please. It's only me.'

Her eyes flew open and her heart raged against her ribs. Rory had his arms wrapped around her chest as he sat behind her. He whispered in her ear, 'Moira. It's me. You are safe. It's only a dream.' His familiar smell of soap and tallow soothed her and his solid strength and warmth anchored her back into the present, far away from the memories of the past and of Peter. She shivered.

'You are safe. I am here.'

But for how long? her mind screamed. Her chest tightened at the knowing she would one day lose him and be alone.

'Just breathe.' His voice eased across her ear and cheek. She took in a breath and released it as her shoulders finally dropped and she relaxed against him.

They sat in the quiet stillness of one another until her heart slowed enough that it no longer drowned out the howling wind. Her gaze settled on the large bank of windows. 'When did it begin snowing again?' she asked.

She felt him smile against her hair. 'Yesterday.'

She stilled. 'Where was I?' Her heart picked up speed and anxiety gripped her.

'You were here. Quite ill. Some sort of fever from being out in the storm. Do you remember? I prayed you would come back to us, and now you have.' His voice was husky and deep as he rubbed her arms and pressed a kiss to her hair.

She turned in his arms. 'Ill? What do you—?' Her eyes widened and she paused at the sight of him. 'What happened to you?' His hair was mussed, his face unshaven, and his clothes were rumpled and worn. She gasped. 'Tell me you have not been by my bedside all this time?'

He smiled and ran his palm down the side of her face. 'Then I shall not tell you.'

'You did not need to stay here. Tressa would have tended to me, and you need your rest.' The worry of losing him sharpened to a fine point and her head throbbed in pain.

He took her hand in his. 'You know I do not sleep, so being here with you was the only place I wished to be.'

A knock sounded on the door. 'Come in,' Rory called without moving.

The door cracked open. 'How is my patient?' a man asked.

'She is awake,' Rory answered. 'Perhaps it's time I introduced you.' He rose from the bed and attempted to straighten his tunic but gave up.

'Moira, this is Dr Wilkes. He has cared for me and

our family for as long as I can remember. Dr Wilkes, this is my wife, Lady Moira McKenna.'

Moira shifted and pulled up the bedclothes. An older man with a full grey beard and rather portly shape came in and greeted her. He had a pleasing smile and laughter in his eyes. 'Pleased to officially meet you, my lady.'

'And I you. Rory has told me much of how you have aided him when he has visited with you in the village. And thank you for coming here to tend to me. I know it must have been a difficult journey in the snow.' She shifted on the bed feeling leery of what she may or may not have said in her sleep. She'd still not told Rory of the letter and—

Blast.

Where was the letter? Her eyes scanned the room in hopes that her cloak or gown from when she was out in the storm was still here, but she knew better. Tressa would have taken it to be laundered immediately.

'Perhaps you could leave us?' the doctor asked.

Rory met Moira's gaze. 'Are you well enough for me to step out?'

'Aye,' she answered.

He hesitated and then finally made his leave, closing the door behind him.

'We have much to discuss,' Dr Wilkes began.

'Oh?' Her cheeks flushed.

'Nothing to fret over. Upon examining you when you were ill, I discovered you are with child.'

She froze. 'What?'

'I could hardly wait to tell you, so you could tell Laird McKenna. He will be so happy and the clan will—'

Moira burst into tears, a sob escaping from her lips.

Now it was the doctor's turn to freeze. 'My lady, I didn't mean to...' He trailed off and stood. 'Perhaps I should leave. Send your husband back in. It was too soon for me to tell you, my apologies.'

She hiccupped. 'Nay. It is glorious news. I am just overwhelmed. I knew I was late with my courses, but I wasn't certain.' She rested her hand on her stomach and worry set in. 'Will the babe be harmed from the fever?'

'Nay. You had a mild case. Nothing to fret over.'

She leaned back against the pillows. 'That is a relief. Thank you, Doctor.'

He smiled down at her. 'I'll leave you a tonic if you need further rest, but otherwise, I'll leave you be.'

'Aye, thank you again.'

'Of course, my lady. And I'll be back to check in on the babe's progress as you wish it.'

She nodded to him, and he left, closing the door smoothly behind him.

Not long after, Tressa entered with two servants behind her to fill the tub with hot water and to bring fresh towels and soaps for a bath. After all was set up and they had left, Rory came in. As he saw her face, his features tightened. He came to her, settling on the edge of the mattress, which shifted under his weight.

Clasping her hands in his own, he took a breath and spoke evenly to her, despite the alarm in his eyes. 'Are you unwell?'

'Nay.' She smiled at him and another tear ran down her cheek.

'Then why are you crying? I don't understand. Did

the doctor have poor news?' He squeezed her hands and a muscle worked in his jaw.

'I am overwhelmed with joy.'

'What?'

'I am with child.'

Rory stilled, his features softening in awe. For moments, he didn't move but just stared into her eyes as tears spilled down her cheeks. His Adam's apple bobbed in his throat. Finally, he moved, resting his hand gently on her stomach, the heat of his touch easing through her thin shift.

'Moira,' he murmured, his voice husky and deep with emotion. 'Such a miracle. I am beyond words. Tressa told me she thought you might be, but it was not official until now.'

His grey eyes were shiny and bright. He leaned forward and kissed her. His lips soft and gentle against her own. 'Thank you,' he whispered as he began to pull away, his breath warm and sweet against her cheek.

'Well, I could not have done it without your help, my laird.' She chuckled.

He laughed aloud and kissed her once more. 'You amaze me, Moira McKenna.'

'Most likely, I offend you. I have been in this bed for days it seems. Help me to bathe.'

He paused, his gaze half-lidded and eager to see if it was an invitation for more.

'You may stay, my laird. I find I have missed you. Perhaps you shall make it up to me in time.'

'Challenge accepted.' He scooped her up in his arms with ease and carried her to the tub. He lowered her feet gently into it and removed her shift in one deft movement. He pulled her to him tightly and kissed her until she could scarce breathe.

'You seem a bit overdressed, my laird,' she murmured.

'Nothing I can't remedy in but a mere moment,' he answered, yanking his tunic over his head.

They sunk down into the warm water and despite being inside a small metal tub Moira felt like she was out in the loch, floating once more along with the current as Rory held her in his arms.

The letter and its contents would wait until tomorrow. All worries would wait until the morrow.

Chapter Twenty-Two

Rory woke with his limbs draped possessively over his wife's body as she continued to slumber. He studied her gentle sloping nose with its sweet tip and her long dark lashes that contrasted her pale, flawless cheeks. Her dark hair lay in rivers of onyx against the cream of the sheets. The woman was perfection.

How in the world had she ever become his?

And now she carried his child. Tressa's speculation was a fact now confirmed by Dr Wilkes. His son or daughter grew even now in her womb. He ran his fingertips over her bare stomach. The miracle of it struck him anew as a wave of reality and sadness banked against it. He would not live to see his child's face or grip their tiny hands. They would never know him, and he wouldn't be around to protect his family. He allowed his palm to flatten and cover her entire abdomen. What he wouldn't give to secure a future with Moira and their child, but such a dream was for another man. He had to face the truth: while he couldn't secure a future *with* them, he could secure a future *for* them once he was gone.

The terms with the Camerons could still be agreed to, and with Moira carrying their bairn, it seemed less of a risk that the clan would lose everything. As long as there was a male McKenna heir, then the Camerons would be allies and protectors against whatever the other clans schemed against them once he passed. Based on the Frasers angry letters, he imagined what they might still be planning would be fierce and horrific. He had quelled Bran with coin, but the Frasers seemed unwilling to back down on their belief that Moira had been responsible for the death of their son.

Rory had no idea what to think.

And then there was *the* letter. The one he could not make sense of. The three lines of script that hummed along in his head in a deadly loop.

I know you killed Peter.
I have proof.
You will hang.

He stared at his wife. Her chest rose in a smooth, even rhythm. Could she have truly killed her first husband as the letter claimed? She didn't look like a killer, and Moira seemed far too intelligent to put herself in such a position to be brought to the gallows. She was no fool. If she killed him, she would have known the risks. It was an offence that could not be defended, at least not in the eyes of the Fraser clan.

He tensed. But Fraser had been a bastard and his

mistreatment of Moira had been fierce based on what she had and had not told him in so many words. Perhaps something worse than he could imagine had driven her to kill him in anger. Nay. He frowned. More likely, it would have been in defence of herself done in a moment of desperation not as part of a larger plan. Moira was a woman who loved life, nature and all that the world possessed. She nursed potted plants and spoke to them as if they were wee babes. She would not have taken anything from this world lightly.

Unless she had been forced to.

His stomach knotted, and he sucked in a breath as pain rippled through him and then abated.

But if she had killed her husband, why not tell him? He could protect her from the Frasers and the courts. Did she not trust him, even now? Had they not grown closer, as a true husband and wife, far beyond anything they might have believed possible when they'd first agreed to marry one another?

Or perhaps such intimacy was only within his own heart. He sighed.

'What has your handsome brow in such a furrow?' Moira asked, lifting a hand to ruffle his hair.

'Nothing for you to worry about.'

'Are you puzzling out how you slept through the night?' She smirked at him.

He propped himself up on his elbow and revelled in her bright blue gaze. 'I did, didn't I? I cannot remember the last time that has happened.'

'Perhaps tending my bedside wore you through.'

He laughed and let his fingertip run the gentle slope

of her nose. 'I think it is knowing that you carry the next McKenna, whether it be our son or daughter, that has granted me some peace.'

Her smile flattened. 'You mean after you are gone.'

'Aye.'

'I will speak with Dr Wilkes. Ask for his most current recommendations for you. I will not give up on you. Please do not give up on us. Agreed?'

He swallowed hard, pressing the lie to the tip of his tongue. 'Agreed. I won't, and I'll drink every horrid tonic you make me.'

'Good,' she added, and threw off the bedclothes. 'No better time than the present.' She gathered her shift and a simple walking dress before disappearing around the dressing screen.

He lay listening to her chatter away about herbs and research and a new finding in one of the volumes from the library, and he prayed that he'd have more mornings such as this, where he could revel in the beauty of his future and the joy of being alive and part of it, despite how long it would last.

How could she tell him?

Should she tell him?

Thistles.

Moira had fussed and fretted in the library all morning after a thorough and heady search of her clothes and enquiry of Tressa about any found correspondence about her chamber. Where had the letter gone? It could be anywhere. Her hope was that it being soaked in the rain and clutched within her hand had made it a blurry, runny stained mess beyond comprehension. Perhaps a servant had found it as such and thought it rubbish. She worried her lip.

Or someone had read it and kept it.

Her stomach lurched and she pressed her hand to it. Now that she knew she was with child, she was desperate to keep the contents of that letter hidden. Nothing would bring her to the scaffold. She'd never admit what she'd done and what part she had played in Peter's death.

Not even to Rory.

Denial was her only option, wasn't it? Telling Rory would only add to his worries, and if she ignored the claims of that one note, wouldn't they eventually fall away? It was one letter, nothing more. It could be a ruse. Why else would the note be unsigned? If she remained calm and focused on her future, nothing more would come of it. Telling the truth would only put her in harm's way, as it would be her word against that of a dead man, and she'd not die for Peter Fraser. He'd already killed enough of her spirit and taken years of her happiness. She'd not give him her life or the life of her bairn now.

Worry threatened to overtake her and thrust her into hysteria, so she released a breath and shook off her suspicion. If someone had it or had read it, they would reveal themselves soon enough. All she could do was wait and focus her energies on healing her husband. The irony of being so desperate for her husband to live when she'd married him because she was assured he would soon die was not lost on her.

She didn't believe in this McKenna curse. There had to be a reason and a cause for his illness and that of the McKennas before him, and she would find it. She would. She and her babe had far too much to lose without him. She found she loved her husband and wished desperately to have the marriage she'd never had with Peter.

Chapter Twenty-Three

Moira rubbed her eyes, stood from the cool window-sill she had sat huddled in reading in the wee solarium, as she affectionately called it now, and stretched her arms high in the air standing on her tiptoes. Staring at the wall clock, she noted she'd lost most of the day reading and making notes for her latest efforts for a tonic for Rory. One of them had to help. Dr Wilkes said it seemed to be an ailment of the gut from some sort of poisoning, but such a broad diagnosis made her work challenging. Propping her hands to her hips, she smiled as she watched the hounds off on a late afternoon walk through the fresh snow. They ran, skidded and collided into one another as Uncle Leo cheered them on. He met her gaze and waved to her. And no one had mentioned the letter. Not yet. She returned Uncle Leo's greeting and smiled. Such a glorious day she could get used to.

As he walked on, her hand slid over her abdomen. Would that be her walking along with her child alone with the hounds in tow to capture some of the crisp winter air after a new snowfall? She liked to imagine Rory alongside them. Her chest tightened. A foolish dream, she knew. His birthday was drawing nearer and with each passing week, she noted his ailments were worsening, but she didn't know why. They shared their meals together and had a similar routine, yet his body seemed to be betraying him day after day. His abdominal cramps had worsened and at times he barely touched his plate, despite his efforts to move his food around to make it seem otherwise. A tactic Brenna had oft resorted to at Glenhaven when Cook had made liver.

Moira's heart still tugged at her siblings' long absence. She missed them. One day she hoped Brenna and Ewan and perhaps even Father would set aside their disapproval of her choice and come see her, if nothing but to at least see their new nephew or niece. She sighed. But she knew her father would do no such thing. Bran Stewart was not one to concede anything, not even the death of his wife. For days he had denied even that until they had come to collect her mother's body for internment in the chapel tombs.

Giving her growing plants a last drink, Moira left her lovely new refuge and went in search of her husband in his library.

'Rory,' she called, entering the study. 'Have you come up with any names yet?' She smiled when she saw him asleep at his desk with his head resting on his folded arms. His favourite chalice sat just beyond his reach and correspondence lay buried beneath him. She shook her head. His multiple afternoon naps had been just another development over the last few weeks, and the early dusk and winter gloom didn't help matters.

She ran her hand along his arm and pressed a kiss to his cheek. 'Love, you've fallen asleep atop your work again.'

He didn't stir, so she shook his shoulder gently. When his head lolled over to the side, and his lips parted, she gasped. Her chest tightened and her fingers tingled. She bent her head down to feel for his breath on her cheek. She did and released a sigh of relief.

He was alive but not conscious. She lifted her skirts and ran from the study down the hallway, grateful she'd donned her boots rather than her dainty slippers this morn. No servants were in sight as dinner and evening turndowns were in preparations. As she reached the main hall, she spied Angus and called for him.

He turned in haste, no doubt hearing the urgency in her high-pitched tone.

'I need help! Send for Dr Wilkes,' she shouted. 'Rory is unconscious in his study, and I cannot rouse him.'

Angus's eyes widened in alarm before he finally responded with a nod. 'Phillip!' he called after a young man carrying a fresh stack of wood to the large hearth. 'Gather the doctor. The laird has taken ill. Hurry!'

'Aye,' the young man answered, his jaw set in determination. The cords of wood clattered to the floor and he disappeared down the hallway running at full speed.

'He'll gather his coat and be off, my lady. He's the fastest rider we have.'

'Can you help me get him back to his chambers?'

Moira asked, worrying the buttons along her dress sleeve.

'Aye. I'll bring two men to assist me, my lady.'

Moira hurried off. She'd hardly been alone with Rory for more than a minute in the study gripping his hand and whispering to him when Angus and two servants came in to carefully support and return her ill husband to his chambers. His head hung forward and the toes of his boots dragged along the floor as the men supported him between them. Seeing him so weak and helpless made her wish to scream aloud. She wasn't ready to be without him. She clutched her belly. Neither of them were.

A day passed and Rory still had not woken. The doctor had come and gone to collect different tonics and medicines for him, but none of them brought Rory out of his endless sleep. Moira rose from the chair she'd pulled to his bedside yesterday and stretched her aching limbs. She'd had little sleep as her mind refused to rest.

'How is he?' Uncle Leo asked, his voice even as if he was already preparing himself.

She met his gaze. 'The same.'

He smiled. 'Well, that is something. I am glad he has not turned for the worse.'

'I suppose.' She stared down at Rory's pale, still form. It didn't seem like much consolation.

'May I speak with you, Moira?'

'Aye,' she said and began to sit.

'Perhaps a walk? I'll be taking the hounds out soon. I thought some fresh air, despite the chill, might do you some good. Rory will have my hide when he wakes if I have not looked after you.'

She chuckled. 'Of course.' She pressed a kiss to Rory's cheek, squeezed his hand and left the room.

They walked silently to the front hall, gathered their hats, cloaks and gloves and found the hounds huddled against the back door awaiting their master.

'These beasts are as good as any timepiece if you ask me. They never fail to remind me when it is time for their morning or afternoon walk,' he teased and opened the door for her and them.

The hounds bounded out in the new snowfall that covered the ground. 'I hadn't realised it had snowed yet again.'

'Began last eve, but you didn't notice. You have been fretting over my nephew instead.' He smiled at her. 'His parents would have adored you and been so pleased by his love match. No one would have expected it, least of all Rory.'

A blush heated her cheeks, and she pulled the cloak tighter around her head. 'Nor did I. It caught us all unaware.'

He smiled at her. 'I thought as much.'

'It is why I am so desperate to cure whatever ails him,' she added, kicking a blob of snow. *And protect him from my past.* 'I simply do not believe in this curse nonsense. It has to be something that we can remedy.'

Uncle Leo threw a stick for the hounds and then kept on. He shrugged. 'I was like you. I didn't believe it before my half-brother, Rory's father, became ill. It was almost identical to what Rory suffers now. We all tried, worked tirelessly with different doctors and healers and medicines to stop the progression, but we could not. While it may not be a curse, it is something that ails all of the McKenna men. No one seems to know why or how.'

Moira nibbled her lip. Did she dare ask? She sucked in a breath and then blurted it out. 'Why have you never become ill? If you are half McKenna, then wouldn't the curse come to you as well?'

'I wondered when you might ask. Although I don't know for certain, I assume that if I haven't already become ill, that I won't. There was a storyteller, a *seanachaide*, in the village decades ago that once told me that the curse was not meant for half-bloods and that I need not worry.' He shook his head and laughed. 'At the time, I didn't know whether to be angered by her insult at my parentage or relieved that she might be right.'

'Interesting. Is this woman still in the village? Could I speak with her? Perhaps she knows something that could help us.' Hope budded up in Moira's chest and loosened the knot there. To do something that might help Rory was a balm to her spirit.

'I'm afraid not. She passed a handful of years ago.'

'Perhaps there is someone else who may know? I could go to the village and ask around.'

'I'm afraid that's another matter I need to discuss with you. It isn't safe for you to travel into the village right now.' He nested his hands in his trouser pockets and the hooked lines of a frown tugged down his lips. The wind whipped up his coattails and ruffled his wavy grey hair.

'Word of Rory's sickness has spread in the village

and beyond. There are other clans encroaching, preparing to try to absorb us in their ranks. With no clear successor, the future here is uncertain.'

Gooseflesh rose along her skin. 'I'm sorry, did you say 'absorb'?'

'Aye. The numbers have been increasing as he edges closer to his birthday. We had expected as much, discussed our options and have prepared accordingly.'

'That sounds dreadful.'

'Has Rory not spoken to you of the proposed alliance?'

Her fingers tingled in her gloves. 'Nay,' she answered, clearing her throat. 'He has told me of the letters from my father claiming that I was stolen away from him. All of it is rubbish and unfounded.' She crossed her arms against her chest and hoped he could not hear the thud of her heart against her chest.

Could he know of the letter from the Frasers?

'Despite whether it is rubbish or not, the Stewarts along with some other clans have found common ground in their dislike of the situation and our clan. Knowing such, we could not leave ourselves exposed.'

'In case Rory dies?'

'Aye.'

'My lady!' Tressa was running to them, waving to gather their attention. She had no coat or hat on despite the snow. The lass looked as if she had gone half mad.

Moira picked up her skirts and went to her. 'What has happened?'

'He is awake,' she cried, joy in her eyes as she grasped both of Moira's arms. 'The laird is awake. Come. He asks for ye.'

'That is wonderful! Uncle, he wakes!'

Moira hurried inside along with Tressa as Uncle Leo gathered the hounds.

Skidding along the stone floors, Tressa hooked an arm through Moira's own. 'Slow down, my lady. I can't have you fall just when the laird is on the mend.'

Moira chuckled and nodded, slowing her steps as they rounded the last corner to the hall of his bedchamber. Moira rushed to his bedside, knelt and kissed him. His laugh on her lips made her smile. 'The moment I leave, you wake,' she chided him.

How glorious it was to have his gaze upon her and to hear his husky laugh.

'Perhaps I knew you were gone, and I did not like it,' he teased and ran a shaky hand along the side of her face. 'How are you? And the babe?'

'Perfect now that you are awake and looking upon us.'

'What happened?' he asked.

'I don't know. I found you slumped over your ledgers in the study. I thought you asleep, but then I could not rouse you.' She leaned back on her haunches and brushed back the damp hair from his forehead. 'You have been asleep for a day.'

His eyes widened. 'A full day?'

'Aye. The doctor could determine no cause. He is due to return soon to check upon you and bring you another draught to try.'

He struggled to sit up, and Moira rose to assist him by tucking extra pillows from Tressa behind his back and head.

'Good to see you up, son. I couldn't bear to read

through one more pile of your correspondence. Dreary, the lot of it.' Uncle Leo smiled, came over to Rory and clapped a hand to his nephew's shoulder. He gave a wink to Moira. 'This wife of yours would scarce leave your side. I had to will her to take some fresh air with the hounds this afternoon after being inside for a full day.'

'Moira, tell me you weren't.'

'Where else would I be?'

'You need to care for yourself and the babe.'

'I have been. You needn't make a muckle fuss over me.'

Rory sat up straighter. 'Blazes. Did you say it's been a full day? Uncle, bring me the agreement. I must sign it and have it returned. I meant to do so yesterday. To think I could have—' He stopped himself, wincing, his brow furrowed as he clenched his jaw and emitted a groan.

'Please. Try to sit back and relax. There is nothing so urgent that it cannot wait until you are better.'

'Nay,' he murmured. 'Uncle?'

The older man nodded and left the room.

'What is it that cannot wait?' she murmured.

His gaze roved beyond her where Tressa still fussed with compresses and clearing the basin of water.

'Tressa, if you will leave us but a moment while I try to get the laird settled.'

Her maid nodded and left the room, closing the door quietly behind her.

'I must sign the document. I should have told you, but—'

The door opened and Uncle Leo came in with a large

rolled parchment, ink pot and quill. 'I have it. Just sign here.'

'Moira, help me sit up, so that I can sign it.'

'Why can this not wait? You are taxing yourself too much. You've just woken.'

'It is for you. Please.'

His eyes were haunted and pleading. She helped him up, set a book in his lap to press upon, while Uncle unrolled the parchment. He gave the ink pot to Moira to hold. She dipped the quill in the ink and gave it to Rory.

He set his name to the line in a sweeping, shaky flourish, fell back against the pillows and released a sigh. 'Have it messengered to them this eve. Do not wait. It must arrive before I am dead.'

Chapter Twenty-Four

Rory heard Moira's sharp intake of breath but chose to keep his gaze forward and on his uncle. He knew what he'd said would hurt her, but he also knew it was the truth, and he didn't know how much time he would have left to prepare her and his clan for a more secure future.

'It will be done tonight.'

'Thank you, Uncle.'

The door to the bedchamber closed and the air thickened. He busied himself with straightening his tunic in a desperate hope that she would let his words melt away in the air.

'Why would you say such?'

Which he knew would never happen.

He faced her then, and the pain in her shimmering eyes and pinched features made him ache to hold her. But touching her would only distract him from the task at hand. He had to make her face the truth. It was better now than later.

'Moira, look at me. I. Am. Dying.'

'Nay,' she disagreed. 'You are not, and besides, you

promised me a few more months. And I plan to hold you to it, Rory McKenna.'

A quirk of a lip helped him see a smile lurked somewhere behind the unshed tears, and he clutched for it. 'That's one of the many reasons I adore you. You hold me to my word.' He steadied himself. He had no time to waste and needed to know the truth. It was the only way he could protect her. 'So I shall hold you to yours. Will you get the wooden box from my desk?'

She rose and gathered it. He ran a hand over the bedclothes, willing himself for the right words, but he knew there were none.

'Open it for me,' he asked when she returned to his side and settled into the chair next to his bed.

He knew the moment she recognised the water-stained letter. The colour drained from her cheeks and every muscle in her body tensed. 'Read it,' he asked, his words softening as they fell.

She stared at it a moment longer and then met his gaze, snapping the box shut. 'I have no need to. I know the words by heart.'

'I found it clutched in your hand that day when you fled out into the storm. I didn't know what to make of it or your fevered confessions at first, but when I pieced some of it together, I didn't wish to ask you. It felt like a betrayal because I *know* you, Moira. I know who you are. You are a good, decent, intelligent woman. The best that I have ever known. What it must have taken for you to…if that is what you did—' He paused as she crumpled into the chair.

The first tremble began in her hand and soon travelled up and along her frame until all of her was a shaking, bent form before him like a beautiful flower crushed by a pounding rain, all of its buds stripped from it. He slid closer to the edge of the bed, clutched her hands in his own and tried to comfort her. 'You can tell me anything or nothing. It is yours to keep or share. I just wanted you to know that your secret is safe with me.'

For moments, she sat trembling, and then she cleared her throat and straightened herself.

'I could never have imagined it. That day,' she began. Her words rang distant as if she had transported herself back to the very day and moment of the event. He ran his thumb over the back of her hand and waited for her to continue.

'It was a gorgeous summer morning. I still remember the fragrant smell of the flowers drifting into our chamber window, so heady, rich and full of bloom. I could hardly wait to be out of doors.'

Rory nodded at her, and she continued.

'After I spent some time in the gardens, I came back into my chambers to find him tearing through my belongings. Letters, clothes and books were scattered about as if they had been thieved and rooted through for coin. He accused me of being with another.' She let out a small chuckle. 'As if I ever wished for any undue or extra attentions in that manner. Not after—' She stilled, the smile dying from her lips. She swallowed and continued.

Steady. He clutched her hand. *Steady.* Rory commanded himself to not react. He would listen and not respond. The rage tightening his chest would not be set free. Not today at least.

'I had learned by then to be calm and still around him when he was in such a state. And so I asked him what had happened to make him think such. I had learned to never refuse his attentions, and spent no time with any other man about the castle. I promised him I had been chaste and loyal to him and that his worries were unfounded.'

She pulled her hand away and nestled her body into the chair, tucking her legs beneath her and wrapping her arms around her stomach, making her a wee slip of herself. Her gaze drifted behind him. 'As you can imagine, he did not believe me, and I was not quick enough to escape his blows. Before I even knew what was happening, I was on the ground scrambling to free myself from his hold.'

Rory clenched the bedclothes tightly in his fisted hands. His heart hammered. His blood thickened.

'He was so angry. I will never forget the rage in his eyes, the hateful words that fell from his lips. I knew in that moment that he truly wished to kill me. That I would die if I did not escape his hold.'

Her hands gripped the material of her dress.

'I kicked him and managed to free one arm. Feeling along the floor with my hand, I found a downed candle-stick and hit him with it. He cursed and relaxed his hold enough for me to free myself and run, so I did. I fled out the back entrance. No one saw me, or so I thought. I disappeared into the gardens and stayed there until nightfall. When I returned for our evening meal, I was told Peter had left on horseback to see my father. I was sick with dread as to what he would relay to him. But the next day, we received word that he had been found dead along the road to Glenhaven. No one knows if he was attacked by thieves or thrown from his horse, but he died that night.'

'How does that make you a murderer?'

'Because I hit him in the head with that candlestick in my efforts to escape. That was by *my* hand. He died because I hit him and left him, allowed him to travel on horse when he was injured.'

'What of the story about him being attacked or thrown from his horse?'

'I believe both unlikely. He was an excellent rider and few thieves were about those parts. It is not a heavily travelled road. What thieves would bother with so few people traversing it?'

'Well, even if it was by your hand, which I'm not entirely sure that it was, he was attacking you. Any man would be justified to defend themselves in such a situation.'

She released a bitter laugh and met his gaze. Her eyes bright with unshed tears. 'But I am no man. Just his wife.' Her tone dropped to a harsh whisper. 'And I had no right to defend myself, even to save my life. Not in the eyes of the law. You know that, Rory. I will hang.'

'Nay. You will not.' He leaned forward, took her face in his hands. 'If it is the last thing I do, I will keep that from happening. You are *my* wife now.'

'But for how long?' she cried, tears spilling down her cheeks.

Deuces.

He didn't know, nor did he want to. He wanted to live, but his body seemed hell-bent on another path. He couldn't answer. He didn't dare utter a lie to her, not now.

Whispering against her lips, he said, 'I am here now. I am here now.'

He hoped that would somehow be enough.

'But who is it that has sent that letter to me? The only person who knew of our fight was Enora. She was my maid, and she cleaned up the disarray in my room. And she would not betray me.'

'Are you sure you even killed him? He could have been attacked by thieves and he could have taken a fall. You don't know if you caused it. He was a fool to ride alone at night,' he countered.

'But I also cannot defend my actions and say with any certainty that I was not the cause.'

'But your intention was also not to kill him.'

'None of that shall matter,' she said.

'Is it possible he told someone of his quarrel with you before he set out?'

Her shoulders slumped. 'Aye. He told his mother everything. She doted on him and he on her. He could have told her all that happened, but I also think she would have accused me then if she knew of it.' She worried her lip and then covered her face with her hands in frustration.

Taking a deep breath, she stood. 'But none of this matters. I wish to focus on you, your wellness and our future…whatever remains of it.' She squared her shoulders and smiled at him, despite the downward pull of the corners of her eyes.

How he loved her.

He froze at the realisation that he did love her. His chest tightened.

'Rory?' Her brow crinkled.

'Aye,' he answered and forced a smile. What a horrible time to realise he had fallen in love with his wife, which had definitely not been part of their arrangement. He ruffled his hair and flopped back on the pillows.

'Will you tell me what that was you signed? Why you were in such a hurry to have it messengered back tonight?'

His eyes fluttered closed. Exhaustion was pressing on him heavy and thick. 'I needed to ensure you and the babe were protected, and such an agreement was the only way. Uncle and I have been in negotiations for a while now with the Camerons. Your note was not the first time I heard of these accusations against you in regard to Peter's death. The Frasers had spread word that you might have been responsible for Peter's death long before they sent you that note. Their claims, your father alleging I had stolen you away and of course my failing health all added to our vulnerability. I had to act. To protect the clan and you.'

'You knew of their claims? Why did you not tell me?' Hurt registered in her features and he cupped her face with his hands, revelling in the soft, smooth feel of her skin.

'Because it didn't matter to me whether you were responsible or not. But I should have told you. There was no reason for me to keep such a secret from you. I'm sorry.' Was he sinking into a cloud? He could hardly stay awake.

'What was in that document?' she asked again. 'What is it that couldn't wait until morn?'

He cleared his throat, struggling to speak. 'I made an agreement with the Camerons. They will be our allies against the Frasers and your father, or any other clans, if needed. Many clans seem hell-bent on watching Blackmore crumble to the ground and will fight over the scraps of what remains. Even now they wait at our village walls for the gossip of my demise. They hope to dismantle us piece by piece.'

She pressed a damp, cool cloth to his forehead and he sighed. He was still sinking further into that cloud, his muscles relaxing. The ache in his abdomen was now a dull throb rather than a roaring pain.

'What did you have to promise them to align with us?' Her fingertips ran through his hair and skimmed along his cheek. 'Knowing the Camerons, they will have asked for something substantial. I am sure of it.'

He sighed aloud at the pleasant rippling sensation along his limbs, an echo of her touch. Her faint scent of roses and dew filled his nose, and he smiled. It seemed little that they asked in order to keep her safe. Very little indeed, especially knowing she was already with child. His beautiful child.

'I promised them Blackmore and with it my men if I had no male heir born within a year of my death.'

Chapter Twenty-Five

The words hit her like a punch to the gut, and Moira struggled for breath. They would lose everything if she did not produce an heir, a male heir at that, within a year of Rory's death? What if she lost her babe as she had before? What if it was not a boy? She froze. He would lose everything and so would his people. The cloth slid from her fingers and down the side of Rory's face. When he did not move, she started and pressed a hand to his cheek. 'Rory? Rory?' No response. She shook his shoulders to wake him. His head lolled to the side.

The door opened.

'Doctor!' Moira rushed to him. 'He was awake, but now I cannot rouse him again.' She clutched the apron around her waist and paced the room.

'If you'll allow me a few minutes,' he asked.

'Of course.' She left hastily and never broke stride as she rushed to the solarium. Once she entered the space with its fresh, green scents and soft florals she released a breath. She walked to the trio of plants now in their larger decorative pots by the familiar bay of windows and sighed.

'Has it come to this, my lovelies?' she asked, stroking the leafy stems with care. 'I have what I long wished for that day at Glenhaven and now I do not want it. Not at all. I want my husband to live. I don't want to be alone. Not anymore.'

As usual, the tiny plants with their waxy leaves did nothing but listen, which used to fill her with solace. All she wished to do now was scream from the cliff side. She had to figure out what ailed her husband and quickly. The truth to what was happening to him had to be somewhere in this castle if he was being poisoned as the doctor had said. She decided to return to their chamber to see Rory and the doctor. Perhaps they could work together and he could help her understand how or what might be poisoning her husband and locate the source. The doctor was packing up his instruments in his satchel when she entered the bedchamber.

'How is he?' she asked.

'Unchanged, I'm afraid.' Sympathy softened his features. 'Best you prepare yourself, my lady.'

'I will do no such thing,' she countered, steeling her spine. 'And I wish for you to explain to me why you believe he is being poisoned and how it could happen here. I'm determined to find the source of it and reverse what ails him.'

He shook his head. 'You cannot expect to reverse such things.'

'Why not? I have read accounts in journals about healing after the source of exposure is removed. And there are several of the family's old journals that reference brief times of recovery of the lairds, usually when they travelled for long periods. Couldn't that mean the poison is here? In this castle? And could we not locate it if we all searched?'

The doctor paused and rubbed his grey beard, considering her words. 'Aye. I do remember the laird's father gaining strength after an extended visit to a cousin in Dundee. There may be something to your theory, but this is a large expansive place and his symptoms are worsening. We may run out of time.'

Tressa came to the door with a set of clean linens and a fresh pitcher of water.

Moira rushed to her. 'I need you to get Angus. Tell him to gather all of the servants, even the cook, and have them meet me in the main hall. We will find this source, Doctor. We will make enough time by working together. Go at once, Tressa. I will explain all when we are assembled.'

A few minutes later the main hall was humming with an odd anxious energy. Low voices and worried faces abounded. Moira entered the room and stood by Uncle Leo. The noise fell to a hush. 'As you all know, the laird is not well, but I refuse to believe that nothing can be done. I also refuse to believe that his sickness is from a curse.'

A hum of murmuring and uncertainty filled the air. Angus came forward and spoke. 'If I may, my lady. I mean no offence, but I have seen it. The way it claimed the laird's father. The McKenna curse is real.'

'Aye,' a few voices concurred.

'I do not dispute the sickness, Angus, just the cause. Dr Wilkes believes his symptoms are from poisoning and based on the many old family journals I have read thus far, there have been times of rebound when the lairds have travelled and been away from here for an extended time.'

'Ye believe someone 'ere is poisoning 'im?' a lad called from the back, crossing his arms against his chest.

Moira shook her head. 'Nay, I know of all of your love and devotion to Blackmore and Laird McKenna. I believe there is some*thing* that is poisoning him, not a some*one*.'

'But what could it be, my lady?' Tressa asked. 'And how can we find it?'

'It must be something only the laird uses or possesses because I am not ill, nor is Uncle Leo, or anyone else in this household.'

The servants looked at one another and some nodded in agreement at her logic.

'So, I have brought you here because you know what the laird uses every day. What he alone might access. I ask you to scour this castle and bring all of the things that you believe only Laird McKenna uses and pile them on these long banquet tables. We will examine them all. We will find this source.'

Uncertainty filtered through them, and Angus dared ask the question even she pushed back from the front of her mind. 'What if we do not find it?'

Moira's eyes welled. She swallowed back the emotion and blinked to keep the tears from falling. 'Then

I will know, *we* will know, that we did everything we could to try to save him, won't we?'

Angus smiled. 'Aye, my lady, we will.'

An awkward silence followed, and then Angus shouted, 'Ye heard 'er! Help us save the laird!'

The servants scattered like ants from the main hall filtering down different hallways and peeling off into other rooms. They loved and respected their laird. With their help, all the items of interest could be gathered quickly and assessed. And maybe, just maybe, they could find the cause of his sickness before it was too late.

'Quite a plan you have here, my lady,' the doctor offered. 'But do not get your hopes up.'

'I know, Doctor. It may not work, but I must try. Can you tell me what might be the most possible of causes for such a poisoning and how you think it might be happening? It may help us sort through the items more quickly. I fear there may be many to consider.'

'That I cannot tell you. It could be absorbed or ingested, especially with how slowly it seems to be working through his body. A stronger or more lethal poison would have taken him already.'

Servants emerged once more and soon the table was covered with items that Rory used and loved. The sight of all of them in one place assaulted her senses and reminded her of all she had to lose: him. She swallowed hard and began to look through them as the doctor did the same.

How could she possibly determine what could be causing his sickness? There were so many items here.

Books, quills, cups, shavers and salves, and more arriving at the tables each minute. She suppressed a groan. Where she had been desperate to begin not long ago, now she feared the process. What if she missed the item making him so sick? What would one even test for and how?

'Doctor, how can one determine what has been poisoned?' She popped her hands to her hips.

'If I knew the answer to that, I would have told you already.'

Her heart sank. Perhaps she was being a fool. How would she know what from this pile of items could be the one that was making Rory so ill?

A servant rushed through them and gave Uncle Leo a note. Upon looking at it, he scowled and sent the servant off. He approached Moira. 'My lady, if I may have a word.'

Gooseflesh rippled along her skin. She followed him to an alcove off the main hall away from the ears of the servants. The edge in his voice startled her. He was a jovial man most of the time, but his tone rang cold like steel. ''Tis your father, my lady. He awaits you outside to take you back.'

Moira laughed aloud. 'What? Now? After months of being here? The idea of it is lunacy. Surely there is a mistake.'

'Nay. The lad tells me he demands entry. I fear he will break down our doors and use what men he has brought with him to battle his way in.'

Of all the times for her father to press in upon her and her life. Anger rippled through her hot and bright. She was no little girl to be bandied about as a possession. She was a grown woman, and she would face him and command his departure.

'I will battle him out of our grounds, my lady. All of us are willing to fight for you. Just say the word.' His body was taut, and in that moment she realised how delicate the situation was. The McKennas were loyal and fiercely protective of those they loved. If she wasn't careful, a battle might break out on the drive in front of Blackmore while her husband's life hung in the balance.

'Nay.' She clutched his forearm. 'I will speak with him. There will be no battles other than the one to keep Rory alive.'

'As you wish.'

She released his arm. 'But I will need ten of your fiercest soldiers at the ready to come with me as I greet him. He responds to force and I want him to know that I am prepared to battle for my husband and for my right to stay here. Blackmore is my home.'

Uncle Leo gave a satisfied smile and thrust his chest out. 'Aye. Consider it done. I will have them accompany you immediately. As shall I.'

'Tressa,' she called.

Her lady's maid set down the laird's chalice along with a comb and soap and hurried to her.

'I am in need of my most intimidating and noble gown. Can you help me?'

Her eyes widened, and she smiled. 'Aye. I have just the one in mind.'

Moira's legs quaked as she walked through the large castle doors and stepped into the arc of soldiers, including Uncle Leo, who flanked the landing. To her pleasure, the McKennas were an impressive and foreboding lot of men with their legs anchored like statues and swords in their waist belts at the ready. Their scowls were fixated on the mirror of soldiers that skirted her father. She paused. And to her surprise, her brother, Ewan.

Thistles.

Betrayal stung her. Why was her brother here? She had hoped Ewan wasn't a part of this, but here he was at Father's side once more. Shoving the hurt away, she summoned the steely rage and caged emotion that years in Peter's 'care' had instilled in her.

'Father. Brother.' Her words carried across the void between them strong and even, and she lifted her chin. A spitting ice storm brewed and the tinny sound of the pellets landing on the smooth drive surrounded them. Her dark cloak and the skirts of her heavy scarlet gown caught the crystals and reflected in the torchlight just as it did off the Stewart men glaring at her. The very men who used to guard and protect *her* now threatened the nest of happiness she had found and created for herself.

Her father and brother didn't answer immediately, but studied her and the men surrounding her.

'Is he already dead, then?' Father asked, his words as brittle and harsh as the weather.

She gripped the fabric of her cloak and commanded herself not to lash out as she longed to. Her father was baiting her, even Ewan knew it. His gaze slid to her and back to their father, interested in who might lose their temper first. The soldiers on each side were taut and eager to battle, but she had little time for base things. She needed to end this and get back to saving her husband's life.

If they wished to, they could attempt to kill one another at a later date.

'I have no time for your baiting, Father. My husband is ill, but he will recover. Just as you will leave me to this life that I have chosen for myself. You have no legitimate claim here. 'Tis only your pride that presses this issue forward. I am surprised my husband's coin did not appease you. It was sizeable if I recall.'

Ewan's eyes widened and several of Father's men shifted on their feet. She had stung and stung hard. There was no other way with Father. She realised that now. He'd never give her grounds for her independence. She would have to be brave and seize it, just like that day of the tournament.

'I have already challenged the legitimacy of your union with Laird McKenna and soon you will hear from the king.' Her father took two steps forward and the McKenna soldiers responded in kind ready to draw down.

Lord above. The king would do no such thing. Her Father's threats were baseless and empty.

But the last thing she needed was a battle on the Blackmore grounds to assuage his bruised ego. She raised her hand to her men and approached her father and brother. 'Then you have wasted correspondence, time and resources. I am not leaving Blackmore. Our marriage is legitimate.' She took another breath and puffed out her chest allowing the hood of her cloak to fall back to rest on the base of her neck. 'Especially now that I carry his heir.'

A few McKenna soldiers sucked in a breath, as if the air had been stolen from them. Most of the clan had not known that she was with child, but this seemed the moment to reveal all, even to her father. It was her last hope of getting him to focus on the future rather than the past and let go of his pride. If he couldn't do that for a babe, for his future grandchild, then there was no hope for any of it.

Laird Bran Stewart, not her father, stared at her, his eyes scanning her face, perhaps in hopes of finding a hint of weakness or deception he could exploit. She held his hard gaze, willing him to accept the truth in her eyes and in her heart. Willing him to see her as his daughter for once rather than the enemy, his property or a prize to be bartered. Sucking in a breath, she risked one more push. 'So you will withdraw your threats as will the Frasers, and you will cease your actions against us. There is no truth to either of your claims. Nor will there ever be.'

'While I will cease *my* claim now that you are with child, I cannot promise the Frasers will do the same.' He started to leave and then faced her once more. 'But I will try to assist you. For the sake of your bairn. He has part Stewart blood after all.'

He turned and left, his men falling in step behind them to mount their horses. Ewan paused and came to her. Moira's heart twisted at the sight of him. He took her hands in his own and kissed her cheek. 'I am glad to see you get what you wanted, sister. Even if it was

Laird Death,' he whispered. He pulled back, winked at
her and squeezed her hands. 'We will come visit once
the babe is born. I will bring Brenna too, no matter
what Father says.'

She choked back the emotion welling within her.
'I look forward to it,' she mangled out in a mixture of
strained tones. She longed to hug him, but she knew
he'd not do so in front of Father. He was soon to be laird
and such softness was frowned upon.

Ewan walked away and pulled up easily on his
mount. She watched the line of soldiers retreat down
the drive until they disappeared through the tree line,
and all she could think was that she'd not said what
was on her heart.

That, despite it all, she missed them.

Chapter Twenty-Six

The weather improved over the next few days, but Moira's nerves sharpened to an edgy point as Rory drifted in and out of consciousness, often awake for only a handful of hours at a time. Usually just long enough to be given tonics, some sustenance and to walk about the halls for a few minutes before needing to rest and drifting off once more to what she hoped was a healing sleep. She'd spent hours every day looking through his belongings excluding one item after another until they were down to one table of possibilities. As each item was removed, so was a parcel of her hope that she would discover the cause of his sickness and he would soon recover.

She'd scoured books and journals, and even begged to rummage through Uncle Leo's study, which he had obliged with good humour. Her mind felt sluggish and jumbled after all she'd read, but she was no closer to discovering the cause of Rory's illness.

Raw energy abounded in Blackmore. Servants bustled about as if their sheer wilfulness to keep Blackmore clean and crisp would keep their laird alive. Moira wished it were so simple and that she had a shred of control over anything. After another night of fitful sleep, she had Tressa help her dress and left for the outdoors. Fresh air had to help her. Nothing inside did.

She climbed along the winding hillside towards the cliffs, but veered off to the woods to visit the chapel. Perhaps some quiet and prayer would help clear her mind and steady her spirit, which had been flagging as of late. She slid into the third pew, the same one they had sat in that morn long ago, and stared at the simple alter before her. They'd been married only a short time, and yet she longed for him and cared for him in every way, far more than she ever had for Peter during their years of marriage. Now, as her marriage was growing stronger, Rory was growing weaker and edging towards the demise she had once hoped and planned for. Her face heated with shame and she rubbed her hands together. How had she ever been so callous? He was a man, a good man, and she had initially married him because he would die.

And now he was.

'Are ye unwell?' Tressa's timid voice rang through the empty chapel.

Moira wiped at her eyes and smiled as Tressa fidgeted with the edges of her cloak. 'Aye. Just feeling a wee bit sorry for myself, that's all. And ashamed. And helpless. Did you have need of me?'

'Nay. Yer uncle asked me to come check on ye. Make sure ye were not alone in case ye had need of anyone. Due to yer condition. With the babe.'

'Please. Join me. I am lost as to what to do.'

Tressa slid into the pew next to her. 'We have finished with the last of the items. The doctor says they are not the cause either. I am sorry.' She looked down at her hands.

Moira sighed. 'I feared as much. It is hard to fathom why we cannot discover it.' She rested her head back against the pew. 'Is there anything else that Angus or one of the other servants prepare for the laird that I do not have? That no one has. If it is not a thing Rory is using that is poisoning him, it must be a food or drink.'

Tressa was silent for countless minutes. 'Oh, my lady! Why did we not think of it before? Angus makes him a drink each night and sets it in his study. In that chalice, the one all the McKenna lairds have drunk from.'

Hope rose and then evaporated. 'Aye, Tressa. But we checked the chalice. It was one of the first items we suspected, remember? The doctor said it was not the cause. And the wine does not seem the cause either. I tried it myself just after I arrived, and Uncle Leo drinks from that same wine decanter, does he not?'

'Aye, he does.' The wisp of a girl deflated and sagged back against the pew.

Moira squeezed her maid's hand. 'But it was a thought. A fine thought.' Then her fingers tingled and she sat up straight to face Tressa. 'Wait. What do you mean by Angus *makes* him a drink? Doesn't he just pour him a cup of wine or dram of whisky?'

Tressa twisted her lips and furrowed her brow. 'Angus always says he's *making* his evening drink for the laird when I see him in the kitchens late at night. I always assumed it was some sort of sleeping tonic. Ye would have to ask him.'

'Then we shall do that at once.'

She smiled, hope puffing up her chest and making her steps back to the castle light and quick. They reached the main hall, and Tressa disappeared in search of Angus. Moira removed her cloak and went to Rory's chambers, their chambers, and settled into the all too familiar chair pulled up to his bedside. She clutched his warm, still hand between her own.

'Do come back to me, my love. All of those days of wishing to be without a husband are behind me. I want to have you with me always.'

He never answered when she whispered this prayer to him, but she never stopped saying it whenever she sat with him as he slept.

The door opened and Angus hurried within with Tressa trailing right behind.

'Ye have need of me, my lady?'

'Aye,' she answered as her heart thudded against her chest. 'Tressa told me that you make a drink for the laird each night. What do you mean? Don't you just pour a whisky or chalice of wine for him?'

'Nay, he likes me to pour him a glass of wine along with the sweetener he prefers.'

'Sweetener?'

'Aye. We've had the recipe for as long as I can remember, and the lairds—' He paused and paled.

'And the lairds what?' Moira enquired as she rose from her chair.

'And the lairds have oft preferred it over regular wine. They say it's sweeter and helps them sleep. I never thought...'

'Fetch it, Angus. I'll find the doctor.'

Moira rushed from the bedchamber in search of the doctor. *Please don't let him have left.* She rounded a corner to the study and found him conversing with Uncle Leo. 'Doctor,' she called. 'Please come with me. We may have discovered what ails him.'

Whether it was her voice or her face, they came to her, following closely as they returned to the main hall where Angus was also returning from the kitchen. He carried a small dark ceramic jar gingerly in both hands as if he now feared its contents. He placed it on the table and stepped back. 'We've had it here at the castle as long as I can remember. 'Tis a sweetener that we get from the village. It makes sour wine taste sweet and fine wine even better, or so some say. I tried it once, but found it far too sweet for my liking.'

The doctor opened the jar slowly, resting its lid on the table. He took a measure of it from the container using the small spoon still resting inside of it. He dabbed a bit on his finger and tasted it before spitting it out on his handkerchief. 'I have a few guesses. I'll need to take it back with me to do some tests in my cottage in the village. I'll return in the morn with answers, I hope. And who is it that you purchase this from?' He wrapped the jar in a large handkerchief and tucked it in his medicine bag.

'Two cottages down from the healer. See her, and

she'll show you the place. I can even go with ye if needed,' Angus stated.

'Nay. No need. I'll go now and be back as soon as I can. Until then, keep the laird comfortable. If he wakes, give him milk and cheese. Nothing else.'

'Aye. Thank you, Doctor.' Moira could hardly stand still. What if they were a day away from discovering the cause of Rory's illness? And they had a chance at a life, a long life, together as a family?

She rushed back to Rory's bedside and knelt. Clutching his hands, she whispered to him. 'I think we've found it, Rory. It is no curse. You will live. Please come back to me. Come back to *us*.'

Moira woke to the shouts of angry men and women from the main hall below. She pushed herself up from the floor and edge of the bed where she'd fallen asleep tending to Rory and rubbed her eyes. It was mid-afternoon based on the sun streaming across his bed, but he still slept soundly. Her heart twisted. Why would he not wake?

And what was going on?

She straightened her gowns, went down the stairs and came to the edge of the hallway near the front entrance and paused. One of the voices became clearer, and she froze. Every fibre of her being remembered that voice. Peter's mother. She had long hoped her mother-in-law would accept her, but that had never happened. Peter had filled her with stories about how disobedient and troublesome she was, and his mother had accepted his words as truth.

But there was another voice she didn't recognise. 'You will bring her to me,' the man commanded. 'She will answer for her crimes against our family.'

'My lady will not answer to the likes of anyone, especially you, Laird Fraser. I know what kind of man your cousin was and by extension I believe I also know you,' Uncle Leo snarled. Rage coloured his voice.

'Then no one will go in or out of Blackmore until she does. I have an army of soldiers in place. Allies you do not have. You are alone, McKenna, and I know your nephew is gravely ill. I will starve you and your people here out of the castle and let your laird die if you do not hand her over to me. Now. The elders have been assembled to hear our case against her, and we will not be denied our opportunity to determine the true cause of my cousin's death.'

Moira shivered. They'd assembled an elders' council to hear her side of the story and to determine the true cause of Peter's death? And now they demanded her attendance or they would blockade Blackmore. Could he do such? Could he starve them out and keep the doctor from returning to tend to Rory? Was it even possible?

She knew the answer. Aye, it was. There was one main road up to Blackmore and one small exit and escape route down the other side of the castle that was large enough for carriages and supplies to be traversed upon. The other trails were smaller and too treacherous this time of year, even for the most experienced of riders. If Laird Fraser dug in and kept their supplies, their men—namely Rory's doctor—from them, then they would eventually starve, but sooner than that

Rory would die. He needed care from Dr Wilkes and quickly. If he'd found out what had made Rory so sick, he might be on his way back tomorrow to cure him. They wouldn't have time for the Frasers to come to their senses or for a battle to wage and end. A day could be the very difference in Rory's survival.

And more than anything, she wished for her husband to live. To continue to care for his clan and have a future. He couldn't do that dead. She went to the door and stepped between two of the McKenna soldiers that blocked Laird Fraser's path.

'What is it you desire?' she demanded.

'You know what I want, my lady. You will join me and answer for your crime against my cousin.'

The McKenna soldiers closed ranks around her, their anger at Laird Fraser vibrating off them.

'And what crime might that be, my laird?' She crossed her arms against her chest and willed the fear that often scampered along her spine when she thought of Peter and his family to hide elsewhere. She had no time for fear. Not today.

'The death of my cousin.'

She scoffed. 'Oh? And how is that? No one has levelled any previous claim against me, and it has been over a year since his death. What has changed?'

'I have a witness.' He called behind him.

A witness? Only she and Peter had been in that room during their fight. Who could he possibly mean?

'Bring her.'

A bedraggled young woman emerged from the carriage that sat at the edge of the drive. Moira gasped when she saw the young woman's face. *Enora.* 'She is no witness. She was my lady's maid. What have you done to her, you brute?'

On instinct, she rushed to her old maid, desperate not only to see her but to help her. Enora struggled to walk and seemed unable to raise herself to standing without assistance. Someone had beat her mercilessly. But why? And how had she even been intercepted by the Frasers?

Unless her father had let her go. She cringed. Perhaps Enora had returned to the Frasers and sought employ out of necessity and, instead of employ, she had been ill used to build a case against Moira instead.

She gritted her teeth. The Frasers had gone a step too far this time.

As soon as her boot reached the bottom step, two of the Fraser soldiers seized Moira roughly by the arms, and she shouted in alarm. In an instant, McKenna soldiers were entangled with Laird Fraser's men, and she and Enora were in a fine crush between them. Moira shoved the Fraser soldiers away attempting to break their hold on her arms, but it was no use. The more she struggled, the tighter their grip became and the more volatile the situation. When one Fraser soldier almost knocked her to the ground, the loud booming voice of Uncle Leo slammed into the air like a hammer.

'Cease! She is with child!'

The soldiers stilled and all eyes fell upon her. A small orb of space opened around her and she reached for Enora, bringing her former lady's maid to her side. 'What has happened to you? Enora, can you hear me?'

'Aye,' she whispered, her voice rough and scratchy.

A far cry from the bright upbeat joy her voice used to hold. 'They forced me to tell them what I knew. I am sorry, my lady. I know ye are not responsible.'

'You have nothing to apologise for. You told the truth, as will I. Then, after the council finds in our favour, which they will as we are guilty of no crimes, then we will come back here and you will join us at Blackmore. You will see.' Her maid's hand trembled against her own. Moira squeezed it and smiled at her even as her own anger and uncertainty consumed her.

Enora nodded in return, but refused to meet Moira's gaze.

'So what is your choice?' Laird Fraser demanded.

'She is going nowhere with the likes of you, Fraser,' Uncle Leo answered.

'Then we will starve you out and block anyone from coming or going from here until she does.'

Moira clenched her jaw. 'I've no patience for your stubbornness and ploys today, my laird. And you will not keep the doctor from my husband. Nor shall there be bloodshed on the drive. I will go with you and answer your questions. You will soon find your enquiry and blame of me false. Your council will realise this is an unfounded, ridiculous ploy manufactured by you.'

Or at least she hoped they would.

'Moira, you cannot. The babe,' Uncle Leo pleaded, approaching her. He clutched her hands in his.

'I refuse to allow Rory to die, and I must answer to these claims once and for all. Otherwise, I shall never be free of the past. I will never be able to move forward. You know that.'

'But you don't know that Dr Wilkes can save him. You may be sacrificing yourself and your babe in hopes that he will live, but it may be too late. You must face that possibility.'

Moira shook her head. 'I refuse to believe such. I also know that Peter's cousin wouldn't dare touch me now that it is known by all of these men here that I am with child. Look at all of these witnesses.' She turned to her mother-in-law and the new Laird Fraser and spoke louder as she held their angry gazes. 'Even you would not dare to hurt an unborn. Would you, Laird Fraser?'

The man shifted on his feet as if he too recalled full well the scene her late husband had displayed and how his actions had caused her to lose their child years ago. He nodded. 'Aye. I would not. I am no brute.'

She wasn't so sure.

'I am glad to hear of such a difference between you and your cousin,' she answered. 'Uncle, send word of our situation to Laird Garrick MacLean,' she said in hushed tones. 'He is an ally and will help us if we have need of it without question.'

Uncle paused, his brow furrowed.

'I know you do not know him, but trust me. Promise me you will do so.' She squeezed his hands.

'Aye. I will,' he conceded. 'I'll send word to him today.'

'Thank you, Uncle.' She smiled and kissed his cheek before releasing his hands.

She glared at the Frasers as she walked past them and into the waiting carriage. A soldier helped her inside and she slid across the bench seat. Enora soon joined her. As the carriage door snapped shut, Moira swallowed hard. Her future depended on how much the Frasers knew and whether she decided to tell all of the truth or not.

Chapter Twenty-Seven

Rory woke with what seemed to be a tiny man with a lochaber axe repeatedly cracking upon his skull. He groaned and shifted on the bed clutching his head.

'Ah. There you are, my laird.' Dr Wilkes rose from his chair and began his usual poking and prodding until Rory swatted him away, as he always did.

'How long have I been out?' he asked, rubbing his eyes and then his face. 'From the length of my beard, I fear it may have been a week.'

'Nay. Not that long. Several days you were in and out of wakefulness, but we were lucky to have you conscious long enough for food, tonics, short walks and some attempts to reverse your illness. Do you not remember?'

He blinked, trying to shake off the fog now that some of the aching in his head was fading. 'Nay.' He stilled. 'Wait, did you say you were reversing my illness?'

'The side effects for now. We discovered what was causing your sickness, and with some luck, time and proper medicine, we should be able to reverse some of the effects of the poisoning over the next few months. Already you seem stronger and have better colour. It may be faster than we had dared hope.'

'What?' he said.

Was recovery possible? Would he live to see and hold his own child? To perhaps even have more children and grow old with Moira. He couldn't believe it. Surely, he had misheard.

'Did you say you can make me well again? That I will live?' He felt light as if he were floating on water, his body buzzing with the news that he might not die. That he could live and have a life as he'd never allowed himself to fully imagine. His chest tightened.

Wait. Where was Moira? He scanned the room, but she was nowhere to be found. Perhaps she was out with Uncle and the hounds again. 'Where is my wife?'

'Aye. You do have your wife to thank.' The doctor rattled on, packing up his instruments in his satchel. 'She never gave up. Insisted we gather every item you used to see what ailed you. We determined it was the litharge you used to sweeten your wine. It seems to contain low doses of lead. Small levels, of course, so not immediately fatal, but over time your body collects it, making your condition worsen. We are working on medicines and herbals to help counteract it in your body and absorb it, so in time you will fully heal.'

Rory stared at him. 'Where is Moira? She is always here by my side.'

The doctor avoided his gaze. 'Much has happened. I will fetch your uncle. He can tell you all.'

Rory grabbed the doctor's arm before he could leave. 'What has happened? You will tell me. Now.'

Sorrow and uncertainty rested in Wilkes's eyes, and a pit the size of a loch opened up in Rory's stomach as he awaited the answer.

'She was taken by the Frasers a few days ago. They claimed she had to answer for her crimes. She is to go before their clan elders today.'

To see to her fate.

The doctor didn't need to say the words for Rory to work that out. He rose from the bed, too quickly, and almost fell face first to the floor. His damned body. It never did what he wished for it to. The doctor helped him regain his balance. 'Get me to my uncle,' he commanded, trying to think. The shock of her not being here cleared his fog. His pulse picked up speed. 'Why did no one stop her? Why did no one protect her?'

None of it made sense. His uncle, his men, would have fought to the death for her. He was certain of it. How had the Frasers seized her so easily?

'Uncle!' Rory called as he gained his bearings and made his way through the hallways. It was taking far too long for him to find him. Where was he?

Finally, he heard his uncle. 'Aye. You're awake!' He smiled and pulled him into a tight embrace. 'To see you alive and well does me good. Does us all good.' His smile faltered as he scanned Rory's face, and his arm fell away from Rory's shoulder. 'I see you have heard of Moira's absence.'

'Absence?' he scoffed. 'You make it seem as if she were away on a trip. Was she taken or did she leave willingly? And why would you have allowed either to happen?'

'Sit,' his uncle answered. They settled into two chairs at the large table in the main hall.

Rory clung to the arms of it to prepare himself. He knew he wouldn't like the answer.

'They came to our door demanding she answer for her supposed crimes against her late husband. They threatened to blockade the roads, hold back any needed supplies and keep anyone from leaving or entering the gates. The men were ready to battle as were we, but...'

'Moira intervened.' Rory scrubbed a hand down his face. He could imagine the scene unfolding. To avoid bloodshed, she left with them. *Lord above.* Why did his wife have to be so noble?

'She also did it to save you. She knew Dr Wilkes wouldn't be allowed in, and we'd just found what we thought was the poison. He'd gone to the village to run some tests on it to confirm what he believed to be true. He was due to return the next morn with the results, which he did. She saved your life in more ways than one that day.'

'How could you have allowed her to go?' Rory pleaded.

'We had little choice. Have you met your wife, my son? She has a mind of her own. There was no stopping her. I could see it in her eyes. She wanted to plead her case and bring an end to their claims against her. She said it was the only way to move forward with her life.'

'What is our plan? We must rescue her and bring her

back to us. To Blackmore. Tell me that you have at least been working on *that* while I have been ill.'

'Aye. We have been planning as you slept, knowing full well that when you woke you would want to do just that. I'll ready the horses and send word to the MacLeans and the Stewarts to join us in route to the Frasers. We can be assembled and ready to leave in an hour's time.'

Rory blanched. 'Wait. The MacLeans and the Stewarts? They have agreed to assist us?'

'Aye. Moira bid me send word to Laird MacLean, as she believed he would offer aid without question, which he did. He said he owed her a debt. And Bran. He is enraged and eager to help now that he is aware that Moira is with child. He will bring a small band of soldiers to join our own.'

'Garrick is a good man to offer such, and I am grateful for the aid from Bran. Rescuing Moira is what is most important. All differences can be set aside for now.' Even if he did despise his father-in-law.

Angus emerged from outside and rushed down the hall to him. 'My laird, I heard ye woke.' He clapped him on the shoulder.

'Aye. I am up and ready to retrieve my wife and child-to-be.'

'Then let me assist ye in getting dressed as they ready the mounts and supplies.'

'And, Uncle, bring anything you believe we will need to barter in case it comes to that. And send word to the Camerons. We may need their assistance yet.'

'Aye. I'll gather coin and send out the messengers

immediately. Let us hope that we rescue her before they can even arrive.'

As Angus helped Rory back to his chamber for a bath and shave, Rory imagined all the ways he would bring the Frasers to their knees for what they had done or planned to do to his wife and unborn bairn.

Peter Fraser would not have his revenge after all, but Rory McKenna would.

'What is our plan?' Enora asked.

'To survive,' Moira answered flatly and then smirked at her lady's maid.

'Anything more specific?' she teased as she styled Moira's hair in a plait down her back. She wished to look as serious and formidable as possible. She could only hope it might work.

Over the last few days, Moira had helped to care for her maid as they were held by the Frasers at the dreary Dunnes Castle she'd fought hard to escape not so long ago. The colour had returned to her lady's maid's cheeks, and she'd gained enough strength to walk un-aided. Moira hoped the same could be said for Rory.

She knew that her risk in coming here had been worth it. Without doing so, a battle could have raged for days between the clans and Dr Wilkes would have never been able to get back to her husband. Hourly, she prayed that he had made it to Rory in time and that her previous wish to become a widow once more had *not* come true.

Enora tugged at Moira's corset once more and then Moira stepped into her gown. 'Soon you won't be able

to fit into this gown, my lady.' She smiled and Moira
grinned back at her reflection in the mirror.

'You are right. An unexpected miracle, don't you
think?'

She nodded.

'I can only hope I am allowed a few more: for Rory
to live and to escape this mess I'm in.'

'The mess *we're* in,' Enora corrected.

Moira squeezed her hand. The lass was right. The
Frasers were after both of them for supposedly conspir-
ing to kill Peter. While that couldn't be further from
the truth, the true cause of Peter's death as well as their
role in it would not be decided by them. The Fraser clan
elders would arrive and ask questions and make their
own decision. Then what came next was a mystery.
They'd never charged two women, let alone a woman
who carried a child, with the murder of a former husband and future laird. Everyone was walking upon un-
charted ground.

A loud knock sounded at the door, and they both
stilled. 'The elders await ye,' a man stated on the other
side.

'I thought we had two more hours before they would
fetch us?' Moira whispered, her heartbeat picking up its
pace in alarm at the sudden change in plans.

Enora shrugged. 'Perhaps they decided sooner was
better.' She finished buttoning Moira's dress.

'I suppose we are as ready as we shall ever be.' Moira
rose, brushed down her skirts and followed Enora to the
door. When she opened it, Moira saw a young man in
Fraser plaid with long brown hair and wide eyes, not a

soldier as she expected. He pushed his way in and closed the door behind him.

Moira moved away from him and pulled Enora by her side.

'We've not much time,' he began. 'But if we leave now, I can get ye out of here.'

Moira stilled. 'What? I don't understand. You wear Fraser plaid. Why would you take such a risk?' she asked, regaining her composure. 'You don't know me. You also know the Frasers will never let this rest. Even if we escape, they would still hound us. This will never be over until we face it.'

'But, my lady, I know ye did nothing.' The lad looked anxiously from her face to the door and back again.

Moira stepped closer. 'How do you know that I am innocent of these crimes against me?'

He blushed. 'I was outside yer window. Nothing untoward, I promise. I was working the garden that day and I heard yer scream. I stopped. I saw him grab ye, what he did. Well, what he tried to do.' He dropped his gaze and began to study the top of his boot. 'It wasn't right. Laird or not, he shouldn't have hurt ye. I was relieved ye escaped.'

Her hands turned clammy and her heartbeat felt irregular, as if it belonged to someone else, and was pounding away in her chest to free itself. 'Did you ever tell anyone this?'

His eyes widened. 'Nay. I wasn't sure it was safe to tell anyone.'

Enora approached. 'So why now?' she asked, popping her hands to her hips and narrowing her gaze at him. Moira was equally suspicious of the timing.

'Ye are kind. I could not see ye and yer bairn hanged. Nor yer maid here.'

'Have we met before?' Moira asked. There was something familiar about him.

He smiled. 'Aye. I'm Cullen. Ye may not remember me, my lady, but when I was a lad, my mother had taken ill after Father died in battle. Ye came to the village just after ye married into the clan and brought us a basket of food and told me to report to the castle for work. That I could be the man of the family now and care for my mother and sisters.'

Her heart filled at the memory. 'I remember now. You had floppy brown hair, and a little dog that nipped at your ankles.'

'Skipper.'

'How is your family?'

'My mother passed a while back, but my sisters are well, and with my work here, I can help care for them until they marry. We would not have fared well without yer kindness. And when the laird bid me bring ye the note, I thought to warn ye, but I lost my nerve. I even followed ye back to Blackmore from the village the night of the storm just to make sure ye arrived home safely.'

She nodded. 'I thought someone was following me that night, but then I saw the stag and thought I was imagining things.'

'Aye,' he said quietly. 'It was me. I should have told ye then in the village of what I knew, but I was worried of what might happen.'

'If the Frasers found out,' she added.

'Aye. But I can help ye escape now. There is still time,' he offered.

She studied him. Could he get them out of Dunnes Castle without any of them being harmed? Uncertainty abounded. It would be a risk.

'Leave and take my lady's maid with you,' Moira commanded.

'Nay. I will not leave ye here,' Enora rebutted.

'It is the best way for you both to escape. I have to face this or I will never be free.'

'Then we all stay and I will speak on yer behalf, my lady.'

'They will cast you out or worse for such an offence, Cullen. And what of your family?'

'I told them of my plan. They wish for me to try to save ye. Without ye, we all would have perished by now.'

She squirmed under his praise. How many more men and women of the Fraser clan had she walked by without a thought? And what of the McKennas? Had she not done the same? She could do more for them all, she knew that. His story was a heady reminder of the power and influence she had as the wife of a laird.

And she needed to use it. She was no wilting violet.

'Perhaps we shall order the Fraser elders to see *us* now?'

Enora smiled. 'Now that is the start of a fine plan. I love the element of surprise.'

Rory had had enough surprises to last the rest of his lifetime. First, his horse had thrown its shoe, and then the Stewarts had been late to join them and the MacLeans at the agreed meeting location. Now they found themselves blocked at every turn by a sprawling sea of Fraser soldiers surrounding the perimeter of the castle walls.

He also felt like the devil.

'They are waiting for us,' Bran stated. 'We'll need to create a diversion, so a few of us can slip in.'

For once, Rory agreed with his father-in-law. 'Aye. What kind of diversion?'

'A big one.' Bran frowned. 'One that will knock their kilts right off. We've got a barrel of black powder to ignite that should do fine.'

Garrick chuckled. 'Sounds good to me.'

'And then, we'll slip in and find them.'

'I'm going with you,' Rory commanded.

'You've just risen from the dead, son. Perhaps you could stand down on this one and let us get Moira and her maid out and to safety,' Bran countered.

'Not a chance,' he muttered. 'She is my wife.'

'And my daughter. And right now, you are a liability. You're too weak to be in the midst of combat.'

'And if anything happens to you, we'll never hear the end of it,' Ewan muttered from behind them both.

'You may be right about that,' Bran agreed.

Rory wanted to charge in, not stay back. But the logic in the back of his mind told him they were right. The one area free of his emotions regarding Moira agreed. 'Fine, then. I'll stay here.'

Bran and his son exchanged a look.

'What?'

'We'd already planned to have to tie you up to keep you here. You've already saved us time.' Bran smirked.

Rory scoffed. 'Glad to hear it. Now what's the rest of the plan?'

'Distraction, we get them clear of the castle, and then run to the copse of trees. You and Garrick can stay with the men who will run behind us to cover us with their targes. With enough shields stacked against one another, Moira will be safe from arrows and blades once she is freed from within.'

At least that was the hope.

'You'll help lead her out with a few men down through the hillside,' Bran continued.

'Then we can split up into small enough groups to fracture their search area,' Rory added.

'And lose us entirely,' said Ewan.

A great deal had to go in their favour for this plan to work, but it was sound. As sound as a plan made in the last day and a half could be.

'Agreed?' Garrick asked.

'Agreed,' Bran and Rory answered at exactly the same time.

Chapter Twenty-Eight

The boom nearly knocked Moira off her feet. She grabbed for the wall to steady herself as the ground trembled beneath and doors rattled.

'What was that?' she asked Enora, glancing out the window. Off in the distance, she could see smoke and a ball of fire. Fraser soldiers raced to the chaos near the border of trees, but Moira didn't have a chance to study the scene further. Their chamber door crashed open, thudding against the wall, and three of Tavish's men rushed in to grab her and Enora by the arms. When the men spied Cullen, they paused but secured him as well.

'You will come with us,' the Fraser soldier ordered. 'The elders will speak with you. Now.' Hope filled Moira's chest. That could only mean that they were nervous. Something was happening and they needed to move their questioning along. *Rory.* The McKennas were coming for them. It had to be. The noise and fire was a ploy. All she and Enora needed to do was to find him and his men. Or to create enough time for the McKennas to find them. She banked on the latter.

The soldiers rushed her, Enora and Cullen along and out of the chamber so quickly that Moira wasn't even sure if her feet touched the floor. Moira caught Enora's gaze and mouthed 'They're coming for us' to let her know what she hoped was happening. That they were being rescued. Enora nodded, and they continued along offering little resistance. Soon they were thrust before a large, wooden crescent-shaped table flanked with five men of advanced age, which she could only assume were the Fraser clan elders.

'You will answer for your crimes,' Laird Tavish Fraser commanded with his aunt by his side. They sat flanked off to the side of the elders in all of their finery. As usual, Peter's mother glistened in her golden gown and jewels while Tavish sat looking rather bored in his plaid and frock coat with its jewelled buttons.

'And what crimes might those be, my laird?' Moira asked, stalling for time. It would take precious minutes for the McKennas to sneak onto the grounds, breach the castle walls and overcome the guards. She and Enora had to provide them as much time as they could.

Tavish scoffed. 'You have forgotten the death of my cousin so quickly? You amuse me.' He nodded and the soldier shoved her so hard she fell to her knees on the cold stone floor before him.

Startled, she lifted her head and glared at him. 'You will have to do more than that if you wish to scare me, my laird. Remember, I was married to your cousin after all.' She leaned back on her haunches and flicked her plait of hair back behind her shoulder.

Enora sucked in her breath behind her. Perhaps

Moira was taking it too far, but she refused to show fear in front of Tavish and her former mother-in-law. She was not the woman she once was. She would speak her mind and stand up for herself. She was Moira Mc-Kenna. The timid Moira Fraser of the past was no more.

Tavish stood and walked over to her. He grabbed her by the wrist and hauled her up to standing, pulling her close enough to him to smell the sourness of his breath. 'Perhaps I am not so different. You will answer the elders' questions in due course or you will be hanged.'

'And *you* will unhand my wife,' Rory roared from behind them.

Moira turned to him, her heart thundering in relief. He was alive. He was here. He had come for her, for them. She smiled at him as tears welled in her eyes. She blinked them back. Tavish released her.

Rory held her gaze. 'Are you harmed?'

'Nay,' she breathed, unable to catch her breath. 'Are you?'

'Nay. I am well. Stronger. And seeing you alive and well is all I need.' He began to approach her, but soldiers set upon him, holding him back from her. She stepped towards him, but he shook his head. She heeded his warning and held her ground.

'She still needs to answer for her actions, Laird Mc-Kenna,' one of the elders stated.

'And I shall,' Moira answered. ''Tis time to face all of it. I am ready.'

'Then may we begin, Laird Fraser?'

'Aye,' he answered and returned to his chair.

'Did you strike your husband and injure him on the

night of his death, Lady McKenna?' the apparent leader of the elders asked.

'Aye,' she answered. 'I did. He believed I had been unfaithful, which I hadn't, but he wouldn't listen. He wouldn't believe me. He attacked me, and I had no choice but to defend myself or die.'

She met Rory's steady and certain gaze. She could do this. Telling the truth would free her, free them. She took a breath, faced the elder again and continued. 'After he dragged me to the ground, I floundered for anything in my reach to free myself. I grabbed a candlestick that had clattered to the floor during our struggle and I hit him. He let go of me and I ran. When he left the room, Enora helped me to straighten it and clean up the blood before anyone else noted our fight.' Relief whispered through her. She'd said her truth.

'You did not check on his well-being later?' he asked.

'Nay. I had learned to keep to myself when he was in such a state. That afternoon, I heard he left by horse to see my father. Most likely to condemn me for my behaviour. The next day I learned of his death.'

Tavish leaned forward. 'You were pleased to hear of his death?'

'Nay, but I was relieved. As you know, he caused me much suffering, as he did many of you.'

'You lie,' refuted Moira's former mother-in-law.

'She tells the truth,' said Cullen, stepping forward. 'I saw him attack her. She hit him to defend herself. He was going to hurt her. From the looks of it, he already had.'

'And how would you have witnessed such in their

bedchamber?' another elder asked, his tone laced with accusation.

'I was in the garden outside their window tending to the weeds, cutting back the bushes and plants. I did not intend to see it. It was her scream that caused me to look. I wish I had never seen it, but I did.'

'Why did you not come forward before now?' Tavish asked.

'I did not wish to put my life and the lives of my family at risk. I was foolish. Scared of what might happen to them, but not anymore.' He straightened up, becoming taller, filling out his space in the room.

'He also lies,' spat Peter's mother.

'You will cease your interruptions, my lady, or be removed from here.' The leader of the elders levelled her with his steely gaze. The woman's cheeks flushed, and she clamped her mouth shut.

'My lady would never hurt anyone without cause, my laird,' Enora stated. 'It is not who she is. She had no choice. I saw the chamber. It was in shambles, and the bruises she suffered were substantial.'

It was Moira's turn to blush. Heat crawled up her neck and into her cheeks. She tried not to feel the shame, but it was there. It didn't matter that she shouldn't. It didn't matter that it was Peter who should have been ashamed by his actions. She was alive, and he was dead. And the shame had to abide somewhere, didn't it?

'Moira.' Rory's voice was kind and tender, achingly so.

She felt the hot burn of tears at the back of her eyes. Did she dare look? She wanted to, but would she want to see what was in his eyes?

Would it be judgment? Sympathy?

'Look at me,' he pleaded.

When she finally did, the longing and ache in his gaze was almost her undoing. She blinked back her tears.

'None of that shame is yours to carry. None of it.' His Adam's apple bobbed in his throat and his voice cracked with emotion.

'I know you're right. You have taught me such.' A tear rushed down her cheek and she wiped it away.

He struggled against his captors, and she ached to touch him, but she had to say all of it. Otherwise, the past would never be over. Peter's memory would linger and taint everything in her world.

She shook her head. 'Actually, what I told you earlier was a lie. I did wish him dead for hurting me, for causing me to lose my child. He was no husband. He was no man to look up to. He was not worthy to be laird. I refuse to say otherwise. Hang me if you wish, but I will tell the absolute truth at last.'

'Thank you, Lady McKenna,' one of the elders stated. 'We will discuss and determine our findings.'

The elders rose and stepped away from the others to discuss what they'd heard. Moira didn't know what they would determine, and the minutes they conversed seemed like seasons. Finally, they returned to their seats at the table and set their steely gazes upon her.

'Come forward, then,' said the leader. 'All of you.'

The three of them nodded and followed their instruction by stepping closer to the table.

'We are not unaware of the passions and flares of

temper of our previous laird.' His gaze drifted to Peter's mother. 'We had also heard reports of his mistreatment of you, Lady McKenna, and the loss of your bairn. We regret no one intervened on your behalf. Therefore, we do not find you responsible for his death. You and your maid may leave. And, Cullen, you may as well.'

'You cannot find her innocent!' Peter's mother protested. 'She admitted to hitting him.'

'Aye, but she did not stab him, my lady. He died by a stab wound, not a head wound. You know that. I am unsure as to why you believed her responsible. And if you felt so, why did you wait so long to bring her to our council?'

Peter's mother fell silent. A feat Moira didn't believe possible.

The news of the real cause of Peter's death startled Moira into silence as well. She'd never been told the truth of it. All this time, she'd never known how Peter had truly died, but had blamed herself. Perhaps that's how his family had wished it. For her to suffer further. The guilt she'd felt slipped off her like a heavy cloak and pooled at her feet. She felt free of Peter and his memory at last and ready to move on from her past. The soldiers stepped away from her and they released her husband as well.

Moira rushed to Rory, crashing into his embrace. Had he ever felt more relief in his life? The feel of her in his arms, her tears on his cheek and her sweet kisses upon his neck filled him with hope. They had no more secrets between them. No more barriers to their happiness, for now. He knew there would be struggles as there always were but for now there were none. There was only unbridled joy and hope.

By all that was holy, she was beautiful speaking her truth. All of it. Even the ugliest parts of it. He was so proud of her. She was no longer hiding in the isolation and the solitude of her plants and books and in the shadows of men. She was no bird with folded-in wings searching for a place to hide for safety. This Moira wanted to live a full, joyful life with him. They would be a family. She was the love match he dared not think possible that day on the tournament fields. She'd fought for a future, and Rory would fight for her in kind. Always. She had saved him when he hadn't even been trying to save himself.

'Daughter,' Laird Stewart called out to them, with his son not far behind.

'You came for me as well?' Moira asked, confusion crinkling her face. 'Together?'

'Believe it or not we did, even though someone, namely your husband, ignored our well-devised rescue plan and charged in here alone,' Bran offered. 'He and I are working on an understanding of one another, but the one thing we agree on is our love and care for you and your bairn.'

'We'll always be here for you, sister.' Ewan hugged her tightly before releasing her again.

'And I you, brother.' She elbowed him in the ribs.

'And if we hurry, we might reach Blackmore by nightfall,' Rory announced. 'You are welcome to break your journey with us. It seems appropriate to celebrate together as a family, don't you think?'

Bran hesitated, but Ewan interrupted him. 'Aye. A fine idea. I've much to catch my sister up on, namely Brenna. And her many suitors.'

Moira shook her head. 'How many this time?'

'You don't want to know. Although one of them comes now,' he whispered as Garrick MacLean approached them with a handful of his men in tow.

Laird MacLean smiled at her. 'I am glad you kept your word, Lady McKenna, and let me know of your need for help.'

'Aye, and I appreciate you offering the aide of your men. It appears our agreement is working out in your favour according to what my brother tells me.'

He nodded and shrugged despite the faint colour rising along his cheeks. 'Aye. It is early days.'

'I wish you well in your endeavours,' she answered.

'I shall need it,' he chuckled and turned to leave with his men.

She laughed and edged closer to Rory as they began to walk out of the castle and return home. He slid his arm around her lower back and she settled into the crook of his arm with her head neatly on his shoulder, exactly where she was always meant to be.

Epilogue

The heavy spring dew filled Moira's nostrils and she sighed aloud. She loved the greenery, the newness and the beauty of these months in the Highlands. Soon bluebells, wood anemones and blackthorns would be in full bloom and the fields around Blackmore would be awash in colour. This was her second spring here with the McKennas, and she could not imagine being happier. Above all, Rory was healthy. The Frasers had been reluctantly forced to publicly acknowledge her innocence in order to avoid isolation from the neighbouring clans, and her family had agreed to come visit in a few weeks to see their new twin boys now that the weather had turned. Rory's wager on having a male heir had been fulfilled in spades, and his alliance with the Camerons had fortified the McKennas' positioning in the Highlands for the better. She smiled as she walked on. Her shoe caught a root, but Rory steadied her.

'Careful,' he urged and she settled in closer against him, savouring his warm and certain presence.

'Where are we going, my laird?' she teased, attempting to lift her blindfold.

He playfully swatted away her hand. 'You shall see. Patience.'

'Fine. I shall behave and go along with your ruse.'

He rewarded her with a kiss to her cheek. 'Good. I would hate for you to ruin your own surprise.'

'I need nothing more, my laird. You and our sons are healthy. My heart and my life are full.'

He paused. 'Should we turn back, then?'

She laughed and tugged on his arm. 'Nay. I wish to see my surprise.'

They travelled up and then along a dirt path. She heard a door creak open, and as they stepped inside, she smiled, breathing in the familiar musky damp air.

'We are at the chapel. You cannot deny it. I know this smell.'

'Right you are.' He untied her blindfold, and she opened her eyes.

She stood stunned and overwhelmed with joy. Before her was her entire family all in one room. Her father, Ewan and Brenna along with Enora, Tressa, Uncle Leo and their beautiful sons, who were close to six months old now. Also present was Laird Garrick MacLean, who had become a firm friend to them both over the last year as well as Brenna's most ardent admirer.

Moira gasped and clasped her hands to her mouth. 'You are all here! Rory, how did you manage this without me knowing?'

He smiled and rubbed her back. 'I have my ways as well as my spies.'

One by one, she hugged them with a final moment with her two boys and Rory. He picked up little Ewan and she picked up his brother, Leo. 'I've one more thing to show you,' he murmured and nodded to the wall of etchings he'd shown her that very first time she'd been in the chapel. She noticed one had been added beside the one of him as a babe with his mother, and she squatted to get a closer look. She smiled and ran her fingers over the etching of them: a man and wife cradling their two sons. 'I adore it.'

'It's hideous,' he offered and smiled.

'Perhaps, but I adore it all the same. I love that you made this for us and that you've allowed yourself to believe you are a McKenna worthy of being on this wall.'

'And I always shall be with you by my side, Moira.'

'Then that is where I will always be.'

* * * * *

If you enjoyed this story be sure to read
Jeanine Englert's
debut Harlequin Historical

The Highlander's Secret Son